The Spyder's Web

I0614784

THE HOUNDS OF ZEUS MC
BOOK 5

BY FAITH GIBSON

THE HOUNDS OF ZEUS

Copyright © 2021 by Faith Gibson

Published by: Bramblerose Press LLC

Editor: Candice Royer

First edition: June 2021

Cover design: Michelle Sewell, RLS Images Graphics & Design

Cover photography: JW Photography and Covers

Cover model: Ryan Lee Harmon

ISBN: 978-1736890011

Dedication

For my little momma – the best biscuit maker ever

"Now hear another monstrous sight: Beware:
The sharp-beaked hounds of Zeus that never bark"

~ Aeschylus, "Prometheus Bound", 5th century
BC

PROLOGUE

Charlotte

"DON'T PANIC, BUT we have a tail. Black truck, three vehicles back."

Charlotte gripped the steering wheel tighter. She waited until the last second to take the exit, but when she glanced in the rearview mirror, the truck was closing in on them. "Shit, hang on." Charlotte took the right at the bottom of the off-ramp faster than she should, barely missing a car merging into her lane. When the other driver laid on their horn, Charlotte muttered, "Sorry." The van wasn't made for speed. Still, she pushed it to its limit. The truck, however, was powerful. Traffic was thick on the four-lane, but Charlotte wove in and out of the cars like a pro.

"Where's a cop when you need one?" Charlotte blew through a yellow light with the truck on her ass. "Seriously?"

"Charlie, you can't outrun them. We need to find somewhere to—" The truck tagged the van's bumper, and both women were pushed forward, their seat belts digging into their chests. "Sonofamotherfucker! Crazy fucking pig licker!" Zedra braced her hand on the dashboard as Charlotte changed lanes then slammed on the brakes. "What are you doing?"

Charlotte made a U-turn in front of oncoming traffic. Cars braked hard. Horns blared. Charlotte didn't let up though. She punched the gas and took off in the opposite direction. "Get someone on the phone. Tell them we need a divers—" A loud pop sounded, and the van careened hard to the right. "Bastard shot my tire!"

"Charlie, look out!" Zedra shouted, like Charlotte couldn't see the light pole they were headed for. Charlotte pulled hard on the steering wheel, but it was no use. She closed her eyes, let go of the wheel, and braced for impact. The airbags did their job, but the seat belt still cut into Charlotte's chest and stomach. The cab filled with a nasty, ashy substance from the airbags deploying, and Charlotte started coughing while waving her hands.

Sirens rent the air, but they weren't close enough for Charlotte's peace of mind. Zedra, still cursing the driver of the truck, released her seat belt. Before Charlotte knew what was happening, an animalistic growl filled her ears as Zedra crawled across the console. Were those fangs? And holy shitballs! Zedra's long hair was no longer auburn. A fur-covered head that looked scarily like a lion smothered Charlotte's face. She couldn't see, but the roar that left her guardian was deafening. Okay, so she'd hit her head and had passed out, because if she'd been conscious, she wouldn't have a lapful of wild animal. That or she was dead. Charlotte didn't think she warranted Hell.

She'd lived a good life.

"Shit, shit, shit." Zedra lunged backward onto her side of the van. Bloody claws retracted, and Charlotte started laughing. Not in a humorous, this-is-funny laugh but a hysterical, I've-lost-my-mind, high-pitched chortle. "Fuck, I'm so sorry." Zedra wiped her hands on her jeans, but the blood wasn't coming off.

"What the fuck are you?" Charlotte managed to ask after her wheezing stopped. Before Zed could answer, Charlotte's door was wrenched open. She screamed as she tried to back away from the door.

CHAPTER ONE

Spyder

"BREATHE, MOTHERFUCKER!" JUDE demanded of himself as he stared at the cracked concrete while begging his brain to get onboard. *You're a fucking Gryphon, for Zeus's sake.* The ear protection did nothing to drown out the sounds of the shooting range, and each fired bullet hammered into his chest. The chest currently having trouble gathering enough air.

"Spyder?" Ryot's voice met Jude's ears right before a firm hand clamped down on his shoulder. "Jude, fuck." Ryker "Ryot" Lazlo, the President of the Hounds of Zeus MC as well as one of Spyder's best friends, grabbed Spyder's bicep and dragged him away from the range and into the building. He continued hauling Spyder by the arm until they were out front. The noise from weapons being fired was still loud, but nothing like it had been standing close to the other Hounds.

"Breathe, Jude," Ryker demanded. Jude stared at his Pres, breathing in through his nose, then exhaling out his mouth until his lungs finally inflated properly.

"Sorry. I thought I could handle it." Jude hated guns. Hated what they could do. After the last job in Texas had gone to shit with Spyder and Havyk going

4

up against the Mexican cartel, Ryker decided all the Hounds should start carrying. Claws and fangs had been good enough for Spyder. Still were. He pulled the ear protection from his head and handed it off. "I gotta get out of here."

"Spyder, wait."

Spyder didn't wait. He left Ryot standing there with no explanation. Instead, he rushed to his bike and straddled the seat, slammed his lid on, and buckled the strap. He cranked his Harley, pealing out of the parking lot. He and Ryker had been friends for a lot of years, but only Hawk was aware of Jude's past. If Hawk had been aware Jude agreed to go to the shooting range, he would probably have kicked Jude's ass.

Instead of heading home, Spyder took the back roads south. He had nowhere to be for the next couple days. He had a Shibari demo Wednesday night at Dominion, the BDSM club where he, Hawk, and Kyllian were Masters. If he hadn't already agreed, he would stay away a few days longer. By the time he rolled up in his mom's driveway a few hours later, Jude's mind had cleared.

The front door opened before he got his kickstand down. Indigo Sterling was shorter than Jude by several inches, but the female was fierce. Indigo wore jeans and a mint green sweater, with her long hair braided down her back. Her bare feet gave no indication it was winter in Upstate New York.

"Hey, Mom." Jude tucked his helmet under his arm as he closed the distance between them. Indigo held her arms open, and Jude let his mother's embrace soothe his soul. It had been the two of them for many years, ever since…

"Come in. I was getting ready to fix a sandwich, but since you're here, I have just the thing." Indigo's feet carried her into the kitchen, where she pulled two beers out of the fridge. Jude set his helmet on one of the dinette chairs, then took the bottle. He didn't bother arguing about her feeding him. It wouldn't do any good.

"Thanks."

He downed the pale ale in one go. His mom swapped the empty for a full bottle before pulling a covered dish from the fridge. When she turned around, she asked, "Do you want to talk about it?"

Jude set the bottle down, dragging the band from his ponytail before redoing it. His mom had a sixth sense where he was concerned, as evidenced by the food heating in the microwave. His favorite cheesy beef casserole scented the air. Somehow, she had known he would stop by and would need the comfort food. Even though she was Gryphon, Indigo rarely ate meat, so the casserole was for him.

"Ryker thinks we need to carry guns on our mercenary jobs."

Indigo narrowed her eyes, then retrieved a cider out of the fridge. After taking a healthy swallow, she leaned against the counter, waiting.

"I thought I could handle it. The sound, I mean. I joined him and a few others at the gun range this morning, and…"

"You had a panic attack." It wasn't a question. His mom knew his past better than anyone. She had lived through it right alongside him. At least she hadn't been there when… Jude swallowed hard. Remembering his sister wasn't a hardship. Reliving the day she had been gunned down still brought him to his knees all those years later.

"Yeah. And instead of working through it, I got on my bike and came here."

The microwave dinged, interrupting their conversation. Indigo checked the food, set the timer for a couple more minutes, then returned her focus to him. "You've been doing mercenary work for a while without an alternate weapon. Don't you all get to choose which jobs you take?"

"We do. For now, I'll only accept those that are quick in-and-outs. I will have to explain to Ryker why though."

"Do you think he won't understand? Ryker seems like a fair male."

"He will, and he is. I just hate talking about it."

Indigo finished getting his plate ready and set it on the table in front of him along with a fork and paper napkin. "Perhaps talking about it will lessen the effect." When Jude's eyes narrowed, his mom held up her hand. "Don't glare at me. I'm not saying you'll forget. But I do know from experience the more you share your story, the easier it is to deal with it internally." She tapped her temple with her index finger. Indigo had seen a therapist after Michelle's best friend's boyfriend gunned her down. His mom tried to get Jude to see her therapist, but he refused. He was a Gryphon. Being such, Jude should be able to handle the trauma on his own. Apparently, he was wrong.

While on the job in Texas with Havyk, Jude had barely kept his shit together. He had gone twenty years without being around guns. Now, those memories of the day Michelle was taken from him were haunting him, thanks to the cartel and the FBI. The report of the pistols that morning was the same as the one plaguing his memories and nightmares. Each caliber gave off a unique sound, and that of a 9mm was forever ingrained in his mind. Jude didn't comment further; instead, he chose to enjoy the food in front of him.

Indigo changed the subject, knowing her son. "I visited with Rory last week and got to meet the twins. You weren't kidding about those two. I about peed my pants when Rory introduced me, and Major asked, 'Where did you go, Indi?' That kid is something else. And Marshall is just as cute in his sweetness."

Jude couldn't help but grin. "You aren't wrong. I want five of each as long as they're all boys."

His mom's smile softened. "It'll happen, Son. Well, maybe not all boys, but you'll find your mate one of these days, and she will be just as special as you are."

Jude didn't consider himself anything special, but his mom had a right to be biased, as did all mothers who carried and nurtured a baby in their stomach for nine months, then popped them out like it was no big deal. He was glad to be a male. Jude couldn't imagine that level of responsibility females carried. They were remarkable creatures. Strong and resilient. Both his father and sister had lost their lives to gunfire – his father trying to stop a robbery and Michelle in a domestic dispute. Despite the deaths of her mate and child, Indigo Sterling had come through both losses and continued living. Next to Rory Lazlo, his mom was the strongest female he knew.

Jude took his empty plate to the sink, kissing his mom on the cheek as he passed her. "You ready for

8

another one?" he asked, grabbing himself a beer.

Indigo downed the few sips left in her bottle. "Yep. I take it you're staying a while?"

"Thought I might." Jude strode into the living room and plopped down on the sofa. "Other than visiting Rory and the twins, what have you been up to?"

His mom sat in her recliner, extending the footrest. "Actually, I've been looking at houses. I think a change of scenery is in order. It's one reason I went to see Rory. There's a cute little cottage close to her house."

"Yeah? That'd be great." Jude loved his mother something fierce. He relished being able to visit when he wanted to get away from life, but having her closer would be even better. "Just let me know if you find a place, and I'll help you move."

"Oh, I'm counting on it. Why pay a moving company when I've got the Hounds at my beck and call?"

Jude tipped his bottle in her direction. "Truth." Like Jude, his father had also been a Hound of the MC. He had been Sutton's VP and one of his closest friends. The two weren't brothers by blood, but the club had brought them together, forging a bond only broken by his father's passing.

Jude looked around his mom's living room. Unlike his own house, there were tons of photos decorating the walls and tables, though few of them were recent. He understood why Indigo kept them, but for him, the reminders of who he'd lost were too painful. He preferred keeping his dad's and sister's likenesses stored away in the recesses of his mind, only bringing them out when he felt strong enough.

9

Jude had helped his mom pack up and move from the house he and Michelle grew up in. It about killed them both, but together, they managed. During that move, his mom had let go of most of his dad's things, only keeping a few items special to her. Jude had inherited his father's motorcycle, which he still rode. Havyk kept it running like brand new. His dad's kutte was framed, hanging above the fireplace in his home. He placed it there to remind him of the kind of male he strived to be. Fearless. Selfless. Heroic. Jude wasn't sure he had achieved any of those things. Truett Sterling left behind some mighty big biker boots to fill, and Jude wanted to do so. He wanted his pop to be proud wherever he was.

For the next couple hours, Jude's mom rattled on about nothing in particular. It was her way of letting him zone out and just be. She didn't ask questions that required his input. When she was talked out, she sat quietly and worked a crossword puzzle. Her presence was enough. When it was time for bed, Jude retired to the room she kept for him. He had spare clothes in the dresser and toiletries in the attached bathroom for those days he stopped by on a whim. Jude wanted to be that type of parent, if and when he ever found a mate and had kids of his own. He wanted to be a safe place to land, even when his children were grown.

As he readied for bed, Jude thought about his conversation with his fellow Hounds while looking for the cult members hunting Rhiannon, Ryker's mate. He didn't think what he wanted in his own mate was asking too much. Someone adventurous, and someone who loved his mother. Jude didn't really have a type. He loved females of all shapes and sizes, but he'd never dated anyone who made his blood sizzle or his beast stand up and take notice. Not since Belinda, but he didn't want to think about her. Jude had lied when he told his brothers he wouldn't accept a female who didn't like spankings. His interests in the BDSM world went only as far as his rope work, but if a woman wanted a little pain, he would dole it out if it were mild. He wasn't a pain master like Kyllian. He wasn't a Dom like Hawk. Jude didn't require true submission, only someone who wanted to be tied up in pretty knots.

Finding a mate in one of the clubs he frequented hadn't happened in the fifteen years he'd been doing demos and playing. Jude had gone out with a couple of Dommes over the years, but he quickly learned he wasn't the submissive type. Plenty of women who were members of Dominion tried to catch his eye, but why give in when he knew he couldn't give them what they wanted or needed? Maybe a mate wasn't in the cards for him.

She's out there.

Maybe. Maybe not.

Well, I'm not fucking giving up.

Jude sighed as he turned out the light and crawled under the covers. *He* wasn't giving up either, although some days he felt like it.

Being around his mother always refreshed Jude. She carried on with her life, not forgetting her husband and daughter, but remembering the good times. Indigo bore none of the guilt Jude did because she hadn't seen either one die. She tried to convince him he shouldn't feel guilty that he hadn't been quick enough to save his sister. It wasn't his fault the man who pulled the trigger had done so. It wasn't his fault Michelle had chosen that day to visit her best friend. Nor was it his fault the gods saw fit to allow it to happen. Jude didn't think Zeus himself ever stepped in to help his children. There seemed to be some predestined plan for each being; whether they be shifter or human, and good or bad, everyone died at some point. One day, Jude would be among those who were no longer of this world. It could be tomorrow or years from now. He could die honorably as his father had, defending a human as he'd been put on Earth to do. Or he could be gunned down by someone who had momentarily lost that part of themselves that knew right from wrong as his sister had. Or maybe Parker just hadn't cared. Jude had come close to visiting the male in prison and asking him why. What made a man so rageful he would attempt to take the life of the woman he supposedly loved?

It had been Hawk who talked him out of going to the prison. Hawk knew Jude's beast would want to shred Greg Parker with claw and fang. No matter what answers the man gave, Michelle would still be gone. Jude had been present when a younger War went after his mate's attacker. The male who took Harlow from War suffered greatly, but in the end, it didn't bring her back, just as speaking to Parker wouldn't bring Michelle back. The best Jude could do was follow his mother's example and remember the good times. If he could only get past the sound of a pistol being fired at close range.

Ryker called Jude to check in with him during his stay at Indigo's. He didn't push, but Ryker did urge Jude to come back for a group ride. Jude loved group rides, especially those that included mates and kids. Sure, they might remind him of what he didn't have, but he wasn't one to shy away from get-togethers for that reason. Any time he could spend with Major and Marshall, Jude took it. He kissed his mom and thanked her as he always did before walking out of her home. He had been blessed with excellent parents, and he would strive to be half as good to his own children. By the time he rolled up to Ryker's house, the others were loading up.

"Hey, Spiderman!" Major called from inside his and Marshall's sidecar. Marshall gave Jude a wave. The twins were bundled up and strapped in.

"Hey, Little Dudes."

Hawk strolled up and held his fist out. "Hey, Spyder. You good?"

Spyder bumped his friend's knuckles. "Yeah. Just needed a little mom time."

Hawk was one of Spyder's best friends. He knew about Michelle. Had been around when she was killed. He had stuck like glue to Jude in the weeks after, making sure Jude didn't do something stupid. Hawk was also a fan of Indigo. Like Rory, Jude's mom took on the role for those whose mothers weren't around.

"I hear she might be moving closer." Hawk straddled his bike and put his helmet on.

"That's the plan. She found a smaller house not far from Rory and Sutton."

"Let her know I'll be more than happy to help lug furniture."

"I'll do it. She'll appreciate it."

"Hounds, let's ride," Ryker called out once everyone was ready.

Family rides were different from when they were in club formation. They still took to back roads, but there were more stops so the little ones could pee and grab a snack. All the kids who accompanied them were good about not complaining, but they could only hold it for so long. Their destination was a state park where they could stretch their legs and enjoy a packed lunch before heading back home. While the adults sat around talking and enjoying the sunshine, the kids ran around playing tag or just chasing one another.

Spyder sat with Kayos and Hawk as they usually did since they were the single males of the group. "I saw the guest list for Intro Night at Dominion. It's going to be a full house," Spyder said.

Hawk swatted at Major when he ran past them, and the little boy jumped out of the way, then did a butt wiggle, laughing. When he ran off after his brother, Hawk leaned his forearms on his thighs. "Silas asked me to be a Dungeon Master. He also asked me to keep my eye on Master R. Silas did a background check and everything was aboveboard, but he feels there's something off about the male."

Silas Cain owned Dominion as well as Transcendent, a gay BDSM club where he and his mate preferred to hang out. Spyder didn't know a lot of gay Gryphons, but he had no problem with them. To Jude, love and attraction were fluid. He had been drawn to males before but never acted on it. He preferred the softness of a female, but he could see the enticement of being with someone who could give as good as they got.

Kayos shifted on the stone bench of the picnic table. "I'll help keep an eye out. I've only met the human once, and that was in passing. Something about him set my Gryphon on edge, but I was getting ready to do a scene, and I was already keyed up."

Whenever Spyder was getting into the right mindset to do his rope work, he meditated beforehand. He had no idea what Kyllian did to get ready to inflict pain, and he'd never asked. It wasn't his business. "I'm doing a demo, but I'll also help watch. The last thing we need on Intro Night is for the human to show his true colors if he isn't who he says he is. Is he a Master with a slave?" In their world, Masters could either be those who were proficient in one or more aspect of the lifestyle, or they could be into the Master/slave kink.

"I didn't see anyone with him, so if he is that type of Master, it's possible he's in search of a slave. If that's the case, he'll be on the prowl." Kyllian stood and twisted at the waist before looking down at Jude. "You want to talk about what happened at the gun range?"

Jude looked around to see who was close enough to listen in. Being shifters, that was everyone. "Not right now."

Kyllian inclined his head and said, "Just know I'm here if you need me." He then started chasing his nephews. Jude closed his eyes and leaned his head back, letting the sounds of his family warm him as much as the sun on his face.

CHAPTER TWO

Charlotte

"THERE HE IS!" Wynter shouted and pointed across Charlotte's face, momentarily blocking her sight. Charlotte pushed her best friend's arm out of the way and corrected the car before she ran over the pedestrians on the sidewalk.

"Jesus H, Wynter. If I wreck, spotting him won't do us any good." Charlotte loved Wynter more than anyone in the world. The two had been best friends since fourth grade when Charlotte transferred to her new school. Tommy Flanders made a smartass comment about Charlotte's wild curls and freckles. Wynter punched him in the nose. They'd had each other's backs ever since.

"Sorry, sorry. You know how I get." Wynter got excited. Then she panicked. Then she got excited again. She had always gone along with whatever hairbrained scheme Charlotte came up with whether she agreed it was a good idea or not. Following this particular man was probably not a good one, but here they were.

"He's in a different car tonight."

"Maybe he traded," Wynter said.

The man in question was Roland Smith. At least that was the name he gave Charlotte's cousin. Elise was older than Charlotte by fifteen years. When Charlotte's mom died, she moved in with her aunt Ellen, Elise's mother. Ellen was a single mom, but she had done well for herself and her daughter, so taking Charlotte in hadn't been a hardship. At least that's what Ellen always told her. Charlotte had always looked up to Elise with a sort of hero worship. Wanted to wear the same clothes. Style her hair the same way. Listen to the same music. Being a wonderful person, Elise indulged Charlotte, and Charlotte's love and devotion only grew over the years, even after Elise moved out on her own.

That devotion had Charlotte and Wynter following Roland. She had never met the man who was trying to get Elise to move away with him, only saw him from her car as she watched him leave Elise's. Elise told Charlotte all about the new man in her life over the phone. While her words were kind and hopeful, something in her tone sounded off. Elise had a string of bad luck when it came to men, so it was no wonder she was leery that he was too good to be true. Elise had changed over the years, going from wild, party girl to devout churchgoer, where she met this man.

In her quest to make sure Elise didn't fall for another loser, Charlotte had set about following the man, which was easier said than done. He rarely left Elise's house until early hours when there was little traffic, and following him was all but impossible. Charlotte and Wynter were on their way home when they noticed Roland walking out of a bar in New Latham. They lost track of him while turning around, but they finally had Roland in their sights. Now if

Charlotte could go after him without Wynter causing a wreck, things would be stellar.

It was easier to follow Roland when he turned onto Highway 9. Charlotte had little experience in tailing someone, but she'd watched enough movies to know you had to be stealthy. If Roland had nothing to hide, he wouldn't expect someone to follow him, but if he did, then he would be paranoid and spot Wynter's car if they were too close. Roland took the exit into New Albany. Since he told Elise he lived in the opposite direction, he had either lied or he was going somewhere else for the night.

Charlotte drove past the parking lot Roland pulled into. She circled the block and parked on the opposite side of the street. The parking served a nondescript, three-story brick structure and was full of high-dollar vehicles sprinkled with a few mid-priced sedans. There wasn't a junker anywhere to be found. No sign outside indicated what was going on inside.

"Whatever this place is, they aren't advertising," Charlotte muttered. Roland had already disappeared by the time they parked, but Charlotte waited. The few people they saw going in were dressed as though they were going to a business meeting, but who the hell had meetings this time of night? "I'm going to get a closer look." Charlotte reached for the door handle, but Wynter grabbed her arm.

"I don't think that's a good idea." Wynter was ever the cautious one. "What if you get caught?"

"I'll just tell them I was looking for somewhere with a bathroom. I'll do a pee-pee dance and bat my eyelashes. You know – the usual."

Wynter rolled her eyes but released her grip. "Be

careful."

With no traffic, Charlotte made it across the street and back in less than a minute. When she slid into the driver's seat, she grabbed her phone out of the cup holder. "There is a small placket with the word Dominion carved into it." Charlotte input the word and street name into the search engine. "Holy shit. It's a BDSM club." She turned the phone around to show Wynter. "I don't see this being the type of place a Godly man would frequent. We need to get in there."

Wynter grabbed the phone. "Says here it's members only." Wynter scrolled through the website with Charlotte looking over the console at her phone.

"Wait, go back up." Charlotte pointed. "There. Looks like we're going to get kinky." She wiggled her eyebrows, and Wynter groaned.

THIS WAS THE best idea ever or the worst one Charlotte ever had.

This was the two of them standing outside Dominion on one of the two nights a year it was open to the public. The owners didn't let just anyone in. According to the website, this night was for women who were curious about the lifestyle to visit in a safe environment. They had gotten lucky when the soonest Intro Night fell on Wednesday the following week. It had taken that long to convince Wynter it was the only way for Charlotte to get close to Roland.

This time Charlotte parked in the attached lot instead of across the street. Theirs wasn't the only vehicle which cost less than fifty grand. They climbed out of the Honda and made their way to the door where a sharp-dressed man waited.

"This is the worst idea you've ever had." Wynter tugged at the short, spandex skirt barely covering her ass, then pulled her winter coat tighter.

"Probably."

Wynter reached under the coat and tugged again, and Charlotte slapped at her best friend's hands. "Why'd you dress like a hooker? Stop pulling at your skirt. You're drawing more attention to it."

Wynter crossed her arms over her ample chest. "I can't believe I let you talk me into this."

Charlotte reapplied her lipstick as they headed across the parking lot. While Wynter chose bright red, Charlotte opted for a subtle pink even though they were going to a club. "I told you I'd come by myself."

Wynter huffed. "As if." She uncrossed her arms, and when she started to tug the tight fabric, Charlotte gave her the evil eye. Wynter stuck her tongue out like a five-year-old, but she left her skirt alone.

Charlotte grabbed Wynter's arm, stopping them a few feet away from the door. "If you want to go home, I'll be fine. You can take the car, and I'll grab a ride later." Charlotte pushed her strawberry-blonde curls away from her face. She didn't want to go in by herself, but she wouldn't dare tell Wynter that.

"It's fine. Let's get this over with." Wynter jutted her chin and marched to the door. Charlotte grinned at her friend's back. Wynter liked to complain about all the things Charlotte conned her into, but at the end of the evening, she would also gush about how much fun she had.

Together, they had read over every piece of information about the club and what they could expect. To be considered, they had filled out a form, paid a not-so-small fee, and received a code when they were accepted. Once inside, they showed their codes and received an armband indicating their intentions. Red indicated they were there to watch. Yellow meant they were open to the possibility of doing a scene, but if they chose green, any of the Masters could call upon them at any time.

Wynter fell adamantly in the red column. Charlotte decided on yellow. She wanted to keep her options open in case Roland happened to be there. Not that she wanted anything to do with him, but she figured getting close to him was the best way to find out if Elise was going to get her heart broken.

A stunning redhead in all leather greeted them. "Welcome to Dominion. I'm Mistress K. Please follow me." Mistress K led them to a table where they were given a list of rules. These same rules had been on the website, but they had to sign an agreement after reading them over. "The first floor is where you'll see the demonstrations. The second floor is reserved for private rooms. Unless you agree to do a private scene, you will want to remain downstairs. Should you agree to a private demo, please know those rooms are monitored as well. We take our clients' safety seriously. Do you have any questions?"

"Do we need a safe word?" Wynter asked.

Mistress K didn't scoff or make fun of Wynter. Her smile exuded understanding. "No. Those are reserved for anyone with yellow or green bands like your friend. Charlotte, with a yellow band, you can say yes to any of the Masters who approach. You can also say no. If you say no, there will be no further discussion. All the Masters have also signed their own agreements to abide by the rules of our club. Safe, sane, and consensual aren't merely words; they are imperative for Dominion to be successful. If anyone were to approach you and not abide by your wishes, please find one of the Masters wearing a blue armband, and they will take care of the situation." Charlotte looked around the room where several men and women wore the blue arm bands.

"Also, with a yellow band, you may not drink alcohol. We can't afford for your judgment to become impaired. Your admittance fee includes all-you-can-drink soda or juice. If you have no more questions, feel free to walk around. Enjoy your evening, ladies." Mistress K gathered their signed waivers and strode to the door to welcome the next patrons. Women filled the other booths and tables signing their own agreements.

"Do you see him?" Wynter asked.

"No, but the time we followed him, he came in later. Come on. Let's look around." Charlotte stood and pulled Wynter to her feet. Groups were already gathering for the various demos being held. Before she began looking into Dominion, Charlotte had never considered going to a BDSM club. She liked sex as much as the next woman but had never had so much as a spanking. Reading about the lifestyle in her romance novels was as close as she got. Charlotte had researched a little about what she might see during

Intro Night, and she had been intrigued by all of it. Wynter had looked over her shoulder at the computer, going on and on about how she would never be into any of it, yet she would tell Charlotte to scroll back so she could get a better look at something. Wynter wasn't anymore a virgin than Charlotte, but her smoking-hot friend loved playing the prude.

Charlotte stopped at the flogging demo where a man in leather pants was strapping a woman to a St. Andrew's cross when Wynter grabbed her arm and muttered, "Sweet baby Jesus." Charlotte turned to see what had Wynter intrigued, and Charlotte had to admit the man her friend was ogling deserved the sentiment. He, too, wore only leather, but his long hair and tattoos were eye-catching. Flogging forgotten, Charlotte crossed the room and joined the crowd for a Shibari demonstration. The blue armband indicated the man was a Master.

"He can Master me all he wants," Charlotte whispered. Like he had supersonic hearing, the man glanced at Charlotte and smirked. Her panties may have gotten soaked with just a look. He returned his attention to the woman he was going to bind, and in that moment, Charlotte would have given anything to be in her place. Well, maybe not. The woman wore only a black thong. Her breasts, as well as the rest of her, were on display for all the club to see.

"For those of you visiting tonight, I am Master J, the resident Shibari expert. For my demonstration, Mistress M will be assisting." His voice was smooth as he explained the history of the art along with the safety measures both top and bottom – top, the one doing the rope work, and bottom, the one being bound – ensured through communication. "It is necessary for the top to be familiar with human anatomy lest they endanger their bottom. I will demonstrate a simple chest harness combined with handcuffs."

Master J grabbed a long length of what he had already explained was hemp. Charlotte was mesmerized as the man deftly wound the rope around his assistant. As he moved front to back, he checked in with Mistress M, assuring the bonds weren't too tight and she was okay. The longer he worked, the more serene Mistress M's face became, as though she were relaxing from a good massage.

"There are two types of bondage – Shibari and Kinbaku. While they are similar in looks, Shibari is more of an art form, whereas Kinbaku is less sensual, and the bindings are tighter. Some bottoms prefer the more intimate bondage, like being held in a lover's embrace, while others prefer a little more pain. It is up to the top and bottom to discuss beforehand the bottom's intentions. Safety is the top's first priority."

Charlotte's eyes tracked the man's deft fingers as he wound the hemp across Mistress M's body, checking the tightness of the rope. Charlotte's eyes may have dropped to his leather-encased ass more than once. As with the craft, his body was a work of art. His muscles bunched and released beneath his ink-covered skin. The moans from a woman being flogged behind Charlotte weren't distracting enough to have her turn her gaze from the scene in front of her. Charlotte had all but forgotten why she was in the club in the first place until a presence at her back was too close for comfort.

"Do you like what you see?" a man's voice

whispered against her ear. She didn't have to turn to know who had asked the question because Wynter's eyes were wide and not in the holy-shit-that-man-is-fine way.

Charlotte ignored Roland, keeping her focus on Master J, but Roland wasn't having it. He placed his hand on her hip, tugging her back against him. She tried to squirm out of his grip, not wanting to interrupt the demonstration or call attention to them, but Roland's fingers on her waist tightened. Charlotte's plan had been to get close to Roland, not push him away, but she trusted her gut, and it told her to get as far away from the man as possible.

"Red," Charlotte uttered the safe word loud enough for Roland and those standing close by to hear. Master J's eyes snapped her direction, then narrowed at Roland before looking across the room and inclining his head to someone.

Roland released her hip, but before he moved from behind her, he whispered, "Later."

Charlotte shivered, and Wynter grabbed her hand. Master J stared at Charlotte, his eyebrows raised. She nodded, letting him know she was okay, even though she wasn't.

Wynter tugged at her hand. "We need to get out of here," she whispered.

Charlotte shook her head. If they left then, Roland would probably corner them. Had he known she had been following him? Or was it a coincidence he chose her to focus his attention on? Either way, Charlotte didn't want to risk moving through the club without getting one of the Masters' attention. She remained where she stood, trying to enjoy the rest of the demonstration. When it was over, those around her didn't clap, but they murmured their appreciation.

"Can we go now?" Wynter asked at the same time a man walked up to them. According to the blue arm band, he was also a Master. The brunet oozed testosterone, but his face was soft.

"Are you okay? Did Master R hurt you?"

Charlotte gasped. "Master R? He's one of you?"

"If you're asking if he's a Master, then yes. Did he hurt you?" the man asked again.

"Master K, is everything all right?" Master J asked. Charlotte had been so stunned to learn Roland was more than merely a patron she hadn't noticed the Shibari demonstrator approaching. He was quite a bit shorter than Master K, but he was still a few inches taller than Charlotte's five-six.

"That's what I'm trying to figure out. Miss...?"

"Charlie..." Wynter elbowed Charlotte when she didn't respond. Charlotte scowled at her best friend for using her childhood nickname, and Wynter rolled her eyes. "Sorry, *Charlotte*. He's asking you if you're okay."

"Fine. I, uh, I'm fine. He didn't hurt me. I was just surprised is all." Charlotte was a terrible liar, and by the way Master J's eyes narrowed at her, he knew it.

"I need to get ready for my demonstration," Master K said to Master J.

"Go ahead. I've got this." Master J waved him off and stepped closer to Charlotte. "Why don't you two ladies have a seat, and I'll get you both some water?"

Still holding hands, Charlotte agreed and pulled Wynter along as they followed the man to a booth. Once they were seated, he told them he'd be right back. Charlotte tracked his ass as he strode to the bar.

26

"Why haven't you called dibs?" Wynter asked.

Charlotte slumped a little in the booth and blew out a breath. "Because you have eyes. That man is so far out of my league we're not even in the same ocean. You, on the other hand, will probably star in his jerk-off session tonight."

Wynter crossed her arms over her chest and scowled. "Just because I'm a little curvier than you doesn't mean anything. When are you going to get it through those thick curls of yours that you are gorgeous?" It was an argument they'd had ever since Wynter had blossomed during puberty. Wynter was everyone's fantasy girl, while Charlotte was cute. It was one reason she acted outrageously early on. It was her way to get attention when all eyes were on her best friend. Over the years, she got used to being looked over in favor of Wynter, but that didn't stop her love of shenanigans.

Master J returned with two bottles of water. "May I join you?"

Both scooted over, but the man chose to sit by Charlotte. He passed out the water, then turned sideways so he had both their attention. "I apologize for Master R. He's new to the club, but rest assured, he will be disciplined."

Wynter paused with the water bottle at her lips. "You mean like whipped?"

"No, like put on probation. We take the safety of our members and guests seriously. May I ask what caused you to use your safe word?" Master J asked Charlotte.

"I overreacted, really. He asked if I liked what I saw, meaning the demonstration. I ignored him, but he

27

put his hand on my hip and pulled me back against his chest. I tried to move, but he tightened his grip."

"It's not overreacting if you were uncomfortable."

"Even though I have on a yellow band?" Charlotte didn't want to cause trouble. She had followed Roland only to see what kind of man he was, not get on his radar.

"Even if you were wearing a green one. No one has the right to lay hands on you without your permission. If I may ask, what brought you here tonight?"

Charlotte and Wynter stared at one another, then Wynter gestured for Charlotte to explain. She looked into fierce blue eyes, and for once in her life, she was stricken speechless. That is until he spoke again.

"Tell me the truth."

Charlotte shivered at the command.

CHAPTER THREE

Spyder

JUDE STERLING WAS smitten. As soon as he'd spotted Charlotte in the crowd, it was all he could do to remember he was giving a demonstration. Mistress M was an experienced rope bottom, but it was still his responsibility to ensure she was safe and comfortable. It wasn't that Charlotte was drop-dead gorgeous, unlike her friend. But the female exuded confidence amid her strawberry-blonde curls and the freckles dotting her cheeks. Before he could forget himself again, Jude had to get to the bottom of the Roger incident. He hadn't intended to use his Gryphon voice on the females, but the way they snapped their gazes at one another when he asked their reason for being at Dominion indicated they were hiding something.

"Tell me the truth."

Charlotte's brow furrowed upon feeling the compulsion. "That man, uh, Master R, I've been following him for months. He is dating my cousin, and I'm trying to figure out why. Not why he's dating her, per se, but what he wants from her. Elise has had a bad run with men, and I don't want her to get her heart broken again."

"And you don't feel as though Master R is a good man?" Spyder got the same sense about the male, but Dominion wasn't his club; therefore, it wasn't his place to investigate the man before allowing him to work there.

"There's something off about him. He lets on like he's this good, pious man, and now I find him here."

That kind of thinking irked Jude. "And you think those of us who live the lifestyle aren't good?" Spyder thought of himself and the other Hounds who liked a little bit of kink in their lives as good males.

"I didn't say that. The way Elise described him to me was as though he was more of a holy roller. Aunt Ellen raised us in church, and I know there are all kinds who are looking for *something* sitting on a pew, but I also know there are those who only go to make themselves look like something they're not. Like her last boyfriend. Fred was a deacon in the church, yet he slapped Elise around whenever she questioned him."

Spyder bristled. It was never okay to strike a woman, even if she struck first. Women could be just as violent, but for the most part, they were weaker by nature. Weaker physically. Mentally, the females Jude knew were stronger than most of the Hounds put together.

"How did your cousin meet Master R?"

"Elise had seen him at church, but never spoke to him. She and Fred had just finished lunch after church one Sunday. When they were walking to the car, Elise asked Fred to stop by the mall so she could pick up some makeup. He had told her more than once not to wear it, and he got upset. Roland – Master R – stepped in and admonished Fred for yelling at her. According to Elise, the two men almost came to blows, but another family from church came from the restaurant, and Fred flipped his switch from pissed off to pillar of the community. He apologized to Elise, but she said Roland seemed like the safer option in that moment. She allowed him to drive her home, and he's been calling on her ever since."

"Are you sure you heard your cousin correctly? Because Master R's name is Roger."

"Pretty damn sure. Those two don't sound alike."

"Okay, it's possible Roger gave us the wrong name. What about him gave you pause?" Nothing Spyder heard so far indicated Roger was a bad male.

"He keeps trying to get Elise to move to wherever he lives. He says it's a wonderful community of like-minded people, living Godly lives. On the surface, it sounds okay, but he's asking Elise to move away from the town she grew up in. Sell the house, give up her job as a nurse, and blindly follow him to parts unknown."

Spyder's shifter sat up taller at the mention of the community. It sounded as though Roger lived in a compound. Whether they were Ministry – the cult the Hounds were trying to shut down – or just one of the ones where people gathered with their own kind, was yet to be determined. Either way, Charlotte had been right to question why a man who lived in that type of community also became a Master in a BDSM club.

Loud voices caught Spyder's attention before those responsible were visible. His shifter hearing picked up on the righteous indignation coming from Roger.

"I know the rules. She was wearing a yellow band indicating she was curious. All I did was ask her a question. That's the problem with this public night.

31

Those who think they want to take a walk on the wild side come in here, see what it's really about, then get their panties in a twist."

"And those who figure out the lifestyle isn't for them don't come back." Silas, the owner, was the most even-keeled male Spyder knew. He was the definition of Zen. "But this night also allows people to sate their curiosity in a safe environment. I'm not saying you did anything wrong, but the young lady didn't feel comfortable. I am pleased she remembered to use a safe word. That means she kept her wits about her instead of allowing the moment to proceed farther than she wanted. Maybe you startled her. Maybe she should have chosen a red band instead of yellow. Regardless, no means no. As a Master, you know this. You have been exemplary up until now. Take the rest of the night off to think about how you could have handled the situation better."

Roger stormed out of Silas's office, and as he strode through the club, his eyes scanned the room until they lit on Charlotte. Spyder slid from the booth and stood with his arms crossed, daring the human to confront the female. Charlotte's friend squeaked. The sound would have been endearing if it weren't for the fear wafting off her. Roger sneered at Charlotte, but he kept walking toward the exit. The male hadn't bothered changing into his street clothes. When he was gone, Spyder returned to his seat.

"Is this going to be a problem for your cousin?" he asked.

"Not unless I tell Elise. Roland has never met me. I have my own apartment, and Roland only visits Elise on Thursdays."

"Are you going to tell her?" Spyder knew what it was like having someone you wanted to protect.

"I will tell her I followed him here, but I won't tell her what happened tonight. She'll freak if she knows I came inside." Charlotte pushed her luscious curls away from her face, and Spyder studied her. Charlotte wasn't as stunning as her friend, but she was gorgeous in her own way. Freckles dotted her pale skin, even though she tried to cover them with makeup. Her eyes were a sea green that sparkled with mischievousness.

"Was following Roger the only reason you came to the club tonight?"

"Yes, but I'm glad I did. That Shibari demonstration has me intrigued," she admitted, and her friend squeaked again.

"Did you see anything else that might intrigue you?"

"We didn't get any farther. When we saw you, we... uh..." Charlotte's cheeks blushed, and she bit her lip.

"Would you like to look around? See what other demonstrations might be of interest?"

"Yes, I would." Charlotte turned to Wynter who was trying to tell her friend something with her eyes. It was clear the other female wasn't comfortable in the club, but Jude wanted more time with his strawberry-blonde. There was something about her that called to him, and he wanted to find out what it was.

Jude stood and extended his hand. Charlotte took it and slid out of the booth. Wynter wasn't as quick to rise, but she did, grabbing Charlotte's other hand in the process. Spyder led the females around the club, stopping at each demonstration to gauge Charlotte's reaction. After observing several scenes, Spyder knew what did and didn't turn her on, and the thought of getting to spank her pert ass had his dick hard. He also realized their hands were still entwined, and he liked it.

"So, what do you think? Is this something you might be interested in?" he asked, mentally holding his breath for her answer.

"The Shibari looks like something I would enjoy, but not if I have to get naked in front of everyone. The stimulation play appeals more than pain. And I'd rather not be gagged. I know I talk a lot, but I can be convinced to stay quiet without having balls shoved in my mouth."

Wynter barked out a laugh, and Charlotte rolled her eyes. "You know what I mean."

Spyder squeezed her hand. "Yes, I do. I tell you what. If you're really interested, how about you and I meet for dinner one night and discuss this further. I can talk to you about what it means to be a member with and without a sponsor."

"I'd like that. I guess you need my number so we can make plans."

"That I do. If you don't mind waiting for me to change, I'll grab my phone and walk you two to your car."

"I'll wait." Charlotte's smile lit up the dim room. Wynter smirked at her friend for some reason.

Spyder led the females to the same booth they'd sat in earlier. "I'll be right back." He was glad he'd only had the one demo that night, or he wouldn't have been able to spend time with Charlotte. The female intrigued Jude, and he couldn't wait to take her to dinner. He prayed to Zeus she wasn't bullshitting with her interest in the lifestyle the same way the waitress over in New Roseville had been. When Spyder hit the locker room, both Kayos and Hawk were there changing out of their leather into their street clothes.

"Hey, Brother. How's your female?" Hawk asked.

"She isn't mine."

Yet.

You calm your tits. Spyder chastised his beast, but he'd had the same thought.

"But she's fine. Actually, there's a story about Master R I think you'll both be interested in. How about we meet at the clubhouse tomorrow, and I'll fill you in."

"Sounds good. Make it noon, and we'll order pizza," Kayos said.

"What about her friend?" Hawk asked. "She looked like she was one swing of the paddle away from passing out."

"I don't know much about either of them, but if I had to guess, I would say Charlotte is the adventurous one, and Wynter just goes along for the ride."

"I'd like to give her a ride," Hawk muttered. Spyder and Kayos laughed at their fellow Hound.

"I can always put in a good word for you," Spyder offered.

"If she's as vanilla as she seems, it would never work." Hawk's shoulders slumped as he tugged his tee over his head.

"Maybe she's just shy in public. You never know until you try. I'm taking Charlotte to dinner soon. I'll inquire as to Wynter's true nature."

"I'd appreciate it. There's just something about

35

those big doe eyes."

Spyder could understand that. He had been entranced by the same type of look more than once, but it wasn't what he wanted or needed out of a mate. He needed someone adventurous. Someone who wanted to be bound. He claimed to be all about spankings, but truth be told, he didn't need that in his life. He wanted someone to give over control while he wrapped them in pretty knots. Jude could already envision Charlotte wearing his ropes.

"They're waiting on me to walk them out. Why don't you come with me, and I'll introduce you to Wynter?"

"Yeah, okay." Hawk stood a little straighter, and the corner of his mouth tilted up. Roman "Hawk" Hayes was handsome when he wasn't smiling, but when he was? Spyder was secure enough in his malehood to admit just how striking Hawk was when the male showed his dimples and straight, white teeth. At six-three, Hawk towered over Spyder, but that didn't bother him. Spyder's attitude made up for his lack of height. After changing into his jeans, white tee, and shit-kickers, Spyder led Hawk to where the females were waiting.

"Ladies, I'd like to introduce you to Roman Hayes. Rome, this is Charlotte and Wynter."

"It's a pleasure." Hawk shook Charlotte's hand, but he kissed Wynter's knuckles. In all his years, Spyder had never actually seen a female swoon until that moment. For a few seconds, he was afraid Wynter was going to faint.

"Let's go get your things, then we'll walk you to your car." Spyder held out his hand for Charlotte, and she smiled as she grabbed hold. When they reached the front of the club, Justin retrieved the ladies' purses without asking their names. The male excelled at his job. Justin was Silas's partner in more than one sense of the word. Their other club, Transcendent, catered strictly to gay men, and that's usually where the couple hung out. On the two nights of the year Dominion opened to nonmembers, the couple was on hand, just in case.

"Here you are ladies. I hope you enjoyed your evening and Master R didn't ruin it for you. To make it up to you both, here is a complimentary pass to return whenever you like. Just give us a call beforehand, and we'll be sure to have armbands waiting. We'll also assure Master R isn't in attendance that evening."

"Wow, that's so kind." Charlotte took the passes and placed them in her purse. "Thank you."

Hawk held open the door, and once the four of them were on the sidewalk, Charlotte pulled out her phone. "If you'll give me your number, I'll send you a text so you have mine."

Spyder rattled off his digits, and Charlotte paused. "Shall I list you under Master J, or can I have your name?"

"Jude Sterling, at your service." Jude bowed deeply, and Charlotte smiled, making her seafoam eyes crinkle at the corners. She was just too cute. Charlotte finished adding his name to her contacts and sent him a text. His phone vibrated in his back pocket, but he didn't pull it out to check it. He would rather stare at the female. Hawk must have sensed that Jude wasn't quite ready to part ways, so he offered his arm to Wynter, and when she hooked hers around it, the two took off toward the parking lot, leaving Spyder and Charlotte alone.

"Do you live here in Albany?" Spyder had been known to drop the "New" from city names over the years.

"No, I live in New Latham. What about you?"

"I live in Troy, so not far at all. How does Wednesday work for you?" Spyder didn't want to seem too eager, but he also didn't want to wait that long to see Charlotte again.

"Wednesday's great. Can I ask where we're going so I'll know how to dress?"

Spyder pulled on one of her curls. "Where do you want to go? Since I don't know anything about you, I don't know what you like. I'm good with dressing up and going to Jacques' or dressing down and hitting a pub."

"You can get into Jacques' that quickly?" Charlotte's eyes danced along Jude's body, more than likely weighing his clothes against how someone who frequented the upscale restaurant would dress.

"Yes. I know the owner. He's an old friend of the family."

"Must be nice to have connections." Charlotte winked at him.

Jude grinned at the playful female. "It is. So, Jacques', and I'll pick you up at six?"

"I'll be ready." Charlotte looked toward the parking lot, and Jude took that as his cue to start walking. He grabbed Charlotte's hand, threading their fingers. It had been years since he felt so at ease with someone so quickly. When they reached the vehicle where Hawk and Wynter were waiting, Charlotte pulled the keys from her purse, and after hitting the unlock button on the fob, Jude opened the door for her. The pull to kiss her was strong, but he refrained. Charlotte leaned in and pressed her lips to his cheek. "Thank you." She slid into the driver's seat at the same time Wynter got into the passenger seat. Hawk closed Wynter's door and walked to the front of the car. They waited until the women were safely on their way before they took off toward the building.

"We need to find out more about Roger. If that's even his name." Jude didn't doubt Silas had checked the male's references, but Jude didn't want Charlotte chasing after the man if he was dangerous.

"Gonna call Lucy?" Hawk waved his keycard over the security panel, then held the door open for Jude.

"Not yet. I'm going to talk to Silas first. Get the man's information and do some checking myself. Lucy's still in New Atlanta. I don't want to take her away from what she's working on. It's too important."

"Truth. After we get the man's address, we can do some old-fashioned legwork."

That was the good thing about having someone like Hawk as a best friend. Jude didn't need to ask for help. It was the way with all the Hounds. They were family first. They strolled through the club toward Silas's office, but the male in question stood at the bar with his partner. When Jude and Hawk approached, Silas kissed Justin, then tilted his head, indicating they should follow.

Once inside his office, Silas ran a hand through his hair, sighing. "You both know I vet anyone who joins either of my clubs."

Jude didn't blame Silas for Roger's behavior. "Of

course, but sometimes people are good at hiding things. It's possible that's the case here. Or maybe he saw the yellow band and assumed Charlotte was closer to green than red."

"Maybe." Silas sat down behind his desk and tapped at the keys on his laptop. After a couple minutes, the printer whirred, producing a single sheet of paper. "Here. I know you have your own means of getting information, but this will be faster. This is all I have on Roger."

Jude took the paper and read over the meager information. Silas wasn't part of the MC, but he was a Gryphon. He and Justin weren't aware of the mercenary work the MC did, but he trusted them with security at both clubs.

"Thanks. We'll get started on this tonight. If he isn't who he claims to be, we'll figure it out."

"I know you will. I put him on two weeks' suspension. That should be enough time to gather the truth." Silas rose from his chair. "Let me know as soon as you find something."

"We will." Jude and Hawk shook hands with the male before heading outside to their bikes. As they walked, Jude handed the paper to Hawk. "Not a lot of information to go on, but I say we start with his home address."

Hawk pulled out his phone and entered the address in a search engine. After tapping the screen a few times, he handed it over. "There's a big box store half a mile away. We can park there and walk in so he doesn't hear the bikes."

"Sounds like a plan."

It had been a solid plan until they arrived on foot

to the neighborhood Roger claimed to live in. The houses were cookie-cutter, each one designed almost identically. The only differences were the colors. The address Roger gave Silas was on a cul-de-sac, and the driveway contained two cars, one a mini-van. The front yard, like those around it, was neatly manicured, but the backyard contained a trampoline, a swing set, and a couple smaller bicycles. For someone who claimed to be single, the evidence said otherwise, unless he had kids with an ex who stayed with him often.

"I'm going to shift and see if I can get a look in the windows." Jude stepped into the shadows of the tall trees toward the back of the yard, removed his clothes, and shifted to his Eagle. Hawk remained in his hiding spot, keeping his senses open to anyone else in the area.

Jude took to his wings and settled on a branch closest to the house. Luckily, the blinds weren't closed, and he could peek into the bedrooms on the back side of the house. A couple slept in one bed, and a young boy in another. Jude launched himself into the air, circling the house. A girl, younger than her brother, was asleep in the front bedroom. Seeing all he needed to, he returned to where Hawk waited.

"There's a couple inside with two kids. It appears Roger Smith isn't happy in his marriage. That, or he's just a cheating bastard." Jude put his clothes on and regathered his hair in a ponytail. "Ten bucks says Smith isn't his last name and the male has a lot more to hide than his sexual proclivities from his wife."

"What now?" Hawk asked.

"Now we call Lucy."

41

CHAPTER FOUR

Charlotte

CHARLOTTE PRACTICALLY BOUNCED in the driver's seat. "I have a date," she muttered for the umpteenth time, while Wynter sang along to the radio. Jude Sterling, a.k.a. Master J, was so far out of her league she still couldn't believe it, but unless he stood her up Wednesday, she had a freaking date! Charlotte's shop was gearing up for Valentine's Day as well as several weddings, but she had two employees who could handle everything if she left early one time. The Blooming Boutique, or BBs as she lovingly called it, was Charlotte's pride and joy. She got her love of flowers, plants, and vegetables from Ellen, helping her aunt in the gardens in the backyard. Their mutual appreciation for growing things brought them closer over the years, especially once Elise moved out on her own.

When Charlotte told Wynter her plan to open a floral shop, Wynter was all for it. Wynter had dreamed of weddings ever since she was five and never strayed from her own plans of becoming a wedding planner. Her customers weren't required to use BBs, but once

42

Wynter showed them photos of past weddings Charlotte had supplied the flowers for, they rarely chose anyone else. No matter the bride's budget, Charlotte could make the least expensive flowers look like something out of a fantasy. Their dreams meshed in a way which was beneficial to them both.

Charlotte parked in Wynter's driveway, still flying high from both her encounter with Roland and from meeting Jude.

"Earth to Charlie." Wynter snapped her fingers in front of Charlotte's face. "Boy, he did a number on you. I'm surprised we made it home in one piece."

Charlotte mock glared at her best friend. "You know I can drive and daydream at the same time." She let herself out of the car, tossing Wynter her keys as they both rounded the hood.

"You want to spend the night?"

Charlotte often stayed over when they were out late, but she wanted to go home where she could revisit her encounter with Jude in private. "Not tonight. I'll see you tomorrow with the Mortons at one." Charlotte hugged Wynter tight. "Thanks for going to the club with me."

"Of course. Try to get some sleep tonight instead of lying awake thinking of Mr. Long Hair."

Charlotte laughed at her crazy friend. "I won't make any promises." Charlotte climbed into her Camaro as Wynter made her way inside the cute house she inherited from her grandmother. Charlotte made the quick drive home to her apartment, which was only a couple miles away. Ellen had left their home to both Elise and Charlotte, but once Elise's life had turned upside down and she began going to church

43

religiously, Charlotte needed space from her cousin. Instead of spending her inheritance from her mom on a house, Charlotte used the money to open her shop. She didn't need a house to be happy; her flowers did that.

Knowing a large beast waited just inside her door to trip her up, Charlotte entered her ground-floor apartment slowly. When she wasn't met with resistance, she closed the door and locked it. "Gibby?" Her twenty-pound Maine Coon was relentless about being the first thing she gave attention to. "Baby boy? Where are you?" Charlotte dropped her purse and keys on the sofa, then got on her hands and knees to search underneath. He was too large to fit comfortably, but he had hidden there once during a violent storm. "Gibby? Here, kitty."

Charlotte then searched every inch of her two-bedroom home until she finally found the cat in her walk-in closet. As soon as she opened the door, he darted out, only going a few feet until he turned and gave her what-for. "There you are." Charlotte dropped to her knees, and Gibby reluctantly came to her. "How the hell did you get locked in the closet?" When she left to meet Wynter, Gibby had barricaded the front door until she picked him up and hugged him tight. It was a game he played whenever she left him alone.

Charlotte looked over her shoulder at the closet. It didn't matter if the door wasn't closed all the way; it opened out, and there was no way the cat could pull it to. Gibby didn't seem to be harmed, only mildly miffed. "You're okay." She stroked his thick, satiny fur, and Gibby's chest rumbled as he began purring. Knowing her beloved pet was okay, Charlotte stood and walked through the apartment checking the doors and windows, but everything was locked up tight. Doing her best to put it out of her mind, Charlotte went about getting ready for bed. She had an early morning at the shop, and she was ready to drop where she stood. The adrenaline crashed hard, and Charlotte briefly thought about Jude before she fell into a deep sleep.

Five o'clock came way too soon. Charlotte stumbled to the kitchen to start the coffee pot, having forgotten to set it up the night before in her search for Gibby. She showered while the coffee brewed, and when she was dressed, she popped some bread in the toaster. Rarely did Charlotte eat a big breakfast, but she liked to have something on her stomach besides caffeine. As she ate her toast, Charlotte looked around her apartment. She had made it her own little haven with bright pops of color here and there, filling most of the space with plants. She couldn't do anything about the bland, beige walls other than covering them with photos and colorful artwork. When Jude picked her up for their date, Charlotte would be proud for him to see where she lived.

Instead of leaving Gibby alone in the apartment, she took him to work with her. He had his own area in the back where he lounged during the day, but sometimes he roamed the shop and interacted with the customers. Margie and Kristoff, her employees, loved Gibby as much as Charlotte did and enjoyed when she brought him.

Charlotte parked in her assigned spot at the side of the building. Kristoff pulled in right next to her, and when he got out of his car, he peeked into the passenger window. When he noticed Gibby's crate, he cooed as he opened the door. "There's my good boy." Kristoff grabbed the handle and lifted the cat's carrier. Gibby answered with his low *"mrawr."*

"Morning, Boss." Kristoff was only a few years younger than Charlotte's thirty-three, but he still hadn't lost his boyish looks. He had the best attitude of anyone Charlotte knew, and he brightened her day.

"Good morning. Are you ready for—" Charlotte froze when she noticed the door to the shop was cracked open. "What the hell?" Charlotte put her arm across Kristoff so he didn't barrel inside.

"Charlie, call the cops. I closed up last night, and I promise I did lock the door and set the alarm."

"Margie probably caught a ride with Benny." Margie's husband often dropped her off when he needed their car. Charlotte cupped her hands around her eyes to look through the windows, searching for anyone who might be inside. Margie stood in the middle of the showroom, her arms hugging her waist. Charlotte's heartbeat dropped back to a normal rate. Pushing through the door, Charlotte looked around. Nothing seemed out of place, but Margie was definitely upset about something.

"I was just about to call you." Margie walked to the front of the shop, pushing on the door after Charlotte and Kristoff entered. They all watched it open a smidge on its own. "The hinge is broken," she said, pointing up. "The alarm was still set, but the door was ajar when I got here."

Kristoff pushed the door closed and jiggled the knob. It didn't help. He bent down to look at the latch. "It doesn't appear as though someone pried it open, but I'm not an expert."

"Yeah, neither am I." Charlotte turned to Margie. "Was anything taken?"

"Not that I can tell, but I've only been here a few minutes. Benny dropped me off on his way to work. Do you want me to call the police?"

"Yes. Even if nothing was stolen, we need to file a report in case it happens again. Damnit, we don't need this today." The orders they had would keep them busy well past closing time. Kristoff worked on the wedding flowers with Charlotte while Margie did the other arrangements. Having the police there would take up a good chunk of her morning, but it had to be done.

Charlotte took a look around, but nothing seemed out of place. There was no cash register out front since most of their business was pre-ordered. Cash payments were practically nonexistent in their day and time. They had a small pad that accepted credit cards, and Charlotte left it in her office each night. She made her way there and checked the safe where she kept a little cash just in case. Nothing had been disturbed in there either. Charlotte sat down at her desk and booted her laptop. Hopefully, the security feed would show their intruder. While she waited, Kristoff entered the office with Gibby in tow. He placed the carrier on the floor by Charlotte's feet.

When Gibby meowed at her, Charlotte stuck her finger through the small window and stroked his cheek. "Sorry, buddy. You need to stay in here for a while. I'll call Aunty Wynter to come get you." Wynter was going to freak, but not as much as if Charlotte hid the truth and Wynter found out later.

"The police are on their way. They said not to

touch anything." Margie's eyes were red as though she'd been crying.

"Like we haven't already touched everything in this place." Kristoff huffed. He wasn't wrong.

Charlotte opened the security app and scanned back to the night before. It clearly showed Kristoff setting the alarm and locking the door behind him. After that it was quiet until... "Shit." At 3:27, the feed went dark and nothing showed on the video afterward. "Somebody messed with the video." Charlotte leaned back in her chair and stared at the ceiling. Who would want to mess with her?

The next two hours were a shitshow. The police took their fingerprints and chastised them for touching the metal between the door and frame that had been jimmied. Charlotte showed them the security feed, and they took the name of the security company to follow up with. Since nothing had been stolen and the only damage was to the door, the officer in charge didn't seem too worried. Charlotte, on the other hand, was furious.

After the cops left, she called a locksmith to fix the door, then the three of them got busy. Of course, the shop had been slammed with walk-ins because why wouldn't it be on top of everything else? Margie did her best to keep up with them, but at one point, Kristoff had to stop working on wedding arrangements to help. Wynter had a mini freak-out when she came to gather Gibby, but Charlotte was too busy to do more than reassure her best friend everything was under control. Wynter took Gibby back to Charlotte's apartment and returned at one with the Mortons. Charlotte didn't have to work too hard to convince mother and daughter she was the best one to handle Courtney's wedding. Charlotte's many photo galleries spoke for themselves. When they left, Wynter remained behind and asked how she could help.

Wynter stayed and answered the phone as well as greeted customers so Margie could work on arrangements. When it was time for her to head off to her next appointment, Wynter promised to return afterward with supper since they were staying later than usual. Charlotte couldn't ask for a better friend. Or better employees. Even with the earlier disruption, the three of them knocked out everything on their agenda for the day. Sure, they had to stay late, but neither Margie nor Kristoff would let Charlotte stay and work alone.

Charlotte locked the door at closing time and turned the radio up. If it had been her by herself, she would have chosen hard rock, but Margie wasn't a fan. Instead, Charlotte found a pop station which played dance music. It, along with the sandwiches Wynter brought, was the pick-me-up they all needed. While Charlotte and her employees worked with the flowers, Wynter printed off the orders they needed to get ready for the following day. Once they were finished, she took them to the cooler. She had helped Charlotte in the early days before Charlotte hired first Margie, then Kristoff. She knew Charlotte's system as well as the others, and her help was invaluable.

"That's the last one," Charlotte announced at close to nine. "I can't thank you all enough for staying. It will be reflected in your pay." Charlotte paid both employees a salary, and whenever they worked overtime, she adjusted their checks to reflect the extra hours.

"We don't stay for the pay, Boss." Kristoff handed the last of his bouquets to Wynter and began cleaning off his table. "But we appreciate it."

"Until we hear back from the police and the security company, I want us all to start work at the same time, and no one will be in the shop by themselves at closing time. Safety in numbers and all that." Charlotte had managed to work without letting the break-in get to her too much, but now that her hands were idle, her mind was anything but.

Wynter came out of the back where the coolers were located. "I just don't understand why anyone would break in and not take anything."

Charlotte wondered the same thing. "Maybe they were looking for money. It's not like they can pawn flower arrangements. Let's hope with the new locks and password change on the alarm it won't happen again. We have plenty of work tomorrow, but let's agree to start at eight. Stay in your cars, and we'll all walk in together."

Everyone waited until Benny picked Margie up to leave. Charlotte and Wynter said goodbye to Kristoff and got in their vehicles. They had already planned to meet up at Charlotte's apartment. As soon as they were inside, Wynter scooped Gibby into her arms, and Charlotte headed to the kitchen to grab drinks.

"What a fucking day," Charlotte muttered as she poured wine for Wynter and a vodka ginger ale for herself. She debated telling Wynter about the night before but decided she wanted Wynter's opinion. "I'm fairly sure someone was in my apartment last night while we were at Dominion. When I got home, I found

Gibby trapped in my closet." She handed over Wynter's glass and sat next to her on the sofa.

"And you're sure you didn't leave the door cracked?"

"It doesn't matter. The door opens out, not in. There's no way Gibby could have closed it. I didn't call the cops because nothing was taken. Kind of like at the shop. Both locks were engaged. The patio door didn't appear to have been messed with."

"Did you check all the windows?"

"Yes. If it weren't for what happened today, I'd chalk it up to some kind of cosmic fluke, but something's going on, and whoever is doing this is sneaky."

"But if they aren't taking anything, what are they after?"

Charlotte took a sip of her drink. "No idea. But I find it rather strange this happened after meeting Roland."

"You think Elise's boyfriend is targeting you?" Wynter stopped petting Gibby, and the cat nudged her hand with his head. "Charlie, I think you should call the cop you spoke to earlier and tell him."

"Yeah, maybe." Charlotte didn't want to admit she was scared. If someone were to break in while she was home alone, she had no way to defend herself other than possibly one of the kitchen knives. She didn't own a gun. She hated them. Charlotte knew a gun by itself wasn't dangerous, but someone wielding one with bad intent was.

Wynter set her empty glass on the end table and took Charlotte's free hand in hers. "I think you and Gibby should come stay with me, at least for the next few days."

"But what if whoever's doing this follows us? I don't want your house to be the next target."

Wynter's eyebrows dipped, her dark eyes boring into Charlotte's.

"What? Why are you glaring at me?"

Wynter wasn't one to hold her tongue. Usually. "Maybe you should call Master J."

"Jude? Why? We haven't even been on a date. And I *really* don't want him to cancel because he thinks I'm too much trouble."

Wynter rolled her eyes. "Charlie, if Jude is any kind of man at all, he'll see this as an opportunity to come to your rescue. You know, be your knight in shining armor."

"Or he could block my number and have the owners of Dominion rescind their offer for another free night."

Wynter clutched her nonexistent pearls. "You're going back?"

"Don't act like you don't think Roman is hot as fuck and you don't want to find out just how kinky he is. I mean, you two with your dark hair and eyes would make some mighty fine babies."

Wynter grinned. "We would, wouldn't we? But we're not talking about me. If someone really is after you, we need to find out who it is, or neither of us will get the chance to return to the club because I'm not going without you."

"But what if it's all something explainable? The hinge was broken on the front door, yes. What if Kristoff only thought it closed when he locked it and a strong wind slammed it open?"

"That's possible, but that doesn't explain the blank video feed. And what about Gibby?" Wynter hugged the Maine Coon tight to her chest.

"Ugh! I don't know. It's all so circumspect. I just hate to call Jude and have him think I'm crazy."

"How about this? Send him a text asking if he knows any security guards. When he asks what's going on, explain about the door. Tell him you're being extra cautious because you don't want your employees in danger, just in case. Maybe don't mention Gibby."

Charlotte swirled her drink, debating whether or not texting was a bad idea. When she didn't respond, Wynter nudged her knee. "When have you ever shied away from a bad idea?"

Charlotte had to think long and hard about that one. She snapped her fingers. "That time J.D. wanted to race for pink slips."

"Only because you were in Aunt Ellen's car, and she would have murdered you."

"Yeah." Charlotte smiled, remembering getting her driver's license and Ellen trusting her with her brand-new Honda. "That, plus J.D.'s Toyota was a stick, and I knew the Honda's automatic couldn't take him. Now if I'd been in Trixie..." Charlotte's Camaro was an older model, but the thing would smoke most cars out there. She had always wanted one, and when Charlotte saved enough money, she could afford a new one with six cylinders, or an older model SS with eight. She chose the latter. Trixie would fly.

"If you'd been in Trixie, J.D. wouldn't have challenged you. He might've acted dumb, but he wasn't. Not when it came to cars. It never ceased to amaze me how that boy could take a pile of junk and make it into something magical, but he never could figure out what a clit was for other than peeing."

Charlotte had just taken a sip of vodka, and it was all she could do not to spit it all over the place. When she stopped coughing, she said, "I bet Roman knows his way around a clit."

"I won't take that bet, because that man is F.I.N.E. And he's a Dom. One command from him and I'd hit my knees so hard the concrete would crack."

"Who are you, and what have you done with my Wynter?"

"What? I'm just saying." Wynter looked off into the distance, fanning herself. When she finished daydreaming, she looked at Charlotte. "So, are you gonna call Mr. Long Hair or not?"

Charlotte groaned, but she pushed to her feet to get her phone. "Here goes nothing."

CHAPTER FIVE

Spyder

JUDE WAITED UNTIL the next morning to call Lucy. She was in New Atlanta with Jonas Montague. Not only was he Tamian's great-uncle, but he was also the scientist who had cloned Tamian from his sister, Tessa. That one act had been the supposed catalyst for the apocalypse brought on by the religious cult known as The Ministry, but The Ministry had to have been planning world destruction long before. You couldn't tear a world apart on a whim. Lucy's great-uncle, Lucius, had been a mad scientist in his own right, studying genetics and performing crazy experiments in the basement of their home. He left behind several journals, and the one Lucy had taken to Jonas held notes on how to prolong human life using shifter DNA.

When Gargoyles mated, whatever was in the bite bound their mate to them, slowing the aging process. Gryphons weren't equipped the same way, and if their mate was human, the human continued aging normally, leaving behind a sorrowful shifter. Lucy and Jonas were hoping to change that with whatever formula Lucius had been working on before his death.

"Good morning, Spyder," Lucy answered.

"Good morning. I'm sorry to bother you, but I need a little computer help." War's daughter, a brilliant geneticist, was also an experienced hacker.

"Tell me what you need." Lucy was busy with the formula, but she never turned the family away. If whatever request wasn't something she could handle, she passed it off to one of the Gargoyles.

Jude relayed everything he knew about Roger Smith as well as what he didn't. "I know it isn't much to go on."

"I've worked with less, but Bishop should be able to handle this."

"Bishop? As in Locke's son?"

"Yes. With me working day and night with Jonas, I asked Ryker to find a Hound who had computer skills. Bishop recently graduated from college, and he's brilliant. He came to New Atlanta for a couple months working with Julian and Henry. It's not that I want to turn the hacking over to someone else, but I don't want the family to be without computer assistance while I'm working on this formula."

"Wow, I didn't know, but that's great. Should I start calling Bishop instead of you?"

"For now, that would be ideal. Julian sent Bishop home with a system comparable to what they have here. I'm surprised Ryker didn't tell you."

"Probably because any hacking we need done usually goes through him. If you'll give me Bishop's number, I'll call him."

"I'll text it to you now. Good luck with this Roger guy."

"Thank you, Lucy."

Jude disconnected, then dialed Bishop and told

him what he needed. The male was excited to have something to work on besides looking for Josiah Talbert. After their conversation, it took all Jude's resolve not to call Charlotte, but he didn't want to bother her at work. They hadn't shared anything about themselves the night before, so he had no idea what kind of job she had. Since he didn't know and didn't want to bother her, he sat down at his computer and put her name in the search engine. A profile came up on one of the larger social media platforms, and he scrolled through the photos. Most were of her and Wynter, but several were of flowers and plants. One in particular showed the inside of a floral business. Jude began searching for florists in New Latham until he found one that matched the photo. When he clicked on the "about us" page of The Blooming Boutique, Jude found that Charlotte owned the business.

"Hmm." Rhiannon, Ryker's mate, had expressed an interest in plants and flowers, thinking she might want to work as a florist. Jude would keep Charlotte in mind if they happened to get along past their first date. Thinking of Wednesday, Jude called his fellow Hound who owned Jacques'. After taking care of the reservation, Jude returned to scrolling through Charlotte's photos. The female was too cute for her own good, and if it turned out she was into Shibari? Jude's cock plumped at the thought of wrapping his ropes around all that pale skin. He didn't care if she never wanted to do a scene at the club. In fact, he would prefer they didn't. His beast rumbled in agreement. He might have a few kinks, but sharing wasn't one of them.

Jude was so engrossed in Charlotte's photos he

jumped when his phone rang. Ryker's name flashed on the screen, and Jude didn't know whether he was glad for the distraction or not. "Hey, Pres."

"Spyder, you up for a job? I think this one is perfect for you."

"Depends on what it is and how long it'll take." He didn't want to miss his date with Charlotte. "As long as I'm back by Wednesday."

"Yeah? Got a hot date?" Ryker's voice was warm. Before Rhiannon, Ryker had been one cold Gryphon. Now that he had the love of a good female, he had lightened up.

"Sure do. And if things with her work out, she might be a good person for Rhiannon to know. She owns a floral business."

Ryker remained quiet for a few seconds. "I've seen the types of females you date. If this one is into all that kinky stuff, I'm not sure I want—"

Jude growled, and his fangs dropped. "I suggest you choose your next words carefully. I love you like a brother, Ryot, but do not start judging someone you don't know for reasons you don't have a clue about. When Kyllian finds his mate, are you going to shield Rhiannon from her too? We don't judge you for what you do or don't get up to in the bedroom, and I would appreciate you extending the same courtesy to the rest of us."

"Fuck. You're right, and I am sorry. If this female is a florist, she probably has the same type of temperament as Rhi. If things work out, I would love to introduce the two of them."

Jude got his beast under control. "Thank you. Now tell me about this job."

After hearing what Ryker had to say, Jude accepted the contract. He texted Hawk and Kyllian to let them know he couldn't meet at the clubhouse, then he spent the next couple hours poring over the evidence. Once he was satisfied of the man's guilt, Jude climbed on his bike and headed west toward New Syracuse. The mark was a judge who had gotten away with abusing his wife and son for years. Quinn Shepherd, the Hounds' new handler, had sent over plenty of evidence, including witness statements and photographs. The man had skirted justice more than once given his position within the system. If the man were only verbally abusive, Jude would be tempted to use his Gryphon voice and encourage him to treat his family better, but he had sent both wife and child to the hospital more than once. Jude had never taken out a mark without first performing his own due diligence. In this case, he would shift and hide outside the family home. Jude's Eagle had an affinity for air, and he would use his element if he needed a distraction.

The O'Reilly home was built on a slope, spreading out instead of up. The house sat on little over an acre, surrounded by mature trees, and had large windows on the back side looking into the den and kitchen. This boded well for Jude. For the judge? Not so much. A thick layer of snow covered the ground and trees, and Jude's white wings would blend in with the environment. He left his bike at a nearby park deserted due to the weather. He grabbed his pouch out of his saddle bag and took off into the woods where he stripped, stowed his clothes in the bag, then shifted. Clutching the strap in one large talon, he launched into the air and flew toward the house. It took a few

59

minutes to find the right one, but the moss-green trim came into view, and Jude landed on a branch.

Walter and his wife, Bonnie, were sitting in the den. Walter kept glancing toward the door and gesturing with an outstretched hand, interrupting his wife as she tried to read a book. Whatever her response, the judge's irritation was clear by the scowl on his face. It took almost an hour before Christopher, a sixteen-year-old sophomore at a private Catholic school, made an appearance, arriving home in a brand-new luxury sedan. He entered the kitchen slowly from the door in the breezeway that led to the garage. The teen moved through the house from a hallway to the kitchen, stopping off at the refrigerator for a soda. Before he could take a sip, his father got in his face. Walter yelled and poked his son in the chest. Bonnie had followed her husband, but instead of trying to intervene, she stood across the kitchen, hugging her middle. Walter yelled at his son, and when Christopher responded, Walter punched him in the stomach.

Bonnie found her feet, rushing over to grab Walter's arm, but he turned and pushed her down. Bonnie landed hard, hitting her head on the island. Christopher charged his father, but Walter caught the teen around the throat. In the photos, Walter's prior assaults had been done to parts of his son's body that wouldn't be seen unless the boy took his clothes off. There would be no hiding these bruises unless the teen wore a turtleneck. Christopher grabbed his father's wrist, frantically trying to remove his hand. When that didn't work, he began slapping his father's face in earnest. He was choking. Bonnie climbed to her feet and jumped on her husband's back, but the smaller woman was no match for the male.

Jude flew from the branch, landing in the side yard where he shifted, dragged on his jeans, and ran to the nearest door. Fuck! He had to hurry. There was no way he would let the kid die on his watch. What a cluster. This was supposed to be recon only, but it had quickly turned into a rescue mission. This wasn't the first time a job had gone sideways. The Hounds didn't have to call Ryker for permission to do what they thought best in the current situation. In instances like this one when a life was on the line, they used their own judgment. Jude ran through the breezeway, praying Christopher had left the door unlocked. He wouldn't be able to erase evidence of kicking it in. Luck was on his side, and Jude rushed through the house to the kitchen.

"Turn him loose," Jude demanded in his Gryphon voice. Walter dropped his son and turned to look at Jude. "Stay there," Jude commanded the man before squatting to check on the teen. Christopher's eyes were red and wet, and he gasped, attempting to get air into his lungs. Bonnie dropped to her knees beside her son. She sobbed as she pushed his hair off his forehead.

"Who the fuck are you?" Walter demanded.

"Sit down, and shut up." Jude pointed to the other side of the island. The judge complied, walking around the counter and taking a seat on one of the bar stools. Jude returned his attention to Christopher. He gingerly touched the boy's throat. Jude wasn't a doctor, but he knew enough about anatomy to know the kid would be bruised for a while. By the sound of his breathing, he hadn't suffered permanent damage. His neck and throat would hurt, but he would heal. Still, Jude wanted the boy looked at by professionals, plus he needed them out of the house. He stood and helped the teen to his feet.

"Bonnie, take Christopher to the hospital. Tell them Walter lost his temper and pushed you. Christopher intervened, and that's when Walter tried to choke Christopher. You hit Walter over the head with a frying pan, then Walter ran outside. You will both forget I was here." Bonnie nodded and ushered her son toward the door. Jude should have told Bonnie to grab a coat, but it would make sense she forgot it in her rush to get her son to the hospital. Walter yelled at them to stop, but they both ignored him as they made their way to the garage. Once the door closed and the car engine started, Jude then turned to the judge. "What did your son do that was so bad it warranted being choked to death?"

"He embarrassed me. He and his faggot buddy got caught making out in the locker room."

Jude hated that word, and he loathed anyone who used it. "And what did he do all the other times you put your hands on him? What did Bonnie do that required broken bones?"

"It's a man's job to keep his family in line. Sometimes that takes a strong hand."

"No! It is a man's job to protect his family. Never to harm them. You've gotten away with beating on your wife and child for far too long, and that stops today. Get your ass up and go outside."

"You obviously don't know who I am." Walter crossed his arms over his chest, smirking.

"I know exactly who you are. Now get up!" Jude let his Gryphon voice surround the judge. Walter slid off the stool and stumbled out the side door Jude pointed to. Once they were outside on the small lawn leading to the trees, Jude said, "Here's what's going to happen. You are going to stand there while I change. When you see a Lion, you will run."

Walter's demeanor changed from smug to confused. "What the fuck are you talking about?" Jude didn't say anything further. He stripped quickly, leaving his jeans where he dropped them. "What the fuck is going on? What kind of sick freak—" Walter stared as Jude let the shift come over him quickly. Walter gasped at the large, tawny Lion. Jude growled deep in his throat, and Walter turned to run. He didn't get far. Jude took a couple steps then launched into the air, landing on the man's back. He could have ripped the human to shreds, but one swipe of his sharp claws against Walter's neck did the trick. Jude shifted back to his human form and squatted beside the male.

"Walter O'Reilly, you will never harm your family again."

"Wh-what are you?" Walter whispered, his hand trying to stop the blood pouring from his neck.

"I'm what you should have been – your family's protector."

Jude remained still until Walter was no longer breathing. Jude shifted to his Lion once again and ran through the trees, leaving paw prints in the snow. It would be hard for the authorities to explain why a big cat was loose in Upstate New York, but the mystery would lose steam eventually. Jude hated that Bonnie and Christopher would come home to find the man dead, but it couldn't be helped. If time had permitted, Jude would have waited until Walter was away from home and made his death look like a mugging gone wrong. Walter took that option away when he put his hands on Christopher. Hopefully, this would help the mom and son be able to move on with their lives. Jude wasn't a therapist. He couldn't remain behind to ensure the two got the help they needed, but they had plenty of money. Jude had to trust Bonnie would use it wisely.

After shifting and putting his clothes on, Jude took a photo of the judge on his burner phone and sent it to Ryker to pass along to Quinn. He then made sure his human tracks meshed with Walter's. He returned inside and found the office. Jude didn't sit. He stood at the desk and brought the computer to life. When it asked for a password, Jude pulled a thumb drive from his pocket and inserted it into the USB port. Lucy had developed a program to quickly hack through simple passwords. Luckily, the judge had chosen his wife's birthday of all things. Jude didn't bother looking through the laptop. He wasn't there to find out what other sins the man had committed. Jude found the app for the security cameras and erased any sign of his presence. Jude wished he could have left evidence of Walter's abuse, but Jude's presence appeared in the video as well.

Jude turned off the computer and wiped his prints. He left the house and once again shifted so he could fly back to where he left his bike. As he did, he wondered who had put the hit out on the judge. He doubted it was Bonnie considering the types of evidence Quinn had received. If it were the wife, Jude hoped she felt vindicated regardless of how the male died. When he landed in the park, his phone pinged with a text.

Ryker: *That was quick and a little unexpected.*

Jude: *It was unavoidable. The mark was choking his kid to death.*

Ryker: *Copy that.*

Jude didn't expect any pushback. Quinn and her father knew the Hounds weren't human. The father/daughter team didn't micromanage how the Hounds did their jobs as long as they got it done. His phone dinged, indicating payment had hit his account. It was going on seven when Jude rolled out of the park to head east. He decided to stop off and eat in New Albany since they had a larger selection of restaurants. After refueling his bike with gas and himself with steak, Jude hit the highway. He had been flirted with by the waitress, and she not so subtly hinted that she got off at nine. BC – before Charlotte – Jude would have been hard pressed to turn the pretty woman down. But he didn't hesitate to say thanks but no. There was just something about the cute florist that called to him and his Gryphon. As he rode the wind, Spyder wondered if this was how it started for the other males who had found their mates.

Jude thought back to the job in South Texas where Hayden felt a pull to Sadie, so much so he refused to even think about taking the female out even though she was part of their contract. Jude was glad Hayden had adamantly believed in the female's innocence without having met her. The same with War when he went searching for Kerrigan. War had never met the female, but something – his beast, most likely – told him to go after her. Charlotte wasn't missing. She wasn't being targeted because of who she had married. No, she was just a regular female looking out for her cousin.

About an hour away from home, Jude's phone vibrated in his pocket. Instead of trying to read the message while on the freeway, he decided whoever texted could wait. It wasn't until he strode into his home and sat down on the sofa with a beer that he checked to see who it was and what they wanted. When he noticed he had a voicemail from Charlotte, Jude smiled. Until his listened to the message.

"Hey, Jude. Crap. I bet you get that all the time. Sorry. Uh, I'm sorry to call so late, and I hope I'm not bothering you, but I was wondering if you know any security guards. I had something weird happen at the shop today. It wasn't anything bad, just the door was open, and the security feed had been erased. Nothing was stolen. Anyway, never mind. I'll figure something out. See you Wednesday. I hope."

Jude's blood ran cold. "Fuck!" He shot to his feet, dialing her number. When it went to voicemail, he didn't leave a message. He hit redial. Voicemail. Redial. Voicemail. "Godsdamnit!"

This was getting him nowhere, so he finally left a message. "Charlotte, this is Jude. Please call me back."

Jude paced the living room, his Lion partially forming. Jude pushed back against the animal. He needed to be human when Charlotte called.

If she called.

CHAPTER SIX

Charlotte

"YOUR PHONE IS going nuts." Wynter stood at the door to the bathroom holding Charlotte's phone. "Seems Mr. Long Hair is desperate to speak to you."

"Gimme!" Charlotte had several missed calls and one voicemail. When she listened to it on speaker, Jude's voice was frantic.

"Wow," Wynter sighed. "I wish someone would panic over me."

Charlotte ignored her best friend and hit redial. Jude answered on the first ring.

"Charlotte? Oh, thank Zeus."

Zeus? "I'm here. Sorry, I was in the shower."

"What's this about security? Are you home? Is someone with you?"

Charlotte cradled the phone between her ear and shoulder while she wrapped a towel around her chest. "I'm at Wynter's." She then proceeded to tell him in detail about what happened at her shop. She even mentioned about Gibby being stuck in the closet. "Though I think that might have been a fluke."

"Give me the address. I'm coming over." Jude's tone brooked no argument from her, so she told him where Wynter's house was located. "Lock the doors, and don't answer for anyone. I'll be there in twenty." Jude disconnected without saying goodbye. If his protectiveness weren't so sexy, she would have been miffed.

"Jude's on his way." Charlotte stood clutching the phone to her chest.

"Yeah? Well, you might want to put some clothes on. Or not. Up to you." Wynter waved her hand at Charlotte's still wet body.

"Shit! He can't see me like this." Rushing around like a chicken without its head, Charlotte dropped the towel and put on the panties she'd brought into the bathroom. She had planned on going straight to bed, so the nightgown wasn't going to cut it. Thank god she hadn't washed her hair. She didn't have time to dry and manage her crazy curls. "Fuck. I need some clothes." Charlotte spent a lot of time at Wynter's, and she had comfy items in the dresser in what she deemed her bedroom.

Wynter left the bathroom to retrieve clothes for her. "Here." Wynter held out an old pair of sweats and a hoodie.

"I need a bra. Where's my freakin' bra?" Charlotte wasn't sure why she was panicking. It wasn't like Jude was coming over for a date. She pushed past Wynter and strode to the bedroom in nothing but panties. The two of them weren't shy around each other. They'd been best friends for so long they were like sisters. They had gone through puberty together, comparing notes on the changes to their bodies. Had taken showers together when they were younger. Shared hotel rooms on vacations. Neither one was shy around the other. When she found her bra, she strapped it on.

Wynter sat on the edge of the bed. "Listen, are you sure you can trust him? You just met him last night."

"You're the one who told me to call him!" Charlotte pulled on her sweats before returning to the bathroom. She slapped foundation on her face, rubbing it in with a sponge. Her makeup routine was probably laughable to a lot of women, but Charlotte wasn't one to spend hours on her face. The rumble of a motorcycle sounded outside, and Wynter ran to the front of the house.

"Holy shit, Batman. Mr. Long Hair is here and looking mighty fine. Did you know he's a biker?"

"Shit, shit, shit." Charlotte fluffed her hair. "No, I didn't. And that wasn't twenty minutes," she groused. If things happened the way she hoped, Jude would eventually see her naked and with no makeup, so she would use this opportunity to see how he reacted to her looking less than put together. If he didn't like what he saw, he would cancel their date, and she'd know he was a shallow man. *Please don't let him be shallow.*

Charlotte padded barefoot to the living room. Wynter opened the door before Jude could knock. He was dressed in a tight white T-shirt underneath a black leather biker's vest, well-worn jeans, and black motorcycle boots. His long hair was pulled back at his nape. Jude nodded at Wynter as he strode by her to get

69

to Charlotte. Jude gently cradled her face, looking her over. The relief was tangible when he sighed and pressed his lips to her forehead.

"Hi," he whispered. Jude's gentleness surprised her, but she didn't hate it. His blue eyes were soft, and she had a hard time looking away from them. When he took a step back, Charlotte wasn't sure what to do with herself.

Wynter didn't have that problem. "Thank you for rushing over here. Would you like something to drink? I have beer and wine."

"Nah, but thanks for the offer." Jude took Charlotte's hand and led her to the sofa. He sat so close their thighs were touching, and he didn't release her hand. "Walk me through what happened again."

Charlotte told him in detail everything, including how Gibby had been locked in the closet. "Like I said, that might have been a fluke."

"If your shop hadn't been broken into, I might be inclined to believe that. But for now, let's assume the two instances are related. I need to know if there's anyone in your life who has a tiff with you. Anyone who would be looking for something."

"Not that I know of. Other than Roland - Roger - I haven't pissed anyone off. I don't date that often, and I don't have any exes who parted on bad terms. My life consists mostly of work, and there haven't been any bridezillas whose flowers weren't what they expected."

Jude scrubbed his free hand down his face. "Tell me more about Roger and your cousin."

"Elise is like a sister to me. She's had her share of shitty relationships, and when she started telling me about this new man in her life, she seemed hesitant.

Like I said last night, they met at church. He visits her once a week like clockwork. It's always at her home, never taking her out on dates. She cooks for him, they hang out, and then he leaves. The one thing that stuck out was he stopped going to church where they met. That and he's trying to convince her to move. That wouldn't be so strange if they had been dating a while, but he showed up in her life, latched onto her immediately, but doesn't date her properly. She thinks it's because he's old-fashioned and is courting her, but now that I know he's a Master of kink, I can't help but wonder what his game is. She's not into the lifestyle at all. Hell, she has no life outside the hospital and church."

"Hospital?"

"Yeah, she's a nurse. She's worked at the same hospital for the last twenty-three years. After..." Charlotte didn't think Jude needed to know the gritty details of what happened all those years before. "After going through a rough spot when she was younger, she started attending church, went to school to become a nurse, and her life became rather boring. She hasn't dated much over the years, and when she does, it's always the same. A man sees her beauty, sees her goodness, and is drawn to her. But when she refuses to sleep with them, refuses to let go of her convictions, they get pissed. It's not like Elise leads them on. She's up front about the type of woman she is." Charlotte shrugged. "It's why she was so excited to meet Roland in church. She thought he would be different."

"Perhaps he truly likes Elise but realized she wasn't going to change her ways to fit into his lifestyle. Just because someone is into kink doesn't mean they can't go to church and lead a somewhat godly life. It just means they don't see what they do as a sin. It doesn't explain why he would be targeting you. Are you sure he doesn't know who you are? If he's been to Elise's house, is it possible he saw photos of you there and realized who you were last night?"

"Maybe, but the only pictures of me in the house are from when I was younger. When Aunt Ellen passed, Elise moved back into the house, and after a while, she remodeled to make it more like her place than Ellen's. Any photos were moved to what she considers my bedroom even though I haven't stayed over since Ellen died. And it isn't like he would have seen the two of us together. I haven't visited Elise since she met Roland. We've only spoken on the phone."

Wynter, who had poured herself some wine, paused the glass at her mouth. "Yes, you have. You met her at Carlotti's for supper."

"But she hadn't met him yet. At least, I don't think she had. She didn't mention him that night."

"You told me she had met a guy at church."

Charlotte narrowed her eyes at her best friend. Not because she was upset with Wynter. Charlotte tried to think back to the conversation with Elise over dinner. "Huh. I guess I put it out of my mind because she didn't make it sound like there was anything there. Other than that one night, I haven't seen Elise."

Jude squeezed her hand. "I don't want to scare either of you, but I think you were right to ask about a security guard. Whether or not it's Roger, someone has broken in twice now. We don't know if they were looking for something or just trying to scare you. I will watch over your apartment, and I'll have one of my friends keep an eye on your business after hours."

"You don't have to do that. I can call a security company." Charlotte didn't know much about Jude. It was possible he was the one in her apartment and business, but for some reason, she trusted him.

"I am in security. It's what our MC does, and I promise you won't find anyone better than we are. We have someone who can monitor your security system. As a matter of fact, I would like for him to upgrade what you have at your shop as well as at your apartment."

Charlotte removed her hand from Jude's and stood. She wrapped her arms around her waist. "Since I don't have an alarm on my apartment, anything will be better than nothing. How much is all this going to cost? The shop is doing well, but I can't afford a new system on both places plus two bodyguards."

"We have some alarms we pulled off another job that were already high-tech, so those won't cost anything. Since I'm invested in your safety, my time won't cost anything either."

"Not that I'm going to agree to you doing this for free, but why are you invested?"

Jude stood and cradled Charlotte's face between his tatted hands. "Because I like you. I know we just met, but I feel a connection to you, and I'd like to think you feel it too."

Wynter cleared her throat. "For what it's worth, I think your offer is amazing, but we don't know you. For all we know, you could have been the one sneaking into her apartment and BBs."

Jude removed his hands from Charlotte's face. "You're absolutely right, and I'm glad to see you are hesitant to trust me. But I can get you proof it wasn't me. After you left the club, Hawk and I returned inside to speak with the owner. He gave us Roger's address so we could begin watching the man. I can show you both the feed from inside the club as well as the GPS on my phone proving where I went last night."

"Why are you watching Roger?" Wynter asked.

"Silas was upset with what happened between Roger and Charlotte. He takes the safety of his patrons seriously, and he won't abide a Dom who doesn't follow the rules."

"So you found his place in New Wilton?" Charlotte asked.

"New Wilton? No, he gave an Albany address. Where did you get that he lives in Wilton?"

"That's where he told Elise he lives."

Jude pulled out his phone. "What last name did Roland give Elise?"

"Smithson."

"At least that's kind of consistent." After typing out a message, he explained, "I have someone looking into Roger. I'm hoping the fact that he told your cousin he lives in New Wilton will help."

Charlotte didn't understand why Jude was so invested, so she asked him, "Do you investigate all Doms who don't obey the rules?"

"Honestly, it's never happened in all the years I've worked with Silas. He is diligent in vetting who he lets in his clubs. Roger acting out of character for a responsible Dom threw up a red flag. When Hawk and I checked out the address on file, Roger was in bed with a woman, and there were two kids in the house. Unless they have an open marriage, his wife doesn't

74

know about his extracurricular activities. I'm wondering what else he's hiding. Then there's the part where he told Elise he's big into church. Like I said before, you can be into kink and still be religious, but it doesn't normally go hand in hand. Most religions frown on exploring your sexuality outside of marriage. Elise obviously had reservations, or you wouldn't have picked up on her unease. Silas has those same reservations. Something about Roger isn't adding up, and I plan on finding the truth. While doing that, I'm going to make sure you are protected. Whether it's him or someone else, I won't let any harm come to you. I think it goes without saying you shouldn't continue following him when he leaves your cousin's house."

Charlotte was conflicted. She felt the connection Jude mentioned, but she couldn't see his interest in her. She was nothing special. Not like Wynter. Someone who looked like Jude – a biker nonetheless – could have any woman he wanted. There had to be all kinds of women at Dominion who would kill to be with a Master who looked the way he did with his sculpted physique, long hair, and tattoos. Hell, she wasn't sure she would enjoy being bound by his ropes, and Charlotte had a feeling that would be a deal breaker.

Jude touched her shoulder. "It's getting late. I assume you're staying here tonight?"

"Yes. I didn't want to come here in case I was being watched, but Wynter insisted."

Jude smiled at Wynter, and Charlotte swallowed the jealousy. "It's good to have friends who care. Wynter, I'm glad to see you have an alarm. I'm going to stay on the sofa tonight, just in case you were followed."

Wynter crossed her arms over her chest. "Do you think that's necessary? I mean, everything you've said sounds great, but we don't know you."

"Would you feel better if a female were to stay here instead? A friend of mine owns a security company. His sister, who happens to be a badass, works with him, and she'd come to watch over you if I called."

"No," Charlotte responded at the same time Wynter said, "Yes." For whatever reason, Charlotte trusted Jude, but it was Wynter's home, and her best friend was already putting herself in danger by having Charlotte there. "Whatever Wynter wants. It is her home."

Jude nodded. "I'll make the call."

While he was phoning this other stranger, Wynter pulled Charlotte out of the room. "Do you trust Jude?"

"Yes, I do."

"What if he's doing all this just to get closer to you? Putting in alarms so he has access to you instead of making you secure?"

"If the situation were reversed and you were in trouble, what if Roman was offering to keep you safe? Would you be as reluctant to trust him?"

Wynter threw her arms in the air. "I don't know. Everything Jude says sounds like he genuinely cares about you, and the way he cradled your face? Gah, that was touching. But you know me, Charlie. I'm the cautious one. I don't trust anyone. And not to sound sexist, but how is a woman going to protect us?"

"He said she's a badass, so perhaps she's got mad ninja skills. I don't know. Maybe we've found ourselves in the middle of a wolf pack, and she's the Alpha's female. His vest says they're Hounds of Zeus."

Wynter rolled her eyes. "You read too many romance novels. Shifters aren't real."

Charlotte grinned. "How do you know? They say all good fiction started from the truth."

"*They* say a lot of things."

"Yes, they do. But we need to decide quickly if we're going to trust Jude. I already do, but like always, I've dragged you into my crazy. I'm really sorry."

Wynter tugged Charlotte into a tight hug. "Eh. My life would be boring without you and your crazy. If you trust Jude, then I do too."

Charlotte kissed Wynter's cheek. "Thank you. I don't know what I'd do without you."

"Okay. Let's not get all maudlin. I'll get blankets and a pillow for our she-wolf."

Charlotte returned to the living room to find Jude staring out the front window. "Is everything okay?"

Jude turned his head, and his face was unreadable. He wasn't frowning exactly, but neither was he smiling. "Yes. My friend is on her way. I think you'll like her. She's spunky, like you."

"You think I'm spunky?" Charlotte had been called worse.

Jude did smile then. "Yes, I do. Listen, Charlie… Is it okay if I call you that?"

Charlotte usually didn't like it, but if she were being honest, she loved it coming from him. "Sure."

"Good, because I think it suits your playfulness. Anyway, I understand Wynter not trusting me. I'm glad she's cautious. But I promise on everything holy I would never hurt you. My club and all those I consider family, we are protectors. Some mythology dictates the Hounds of Zeus were Harpies, but the true Hounds were created by Zeus to protect humans, not harm them. I don't want you to take my word for it, though. I will prove by my actions what I say is the truth." Jude looked back out the window. "Zedra's here."

Charlotte expected a Lara Croft type or possibly someone decked out in all leather, but the woman who walked in the door was neither of those. Zedra was tall and slender, dressed in regular jeans and a chunky sweater. Her auburn hair was piled on top of her head in a messy bun, and she exuded sweetness.

"Spyder," a deep voice said. Charlotte had been so fixated on the woman that she hadn't noticed the man with Zedra.

"Hey, Zander. Thanks for bringing Zed." The two men bumped fists. "Zedra, this is Charlotte. Charlie, Zedra and Zander Andino. I explained to them what was going on, and Zedra agreed to be your shadow until we figure out who's trying to scare you."

Zedra stepped up to Charlotte. Instead of holding out her hand, she pulled Charlotte into a hug. "Don't you worry, Charlie. We'll get your mystery sorted quickly, and then you can get back to life as you knew it." Zedra stepped back but kept her hands on Charlotte's biceps. Her smile was genuine. "We won't let anything happen to you." Zedra's eyes narrowed, and if Charlotte didn't know better, the woman sniffed the air. "Well, hello there. You must be Wynter."

Charlotte turned to find Wynter frozen at the edge of the room, her arms full of blankets and a pillow.

"Wynter?" Charlotte worried her friend was about to run out of the room by the look on her face.

"Yes, right. Zedra. Uh, good to see you. I mean meet you. I have bedding for the sofa. I'll just…"

Wynter tossed the items on the sofa, then thumbed toward the hallway. "I'm sure you have things to talk about, so I'm going to call it a night. Charlie, you'll lock up?" Wynter didn't wait for her to respond before hightailing it to her bedroom.

"Sorry about that. She's…" Charlotte had no idea what was wrong with Wynter, but she had other things to worry about, like the fact that she was pretty sure Zedra had growled when Wynter ran off.

Maybe Wynter was right, and Zedra was a she-wolf.

CHAPTER SEVEN

Spyder

JUDE LAUGHED AT Charlie's and Wynter's conversation they thought he couldn't hear. They were closer to right than either of them knew in calling Zedra a wolf. As a Gryphon, Zander's sister was strong. When Zedra sniffed the air, though, it reminded Jude she truly was the best female to watch over Charlie. Zedra was one of the oldest Gryphons in the area. As far as he knew, she had never found a mate while living on the West Coast. Zedra relocated to New York several years back to work with her brother.

Jude didn't miss the way she stiffened when Wynter entered the room. He would have to ask her later what that was about. For now, he would step outside where he would spend the night. Not that he didn't trust Zedra; he did. That was why he called the female. But an extra body wouldn't hurt anything. "Charlotte, I'm going to let you and Zedra get settled. I'll see you in the morning." It was all Jude could do not to pull her into his arms and give her a proper kiss goodnight. By the gleam in Zedra's eye, she knew it.

"Charlie and I will be fine." Zedra waved Jude and

Zander off, then turned to Charlie. "You can pretend I'm not here if you like. I'll be right here on the sofa, guarding the door."

Jude left the females to it, and he and Zander stepped outside. He hadn't lied exactly when he told Charlotte he provided security, but he needed to get his hands on an alarm system. That he had lied about, but it was also one reason he called Zander.

"What can I do to help?" Zander was a larger Gryphon, standing almost a foot taller than Jude. Instead of being a mercenary, Zander had formed a security company, enlisting the Gryphons in the area who would rather watch over humans than take out the evil ones. Zander had offered Jude a place in his company, but Jude enjoyed taking out the trash.

"I promised Charlie I'd get an alarm set up on her apartment. She has one at her business, but I'd like for you to take a look at it. See if it needs upgrading. I'd also like for your company to take over monitoring both."

"I just need an address. I'll get her apartment kitted first thing in the morning, and then I'll swing by her shop and take a look. Can I assume Charlie isn't just some female?"

"It's too soon to tell, but there is something about her that calls to me. I want to spend time with her and see if we're as compatible as I believe we are."

"Do you need help looking into this Roger Smith?"

"I have Bishop looking into it, but if he can't find anything, I'll let you know."

"Locke's son, Bishop?"

"Yes. He spent some time down in New Atlanta with Lucy and the Gargoyles. According to Lucy,

81

Bishop is quite adept at hacking. Who knew?" Not all the Hounds were aware that Lucy's mate and his family were Gargoyles, but Zander had enlisted Lucy's help on occasion in his business.

"That's wonderful, actually. It'll take some of the responsibility off Lucy." Zander clapped Jude on the shoulder. "Okay, I'll head back and get a system together for Charlotte's apartment. Text me the address and I'll get it installed first thing."

"Thanks, Brother." Jude waited until Zander drove off before he walked around Wynter's house and settled in, hiding in the shadows. If whoever was targeting Charlie had followed her to Wynter's, they likely wouldn't hang around the area with Jude's bike in the driveway. But if they had followed, now Wynter was also a likely target. Jude pulled out his phone and sent Hawk a text, letting him know what was going on. He didn't have to wait long for a response.

Hawk: *I'll gladly keep an eye on Wynter. There's something different about her. Not like you feel for Charlotte, but like a scent.*

Spyder: *Zedra sniffed the air when Wynter walked into the room, so you might be onto something.*

Hawk: *Since Wynter isn't trusting, I'll follow her and watch from a distance.*

Spyder: *Sounds good. I'm going to do the same for Charlotte even though she'll have Zedra as a shadow.*

The two males made plans to meet up the next morning and said goodnight. Jude brought forth his Lion so he could listen in on the females. When he didn't hear voices, he assumed they had gone to bed. Zedra would be alert even in sleep. Plus, she knew Jude remained outside watching over them all. Jude would need sleep at some point but not until Charlotte was safely at work.

Jude used his Eagle's keen vision to check the shadows surrounding the other houses. It was a little past one when he caught movement from a second-story window at one of the houses on the street behind Wynter's. If it weren't for his Eagle, Jude would have missed it. A silhouette was barely visible in the dark room, but it was clearly a man looking out. Jude froze, keeping himself hidden. The figure gestured with one arm, and another, smaller figure appeared next to him. From where he stood, it looked like a couple embracing. Jude had his own kinks, but voyeurism wasn't one of them, so he left the couple to whatever they were getting up to in the early morning.

The hours dragged on with Jude keeping his senses open to both his surroundings and the three females inside. He pondered his intense interest in Charlotte, having only met her the night before. Jude had taken many females to bed over the years. He wanted a relationship. Wanted to find his mate. He thought he'd found that once before, but Belinda had chosen someone else over him. It had been a kick to the nuts because he felt he was the better male, but obviously she had been looking for something different than what he offered.

That had been almost twenty years ago, right after Michelle had been taken from him. Maybe his grief had been too much for Belinda to handle, or she didn't want the lifestyle of a biker that had drawn her to him in the first place. Jude didn't know Charlotte. Didn't know what type of male she usually dated. Hell, they hadn't even been on a date, and he was already thinking further into the future. But he felt a connection with her he'd never encountered before, not even with Belinda. Was it fate intervening? Had destiny brought them together to help in his quest for the one who completed him?

Those thoughts kept his mind occupied, and when the sky slid from inky darkness to the brighter shadows of dawn, Jude had no answers. He was ready for Charlotte to go to work so he could work on securing her business as well as her home. The front door opened, and Zedra stepped out looking as put-together as she had when she arrived the night before.

"Good morning. All clear out here?"

"Good morning, and yes." Jude studied the female a few seconds before asking another thing he'd pondered during the night. "You want to tell me about Wynter's reaction to you?"

Zedra gave him a sad smile. "Not really, but let's just say she and I met when I first moved here and leave it at that. It won't be a problem."

"That's all I needed to hear. I want you to ride with Charlotte to the shop. I'll follow and make sure the place is secure. Then I'll leave you to it while I help Zander get her apartment secure."

"Sounds like a plan. I'm going inside to freshen up. We should be ready to roll in thirty."

"I'll be waiting." Jude sat down on the steps, propping his arms on his thighs. A few minutes later the door opened again. He expected Zedra, but Charlotte appeared with a cup of coffee.

"I wasn't sure how you took it. If you don't like it black, I can go back and doctor it up."

Jude took the mug, smiling. "Black is perfect.

Thank you."

"You're welcome. Zedra said you need to get into my apartment." Charlotte held out her hand. "Here's the key. I'll text you the address."

"Thank you. Are you sure you trust me to add the alarm without you there?" Jude took a sip of coffee and relished the liquid. He didn't need the caffeine, but he was used to starting his day with it.

"I do." Charlotte sat down beside him and leaned against his shoulder. When she looked up at him, her seafoam eyes were sparkling in the early morning sun. "Zedra and I had a brief chat about your MC and your family. She told me how you go after cults and rescue those who are kept there against their will. She also told me about the women who have become partners to some of your MC members. I figure a group who rescues people has to be trustworthy."

Jude cradled the cup between both hands so he wouldn't be tempted to touch the female. He wanted to prove to her he was trustworthy, and moving too quickly was probably a bad idea. "I'll follow you and Zedra to your shop and make sure it's secure before heading to your apartment."

"I'd appreciate that, but I'm worried about Wynter. What if whoever is after me followed me here? I don't want to leave her to fend for herself."

"Hawk is going to shadow her. He won't get in her way, and she won't see him, but he'll see her."

Charlotte scrunched her nose. "Yeah, I don't think that's a good idea. She's already leery, so it would probably be best if you told her she'll have a shadow. That way, if she feels she's being followed, she won't be paranoid."

"You know her better than I do, so if you're sure…"

"I do, and I am. I'll go give her a heads-up. She doesn't need to leave for another couple hours, so maybe you can have Hawk come here and watch the house since we need to get a move on."

"I'll do that." Jude wanted to lean in and press his lips to Charlotte's, but she stood and squeezed his shoulder before he had the chance. Shaking his head, he set the mug down and called Hawk.

Twenty minutes later, Charlotte and Zedra were climbing into Charlotte's Camaro, and Hawk had taken Jude's place on the porch. Wynter had been reluctant to have Hawk watch over her, but after a lot of begging on Charlotte's part, her best friend gave in.

Jude straddled his bike and followed the females through town. When they pulled into the parking lot next to BBs, two cars were waiting on them. As per their earlier conversation, Charlie didn't get out of her car. She had already called her employees to let them know to wait until Jude checked out the shop before exiting their vehicles.

The front door was locked up tight. The track lighting illuminated the showroom, and from what Jude could tell, nothing looked out of place. He opened his senses, searching for any sign of someone hiding inside. When he found no one, he motioned for Charlotte to get out of her car. Her employees followed suit, and Charlotte introduced everyone. Margie was huddled under her husband's arm, and Kristoff was eyeing Jude like he was two seconds from jumping him. Jude smiled at the young man, and Kristoff let out a little "*eep*." Turning to Benny, Jude held out his hand.

86

Margie's husband wasn't a small man, and he sized Jude up. While Charlotte unlocked the door and ushered everyone inside, Benny remained outside.

"My whole world just walked through that door. Can you guarantee my wife will be safe?"

Jude appreciated a man who knew his woman's worth. He wanted to know what that was like. To have the love of a good female he would do anything for. "Nothing in life is a guarantee, but I do vow I will do everything in my power to keep Margie as well as the others safe." Just then, two motorcycles rumbled down the street and turned into the lot, parking beside Jude's bike. He had texted Ace and Ripper, enlisting their help in watching over Charlotte while Jude went to her apartment. The two Hounds spent most of their time helping Sutton chase down The Ministry. With Josiah Talbert in the wind, things on the cult front had been stalled for the past couple months. They strode to where he was standing. "Benny, this is Ace and Ripper. I trust them with my life; therefore, I trust them with Charlotte's and Margie's."

"But not mine?" Kristoff asked. He stood half in the door, looking the Hounds up and down.

"Kristoff, get your ass in here and stop ogling the bikers!" Charlotte yelled.

Jude grinned at the young man. "The question is, can I trust their lives with you?"

Kristoff cocked his head to the side. "I'll watch them like a hawk."

"Kristoff!" Charlotte yelled again.

"Coming," Kristoff sing-songed and retreated inside. Just before the door closed, he asked Charlotte, "How am I supposed to work with all that hanging around?"

Ace and Ripper chuckled while stepping up to shake hands with Benny. Ace sobered as he spoke for the duo. "No one is getting near your female. That is a vow."

Benny looked through the window where Margie was talking to Zedra. "I'm holding you to that. If I didn't have to work, I'd be the one watching over her. And Charlotte. That girl is like a daughter to us."

The man's words warmed Jude's heart. "I'm glad to hear that. Family is important, and we will watch over all of them." Benny hesitated a few seconds before walking off to his car, looking back through the window as he did.

"Come inside, and I'll introduce you." Jude led the others into the showroom. Zedra greeted the Hounds, and Margie visibly relaxed.

Charlotte appeared through a door at the back of the room. Her curls were now held back in a colorful bandana. She sidled up next to Jude and held out her hand. "Thank you both for offering to help out. I'm Charlotte."

Ace and Ripper shook her hand, offering their real names. Asher "Ace" McMurray and Ripley "Ripper" Davidson were large males, and adorned in their biker kuttes were intimidating, but Charlotte was relaxed in their presence.

"Ace and Ripper are going to watch the perimeter while Zedra hangs out inside. I'm headed to your apartment to let Zander in. As soon as we're finished there, we'll come back here unless you'd rather he waited until you finish for the day."

"Sooner is fine." Charlotte gripped Jude's hand.

"Thank you. For everything." Jude wanted badly to kiss her, but they had an audience. He did the next best thing and lifted her hand to his mouth, brushing his lips across her knuckles.

"Then I'll see you in a few hours." He inclined his head to the door, and Ace and Ripper followed.

"I appreciate you both helping me." Jude leaned against the side of the building, propping one booted foot on the brick. "Bishop is looking into Roger Smith. Everything in my gut tells me Smith isn't his real name. He told Charlie's cousin his name is Roland and that he lives in New Wilton, yet he put an Albany address on his paperwork at Dominion." Ace and Ripper weren't into the lifestyle, but both males had worked security on occasion for Silas over the years. "When Hawk and I checked out the address, he was there with a woman and two kids. If that's his family, he's not only a Dom but leading Elise on."

"That's Charlotte's cousin, right?" Ace asked.

"Yes. He met her at church, and after they started seeing one another, he stopped going. According to Charlie, the male is trying to get Elise to move to New Wilton, yet he only visits Elise one night a week. Stays until one or two, then heads out. Charlie was looking out for her cousin and decided to follow Smith to see where he lives. Instead of going home, she followed him to Dominion. She and her best friend bided their time until Intro Night, and that's when all this shit started." Jude explained how he was giving a demonstration and Roger approached Charlotte.

"It sounds as though Smith is leading a double life, and Charlotte is right to worry about her cousin." Ripper cracked his knuckles. "This could get

89

interesting."

Jude pushed off the wall. "It already is. Zander is waiting for me, so I'm headed to Charlie's apartment. We'll be back as soon as he gets the system installed." Jude bumped fists with both Hounds, thanking them once more for their assistance, then got on his bike and headed out.

Charlie's apartment was everything Jude expected – colorful, inviting, and full of plants. Cat paraphernalia littered the space. Charlie mentioned Gibby going to the shop most days, but she had opted to leave her pet at Wynter's since Wynter didn't have a full day planned. The large Maine Coon, named after the Gibraltar Campion, a rare flower, had been suspiciously okay with Jude.

Zander placed a box on the kitchen counter. "I figured out where the intruder got in." He pointed to the sliding-glass door. "All it takes is a flathead screwdriver." Zander slid the door open, and Jude followed the Hound outside. "You can see at the bottom here." Zander squatted and pointed to where the white paint was chipped. "At the very least Charlotte should have something wedged between the door and jam. I didn't bother dusting for fingerprints. If whoever broke in was good enough to pop the lock, they were probably smart enough to wear gloves."

That didn't bode well for them figuring out who had broken in. Jude looked around. Charlotte's apartment was in a nice complex. The apartments over hers had balconies above the small patio off her kitchen. The rails boxing the patio in were low enough most adults could climb right over. Gorgeous landscaping surrounded the property with a row of evergreens between her building and the one behind it. While it gave Charlotte privacy from the apartments directly across from hers, it also gave an intruder that same advantage. And with Charlotte's unit being on the end, it was too easy for someone to slip over the railing unnoticed.

Jude texted Charlotte and asked if she had a tape measure. He didn't want to pilfer through her drawers without her permission.

Charlie: *Junk drawer on the right side of the stove.*

Jude was surprised when he opened the drawer. It wasn't full of junk. Instead, it held a variety of tools. He measured the length and width of the space between the door and frame, then sent a text to Hayden. Instead of finding a length of wood, Jude thought a piece of metal piping would be stronger. Charlotte could also use the pipe as a weapon if need be. Hayden not only built stunning bikes, but he also made intricate designs welding chains and sprockets together. Jude explained what he needed, then tucked his phone in his pocket.

When Jude offered to help Zander, the male waved him off, so he walked back outside and looked around. The complex was upscale with a large pool, tennis court, and a covered patio where comfortable-looking chairs surrounded an outdoor fireplace. A pavilion sat off in the distance, courting patio tables and grills. A walking track circled the outside of the property. The setup was nice. The property even boasted a gated entrance where a guard checked each car. All Jude had to do was tell the guard he was there to install a security system, and the man waved him through. He would be talking to Charlotte about that.

Once back inside, he compared her home to his

own. He had bought a three-bedroom split-level close to several other Hounds when he first moved to New Troy. The neighborhood was nice and quiet, just the way Jude liked it. He liked being able to walk outside and enjoy the night air on his back deck without having to share it with a bunch of others. He couldn't imagine living in a complex with so many people using the common areas. He also enjoyed having an attached garage where he could park his bike out of the weather. Jude had an SUV, but he only drove it when he absolutely had to. Like when he took Charlotte out to dinner. There was no way he would pick her up on his Harley for a night out at Jacques'.

By the time Zander finished installing the alarm, it was time for lunch. Jude didn't want to bother Charlotte in case she was busy, so he called Zedra.

"Hey, Jude. Everything's quiet here."

"I didn't figure with Ace and Ripper standing guard outside someone would approach the shop. Your brother and I are headed that way. Will you ask Charlotte if she wants us to pick up lunch?"

"Oh, we just called in an order at the deli down the street. Do you and Zander want me to add to it?"

"Zedra ordered from the deli. You want anything?" Jude asked the other Gryphon.

"Pastrami on rye with extra pickles. Plain chips."

Jude relayed Zander's order, then added his own. "Thanks, Zedra. We'll be there in about fifteen."

"See you then."

CHAPTER EIGHT

Charlotte

ACE AND RIPPER had gone home to rest while Jude and Zander were at the shop. They returned at closing time to stand guard. Instead of remaining outside, Charlotte offered for them to sit inside where they'd be more comfortable. The men declined, but thanked her for her generosity. Benny arrived to take Margie home, and Kristoff got in his car after waving goodbye to Ace. Charlotte laughed at her friend's overzealous flirtation even though she'd told him not to scare off their security guards. Thankfully, Ace shrugged off Kristoff's playfulness.

"Sorry about him," Charlotte told Ace as Jude walked her and Zedra to Charlotte's car.

"Eh, he's harmless." Ace's eyes followed Kristoff's car until it was out of sight. Charlotte didn't know the biker. Didn't know if he was completely straight. It didn't matter, and she had enough to think about with whoever had disrupted her life without worrying whether or not the handsome man might be interested in her employee.

Jude opened Charlotte's door after she unlocked it.

"I'll see you in a few." Jude waited until Charlotte buckled before closing the door. She started the engine while watching him walk to his bike and climb on.

"I'm impressed," Zedra said. "You have a great thing going here with your business. Your work is stunning, and your employees love you."

"And I love them." Charlotte pulled out of the parking lot and headed home. "They're family."

"Are we going to stop by Wynter's and pick up Gibby?"

"No. Wynter's keeping him another night."

"Oh." Zedra sounded disappointed.

"Can I ask you something?" Charlotte was curious as to Wynter's reaction the night before. Zedra *hmm'd*, so Charlotte continued. "Do you know Wynter? I mean, have you met her before last night?"

"I think that's a question you should ask your best friend."

"So that's a yes." Charlotte reached up and removed her bandana, letting her curls free. She fluffed her hair before settling her hand back on the steering wheel. Charlotte's mind was abuzz thinking about Zedra and Wynter together. Wynter had never mentioned being bisexual or even bicurious, but that didn't mean she wasn't or hadn't been. There was nothing Charlotte kept from her best friend, so it didn't make sense if Wynter had kept secrets. Charlotte prayed Jude and his friends figured out who had broken in sooner rather than later, because she didn't want to go too long with Wynter staying away if she were in fact avoiding Zedra. Maybe she should ask Jude to stay instead.

Zedra bit the side of her thumb as she stared out

the side window, so Charlotte let the other woman have her secrets. She'd get it out of Wynter. Eventually. Charlotte stopped at the gate and waved at the guard. The barrier swung open, and Charlotte pulled through with Jude on her tail. The man was too sexy on his black and chrome bike. She parked outside her unit, and Jude coasted the bike in next to her. She ogled his muscles, the way his white T-shirt stretched around his bulging biceps. All his ink was on display...

Charlotte got out of the car. "Are you not freezing?" It was February in Upstate New York, and the temps at night got downright chilly.

"Nah. I'm hot-blooded." Jude wiggled his eyebrows as he placed his helmet over one of the mirrors, and Charlotte laughed at his cheesiness. "Come on, and I'll show you the upgrades." Jude slid off his bike with ease, and Charlotte lagged behind so she could admire the way his jeans hugged his tight ass and thick thighs. When said ass stopped abruptly, Charlotte didn't have time to halt her feet and ran into his broad back.

"Umph." She grabbed onto his arms, and Jude grinned at her over his shoulder.

"My eyes are up here."

"And what pretty eyes they are." Charlotte batted her eyelashes at him.

Zedra stepped up next to Charlotte. "You two are ridiculous."

Jude held out his hand. "Keys, please." Charlotte passed them over, and Jude unlocked the front door. He held it open so the two women could enter the apartment, then closed and locked it behind them. He pressed some buttons on the new alarm panel, and it beeped. "You'll want to change the code."

"You can show me later. Right now I'm hungry, so I'm going to cook. Is spaghetti okay with you two?" Charlotte loved to cook, and on her days off, she spent time in the kitchen cooking and baking for her and Wynter. "It's not fancy, but it's quick."

"I'll eat anything," Jude responded.

"Me, too. Can I help?" Zedra offered.

"Thanks, but like I said, it's easy. Help yourself to whatever you want to drink." She dropped her purse onto one of the chairs at the bar and washed her hands before pulling the ingredients out of the fridge and pantry. Once she had the meat cooking, she set the water to boil.

Jude pointed to the corner of the room. "Zander set up several cameras. That one points to the front door. The one over there by the window is aimed at the back door, and there are two more outside. There are sensors on all the windows as well as the sliding glass door, and it is armed with a separate panel." Jude indicated the white box on the wall. Charlotte was impressed with how quickly they had set up the new system. There was no mess she needed to clean up from where they drilled into the drywall. "If for some reason you forget to turn the alarm off when you come in, you'll receive a phone call. If you don't answer, someone will be sent to check on you, and a call will go out to the police. If either alarm is tripped, Zander's company will check the feed from the cameras, and again, the police will be notified."

"What if I want to open a window? I know it's cold right now, but I like having my windows open in the spring."

"They're motion sensors and are on the outside, so unless you remove the screen and stick your hand out, you'll be okay."

Charlotte whistled. "That's some high-tech stuff. I can't afford all this."

"Don't worry about the cost. I've got it covered." Jude stepped back into the kitchen. "Why don't you let me handle the spaghetti and you get comfortable?"

"He's gorgeous and cooks too," Charlotte whispered to the man's retreating back.

Jude turned and winked. "You haven't seen anything yet."

Charlotte added superhuman hearing to Jude's attributes. Before she could further embarrass herself, she turned around and disappeared into her bedroom to change clothes.

And hide.

Spyder

"YOU SURE YOU want me to hang around tonight?" Zedra asked. "I feel like a third wheel."

Jude dumped the pasta into the boiling water. "I'm sure, unless there's something else you need to be doing. I want to be able to leave if Bishop finds anything on Roger, and I don't want Charlotte left on her own." Jude stirred the noodles, then set the long spoon on the counter.

"No, I have nothing else going on right now. I just came off a big case, and hanging out with Charlotte at BBs was actually nice. I just thought you might want to be alone with her tonight." Zedra rummaged through the cabinets until she found the plates. She pulled three of them down and placed them on the counter.

"There'll be plenty time for that later. I want to keep her safe and figure out why she's being targeted first." Jude looked down the hallway to make sure Charlotte wasn't within earshot. "There's something special about Charlie."

Zedra pulled open a drawer. "Aha." After picking out three sets of cutlery, she asked, "Like mate special?"

"Yes. I know it's really too soon to tell. We may be compatible on the surface, but knowing if she's the one I want to claim will take time. At least for me. It always amazes me when others see someone and just know they want to spend their lives together."

"What's your Gryphon saying?" Zedra pulled three paper towels off the roll and folded them neatly.

"It's saying she's the one. And honestly? It's never voiced an opinion so strongly before. Well, it has, but always in the negative. It's even pickier than I am."

"Then I'll go ahead and say congratulations. If your beast is onboard…" Zedra picked up the wine she had neglected in order to help and raised the glass in a salute.

Jude wanted a mate more than anything. Wanted to have someone to come home to at night and talk about their day. Someone to have children with. Grow old with. Even though he wasn't old by Gryphon standards, he wasn't getting any younger, but he wouldn't settle with a female less than perfect for him. Or him for her. His mate would have to be okay with his lifestyle as well as his mercenary work. He wouldn't hide either of those things from his partner.

Charlotte padded into the kitchen on bare feet, and Jude's heart stuttered. Charlie had taken his advice and dressed in flannel pajama pants adorned with kittens and a pale blue hoodie. She stopped to pick up one of Gibby's toys and pressed it to her chest.

"Do you want me to go get Gibby?" Jude asked.

Charlotte tossed the toy into a box beside the sofa. "No. He'll be fine with his Aunt Wynter." Charlotte's tone was sad though. "What can I do to help?" she asked, shaking off her melancholy.

"Everything's ready. I just need to strain the pasta."

Charlotte moved to his side and bumped Jude's hip with hers. He stepped out of the way, and Charlotte opened the cabinet to retrieve the colander. Instead of taking it from her, he let her finish getting the food ready.

"Would you like a glass of wine?" he asked, wanting to be helpful.

"Ugh, no. I can't stand the stuff. I will take a glass of milk though." Charlotte reached into an overhead cabinet and pulled down a tall glass, handing it over with a smile. "Thank you."

Jude didn't comment on her drink choice, but Zedra spoke up. "Why do you have several bottles of wine if you don't drink it?"

Charlotte dumped the noodles into the colander. "Jude, while you're in there," she said, pointing at the fridge, "would you please grab that big, covered bowl and the dressings? I keep salad made for nights I want something light. Wynter loves wine, so I keep it on hand for her. If I'm going to drink, I prefer vodka. I can handle some of the fruitier beers, but honestly, I don't drink all that often. I tend to partake too much when I do, and I hate hangovers. Sorry I don't have any French bread to go with the spaghetti. I never cook for anyone other than Wynter, and we usually just toss some sandwich bread in the toaster. I can do that, if you'd like?"

Jude loved the way Charlotte switched gears between topics. "None for me, thanks." He put three different types of dressing on the four-person table after setting Charlie's milk down on one of the placemats.

"Help yourselves." Charlotte didn't bother putting the food on the table. They fixed their plates and salad buffet-style, which suited him fine. He took note of which dressing she preferred as well as how she put her salad on the plate instead of using a bowl.

"Did you make this sauce?" Zedra asked. Jude wondered the same thing when he noticed the jar didn't have a label on it.

"Yes. It's one of the things Aunt Ellen taught me how to cook. I usually make a large batch on my days off for the following week. Spaghetti is quick, and I get plenty of sandwiches during the day. If I have to work late, I usually end up eating cereal or salad before crashing." Charlotte shrugged like her choice of meals was no big deal, but it hurt Jude to think of her not eating better at night because she was tired. If things between them ended up working out, he vowed to

100

change that. He would gladly cook supper for her every night.

They were quiet after that as they enjoyed the simple meal until someone knocked on the door. "Are you expecting someone?" he asked.

"No. Wynter would have texted if she were coming over."

Jude rose from the table. "I'll see who it is." He hadn't taken the time to get the app installed on Charlotte's phone that connected to the camera. He chastised himself for it. Jude braced himself as he unlocked the door. When he cracked it, an older woman waited there holding an envelope.

"Hello. This was left at my door by mistake." She held the package out, and Jude took it.

"Thank you."

The woman walked away, and Jude watched her until she entered an apartment a few doors down. The envelope was made out to Charlotte with the correct address, but there was no postage on it. Jude's Gryphon grumbled.

I don't like this.

Neither do I.

Charlotte was standing in the living room. Her apartment wasn't large, so she would have been able to hear the exchange even if she'd remained in the dining area.

"Charlie, I'd like your permission to open this. It has the correct address, but there is no postage, so I have a feeling whoever left it with your neighbor did so on purpose."

Charlotte sat down on the sofa and pulled her knees to her chest. "Yeah, go ahead."

If the neighbor hadn't already handled the envelope, Jude would've been more careful about getting fingerprints all over it. He ripped it open and peered inside. "It's photos." He turned the envelope over and several pictures slid out into his hand. He knew from the one on top the rest were going to piss him off. He was right. Every one of them were of Charlotte, and a couple showed Christmas decorations in the background. A few included Wynter, and those were from the night they'd visited Dominion.

"Whoever this is has been watching you longer than we expected." Jude handed the photos to Charlotte's outstretched hand. Zedra sat down next to Charlotte and put her arm around the female. Charlotte's hands shook as she flipped through each one. She neatly stacked the photos and handed them back to Jude. "This doesn't make sense. Roland, Roger, whoever the hell he is, shouldn't have known who I was."

No, it didn't, but Jude wouldn't rule the male out yet. He sent a text to Zander and told him what was going on. It was possible the camera by Charlotte's front door had picked up whoever delivered the package. Since it wasn't delivered directly to her door, had they been close by when Zander and Jude were there earlier? If so, they were aware of the cameras being installed.

"It doesn't make sense Roger would be after you, if it is him. If it isn't, we need to figure out who would have something to gain by trying to upset you. Are you sure you don't have any disgruntled exes?"

"I'm sure. I haven't had any long-term relationships that ended badly. The few men I have dated were mostly casual, and the men were the ones who ended things when I wasn't available every night because of my business. I spend a lot of hours at the shop, and on my days off, I like to chill in my pajamas. Not very glamorous, but that's my life." Charlotte jutted her chin up, and Jude wondered if she was preparing him for what he had to look forward to. Or maybe she was challenging him.

Challenge accepted.

"Then those men weren't right for you. You have built an amazing business, and it takes time and effort to keep it successful." Jude winked at her, and Charlotte relaxed. "Okay, no past boyfriends. And you said there haven't been any disgruntled customers. No bridezillas."

Charlotte laughed. "Oh, there have been plenty of those but only in the beginning. I've been doing this long enough to pick my battles. When a bride says she wants some crazy color scheme, I put together one small arrangement to show them what they'll be getting. Nine times out of ten they realize it isn't what they really want. Then I show them something different. Something less chaotic, and they make the right decision. Those who insist their ideas are the best love what I put together even though I think it looks like crap. I've never received a bad review. Never had anyone come back after the fact and complain. Most of my wedding business is from word-of-mouth. Someone whose Aunt Edna attended a wedding and told her niece or nephew they should use my shop, or the maid of honor remembering me when it was her turn to get married."

Zedra turned and tucked her leg underneath her

butt. "Could this be someone from Wynter's past?"

"Why would they target me though? Why not her?"

Zedra held up her hands. "Just thinking out loud here. People do crazy things when they feel slighted. Maybe by going after her best friend, they feel it will hurt her too."

Charlotte glared at Zedra. "Wynter doesn't have anyone from her past who would want to hurt her either."

"And you know every single person your best friend has ever gone out with?" Zedra challenged.

"Are you saying I don't? Is that what this is between the two of you? You dated Wynter, and she didn't tell me? If you think you're being coy, you're really not." Charlotte was fishing, but she would never admit it.

Zedra stood from the sofa and looked down at Charlotte. "I'm saying you never truly know every single thing about someone else. You might think you do, but everyone has secrets, Charlotte. Everyone." Zedra strode to the dining area and began cleaning off the table. With the neighbor interrupting their meal, none of them had finished their plates.

"Do you want me to reheat your spaghetti?" Jude asked.

"No, thank you. I've lost my appetite." Charlotte leaned her head back and closed her eyes. Jude studied the female. Her face was devoid of makeup, and she was still pretty. Her freckles were more pronounced, and he wanted to map every single one of them. He also wanted to take away the stress she was under, and the best way to do that was to figure out who was targeting her. But if she had no enemies…

"We need to talk to Elise. If Roger visits her every week, there has to be something he's told her that would indicate what he's after."

Charlotte opened her eyes. "I'll give her a call tomorrow and ask her to meet for lunch after church Sunday. Hopefully by then I'll figure out exactly what to say to her." Charlotte turned toward Zedra. "Leave the dishes. I'll get them later."

Zedra waved her off. "No, I got them." Jude could feel the tension between the two females, and that wouldn't do if Zedra was going to continue watching over Charlotte. He had no idea what happened between Zedra and Wynter, but something had. Zedra said it was when she first moved to the area, and that had been about fifteen years ago if he remembered correctly. Before he could figure out how to fix things, Charlotte rose and padded to the kitchen.

"I'm sorry, Zedra. You're right about people having secrets, and if you and Wynter did go out or whatever, it's none of my business." Charlotte began helping the other female clean up.

"I'm sorry too. If you want to put the leftovers in containers, I'll handle the dishes."

Jude shook his head, proud of how the females quickly got themselves back on an even keel. He wondered what secrets Charlotte had and if he would ever discover them. If they were something that could help with finding who was stalking her, he hoped he found out sooner rather than later. He also prayed they weren't anything which would keep them from moving toward having a relationship. Charlotte was aware of his lifestyle. She had agreed to a date knowing his kink. Perhaps even because of it. It wouldn't be the first time a female had shown interest because of his status as a Master. She mentioned casual relationships, but Jude didn't want to think about her with anyone else. Yes, that was hypocritical, but he couldn't help it.

With Roger being their only suspect, they needed more information on the male. Why would he tell Elise he wanted to be with her but only show up one night a week? Was his own kink keeping him away the other nights? Whether or not he was the one targeting Charlotte, the male was hiding something. Jude vowed to figure out what.

"I'm going to step outside," he said. The females waved him off, so he unlocked the back door and slid it open. The air was brisk. If he weren't a shifter, he would need a coat. Jude loved winters in New York. He relished the colder temperatures. If Charlotte was going to be his, he needed to make sure she had the appropriate gear for riding during the colder months. Jude couldn't wait to get her on the back of his bike and take off on a road trip. But that couldn't happen anytime soon. Not with her being in the middle of a busy season. Charlotte mentioned her previous relationships failing because she didn't have a lot of free time.

Jude could envision having supper ready for her when she got home from a long day at her shop. He would run her a bubble bath and give her massages to relieve the tension and stress from standing on her feet all day. He understood about work getting in the way of relationships. With him doing mercenary jobs, he was often gone for days at a time. At least Charlotte wouldn't be sitting home waiting for him to return. She had her own business to keep her busy while he was away. Jude gazed at the moon, realizing he was thinking about a future with Charlotte like it was a done deal. It had been a long time since he felt like he might have found his mate, and he wasn't going to let the past tarnish his hope.

When he went back inside, Jude had Charlotte install the app on her phone that allowed her to access the cameras. He also had her change the passcode on the alarm. When that was done, she announced she was ready for bed.

"I'll take the sofa, if that's okay with you. Zedra can have the spare bedroom. Then tomorrow, I need to head home for a few hours, but I'll be back before you close up for the night." Jude wanted nothing more than for Charlotte to invite him to her bed, but with Zedra there, that would be awkward.

"I can take the sofa," Charlotte offered.

"That's not necessary. Your couch is plenty comfortable."

Zedra settled the argument by sitting down. "*I'll* take the sofa." She grabbed the soft-looking blanket folded over the back of the couch and stretched out before Jude could argue.

Charlotte took Jude's hand. "Okay then. You get the spare room." She led him down the hallway and stopped in front of the open door. "Thank you for everything." Charlotte leaned in and pressed her lips to his. He wanted to deepen the kiss, but she pulled back and walked away. He admired her ass in the cute sleep pants. When he noticed her ass wasn't moving, he raised his eyes to find her grinning at him. "My eyes are up here."

"And what pretty eyes they are." They laughed at the reversal of positions from earlier.

"Goodnight, Jude."

"Night, Charlie." Jude didn't bother taking off his clothes. He did remove his kutte and boots before lying down. Having not slept the night before, Jude was tired. As a Gryphon, he could go days without sleep if need be, but he didn't fight it when his eyes became heavy. He hoped his dreams would be filled with freckles and curly hair instead of guns and blood.

CHAPTER NINE

Spyder

BEING PRIVY TO Charlotte's morning routine thrilled Jude. She woke early enough to have a piece of cinnamon toast and coffee before getting dressed for her day. She was either unaware he was watching, or she didn't care as she danced around the kitchen, singing off-key to the music playing on her phone. Jude took the opportunity to observe Charlotte from the hallway. When she caught him watching, she just smiled.

"Good morning. Coffee?" she offered.

"Yes, please." He crossed the space and stood close enough to catch her scent. It was probably a good thing Zedra had stayed, because Jude didn't think he would be strong enough to resist Charlotte's cuteness otherwise. "Thank you," he said when she handed him the mug. Jude snagged her wrist before she got too far away. Pulling her to him, he pressed a kiss to her forehead. "Good morning."

"Can I fix you something to eat?" Charlotte asked, staring at his lips.

Jude set the mug down and wrapped his arms around her waist. Kissing her was a bad idea, but he needed a small taste. Moving one hand to her curls, he cradled her head and pressed their lips together. Charlotte opened for him, tasting of coffee and cinnamon sugar. She slid her hands up his chest, around his neck, and held on tight. It was a slow, sensual dance of tongues and lips. They tasted and teased until Zedra cleared her throat.

"Don't mind me. I'll just hang out over here and enjoy the show." Zedra stood at the counter with a full cup of coffee. Jude had been so into the kiss he hadn't heard the female enter the room.

"Show's over." Jude kissed Charlotte's nose before releasing her to pick up his own mug.

"No wonder you go to bed so early." Zedra yawned, twisting her waist. "I would too if I had to get up at the crack of ass."

Charlotte laughed. "It's not always like this, but it is my busy season. Well, one of them. Once Valentine's Day is over, there will be a small lull until wedding season. It used to start in June, but for me it begins in May. I can have as many as three or four weddings per weekend. Then things start slowing down again afterward. After years of having my own business, I'm used to it."

"I'm going to run through the shower, and then I'll be ready to go." Zedra grabbed some clothes from her go-bag and disappeared down the hallway.

Charlotte leaned her hip against the counter. "Am I taking Zedra away from her job? I didn't even ask what it is she does or how she could drop everything to babysit me."

"She works with her brother in their security business. Mostly she handles the admin part of it, but if

110

needed, she does security like she's doing with you."

"Is she trained in martial arts or something? Don't get me wrong. I appreciate her help, but she doesn't appear like she could kick anyone's ass."

"Looks can be deceiving." Jude finished his coffee, rinsed his mug, and put it in the dishwasher. When he turned around, Charlotte was standing close enough to touch, so he did. He snagged her around the waist and pulled her to him. Brushing her curls off her shoulder, he studied her freckles. Charlotte leaned in and pressed her cheek to his chest. Jude tightened his grip, and they embraced quietly for a few minutes.

"Thank you for making me feel safe," Charlotte said against his neck. Her warm breath had his cock twitching, but it wasn't the right time to get a hard-on.

"You're welcome. Thank you for calling me. I'd hate to think of someone else guarding you."

Charlotte leaned back, smiling. She was so fucking cute he couldn't resist a small kiss.

"I'm ready," Zedra said, interrupting once again.

Jude pressed his lips to Charlotte's temple before releasing her. "Then let's ride." He helped Charlotte into her coat, then followed both females to the parking lot. He scanned the area but didn't see anyone else out that early. There was little traffic, and they made it to Charlotte's business quickly. Kristoff and Margie arrived within minutes. If Jude hadn't already borne witness to the dynamic between Charlotte and her employees, he would wonder what made them work such long hours. It was apparent the two workers not only loved what they did but Charlotte as well. They were like family, and Jude wanted to keep them all safe. He wanted to ensure Rhiannon had a safe environment if she ever had the chance to come work with Charlie.

Kristoff exited his car, his hands full of two pink baker's boxes. "I come bearing gifts." Jude didn't know what was inside, but by Charlotte's smile, it was something she enjoyed.

"Two boxes? What gives?"

"There are two hunky men watching our asses. They deserve their own box."

"You wish they were watching your ass," Margie sassed. It was the first time Jude had heard the other woman make a joke. Charlotte laughed, and Kristoff wiggled his butt. Kristoff was gorgeous with his shoulder-length, dark hair and bright blue eyes. He had an average build and was several inches taller than Jude, but his ass did fill out his jeans nicely.

"See? Even Jude can't keep his eyes off my ass." Kristoff blew Jude a kiss. He handed one box to Charlotte before heading Ace's direction with the other. "Good morning, my Ace of Hearts. I brought you and the ripped one breakfast."

Ripper grinned at Kristoff's play on words. "Please tell me there are eclairs hiding in there."

"Of course there are. And this box is for you two to share. Enjoy." Kristoff handed the treats over and retreated inside with no further flirting. Jude liked that about the man. He was just playful enough to make the Hounds feel good without crossing any lines.

With Ace and Ripper on guard duty, Jude didn't worry about leaving Charlotte and the others alone while he returned home to shower. He didn't kiss Charlotte goodbye the way he wanted. She had a business to run, and he had people he needed to talk to.

Jude headed to his home on Beecher Street, where he showered and changed in record time, ready to get to Zander's office. It was still early, but Zander was waiting for Jude when he arrived.

"Morning, Spyder."

"Good morning. Thank you for meeting me so early." Jude handed the envelope of photos over to Zander.

"Son of a bitch is smart," Zander said as he looked at the pictures. "And whoever it is has been watching Charlotte for a while." Zander scrubbed a hand down his face before tapping away at his keyboard. "Where does the neighbor live who delivered the envelope?"

"Four doors down."

"Okay, let me take a look."

Jude sat in one of the leather chairs across from Zander's desk and waited. "We don't know when these were delivered, and we don't know which cars belong in the area and which don't. Let's get Bishop on the line and see if he can help." Zander dialed Bishop for a video chat. The male answered, sitting at his desk.

"Good morning, Zander."

"Bishop, I have Spyder here with me. Someone dropped an envelope full of photos off at one of Charlotte's neighbors yesterday. I went back through the video recording from her front door, but there was no one on foot. Several cars entered the parking lot, and most of those were quick in-and-outs. They could belong to whoever delivered the package, or they could be residents. Is there any way you can tap into the camera at the guard shack? If we can see who stopped to ask for entrance, we can narrow it down."

"I should be able to. This new system Julian Stone hooked me up with is amazing. It's also fucking scary. It makes you wonder who else in the world has these capabilities and how much privacy we actually have."

Jude leaned his forearms on his thighs. "Truth, but like the Stone Society, you're using it for good, not to perv on some unsuspecting female."

Bishop snorted and shook his head. "Nope. No perving here. Spyder, if you would, please ask Charlotte what kind of vehicle Roger drives. That may help in finding where he actually lives as well as see if his car is one of those coming in and out of her complex."

"I already have that info from when Hawk and I drove by his home."

"What if he doesn't use the same vehicle? He might drive the wife's car sometimes."

"Truth. I'll call her now." Jude pulled out his phone and dialed her cell. When it went to voicemail, he then called the business phone.

"Good morning. Thank you for calling The Blooming Boutique."

"Margie, it's Jude. Can you put Charlotte on the phone please?"

"Sure. Hang on a second." Margie's steps were muffled as she walked across the tile flooring in her sneakers. Jude rattled off the make and model of Roger's car while he waited. Margie's footsteps halted. "It's for you. It's your man."

"Margie!" Charlotte must have placed the phone against her body, because her next words were muffled. Was she saying Jude wasn't hers? When she did answer, Charlotte's voice was breathy. "Hello?"

Jude wanted to hear that tone when they were alone. And naked.

"Hey, Charlie. Sorry to bother you, but we need to know what kind of vehicle Roger drives. I should have already asked you this."

"You aren't bothering me." Charlotte rattled off the make and model as well as the license plate number. They were different than either one in Roger's driveway.

"Damn, that's impressive." Jude relayed the information to Bishop. "Thanks, Love. I'll let you get back to work." Fuck, he hoped Charlie didn't look too closely at the endearment. He didn't want to scare her off before they even had their first date. Yes, he spent the night in her home, and yes, they had already kissed. But sometimes his mouth overrode his brain.

"Talk to you later." Charlotte's tone was warm. Damnit. He also wanted to hear that voice when they were alone. After they'd been naked. Coming down from mutual orgasms.

"Spyder?" Zander was smirking at him.

"Sorry. She's just... Yeah. I'm here." Jude felt like an idiot. He was almost fifty, and his libido was wrecking his brain.

Zander grinned. "I get it, Brother. Farrah still makes me forget myself after all these years." Zander had been mated long before Jude met the male. He and his female grew up together as kids, and as soon as they hit puberty and came into their Gryphons, that was it. Farrah was a blonde bombshell like the actress she had been named for, and she had given Zander five offspring who ranged in ages from thirty-nine down to ten. Erik, the oldest, worked with his dad at the security firm. Farrah was much more than her looks. The female could build anything her mind created. She mostly built furniture, but sometimes she carved wooden creatures that were beyond realistic. They were fantastical. Several of her carvings were placed around Zander's office.

"Okay, let me get busy," Bishop said from the screen. "I'll call you as soon as I have something."

"Thanks, Brother." Zander disconnected the call. To Jude, he said, "I've never seen you so taken with a female."

"Charlie's different. There's something about her. Something I can't put my finger on. I mean, we just met, for Zeus's sake, and not under the best circumstances. If she were anyone else, I'd say I feel protective because someone's after her. If I didn't know better, I'd say I've known her for a long time. She's that familiar to me."

"Then let me be the first to say congratulations. It seems you've found your mate."

"Technically, you're the second. Your sister said the same thing last night. But I really think I have. She's—" Jude's phone rang, and he smiled when Charlie's name flashed on the display.

"Hey there. Did you think of something else?"

"I called Elise to ask her to meet me, but her phone is going directly to voicemail without ringing for some reason, so I called the hospital even though she doesn't normally work on weekends. Jude, her supervisor said she turned in her notice and no longer works there. I have a bad feeling about this. Why wouldn't she call me and tell me?"

"Do you want me to drive by her house and check

116

on her?"

"Would you? Please? I have to get this wedding order over to the venue by noon."

"Text me the address. I'll go over there now." Jude had a bad feeling about Elise, but he wasn't going to share it with Charlotte. He didn't want her any more worried than she already was.

"Thank you. Please call me back if you talk to her."

"Will do." Jude hung up without promising he'd find her cousin. He honestly didn't know what was going on. "Elise's phone is going straight to voicemail, and she quit her job at the hospital. I'm going to ride by her house."

"You want me to go with you?" Zander asked.

"Please. Two sets of eyes are always better. If you don't mind, let's take your SUV. It's less noticeable than my bike."

"Of course." Zander closed his laptop and rounded the desk. Erik stepped into the office as Jude turned to leave.

"Hey, Spyder, long time, no see." Erik held out his hand, and Jude shook it. "How's it going with the florist?"

"Frustrating. Not us, or her. Uh, the case. It's slow-going."

Zander shook his head. "We're headed out to check on the cousin's house. If Bishop calls, patch him through to my cell."

"You got it." Erik clapped his hand on Zander's shoulder and gave Jude a chin lift. The male was the spitting image of his father. Anyone who met the two mistook them for brothers.

Once in the SUV, Zander asked for the address. He

punched it into the navigation system, then drove toward the freeway. "I filled Erik in on the case last night. He was already aware that Bishop had been in New Atlanta with Lucy. I knew the two of them hung out, but I didn't realize they were as close as they are. Erik keeps things close to the vest. When we're at work, he's strictly business."

"He is an adult. I don't talk to Indigo about what Hawk and I get up to."

Zander grinned. "Yeah, I would hope not. *Hey, Mom. Would you like me to show you my fancy rope work?*"

Jude laughed at Zander's high-pitched voice. "Wait. How do you know about my rope work?"

"I have my ways." Zander kept his eyes on the road, but his mouth was pulled up at the side. When he glanced at Jude, he shook his head and sighed. "Erik might be tight-lipped, but Jackie isn't. She tells her mother everything. She visited Dominion last year on that night they let anyone in and saw you, Hawk, and Kayos there." Jaclyn was Zander's oldest daughter. Katie was their youngest. Farrah thought it would be cute to keep the "Charlie's Angels" theme going with their names. He put his foot down with their sons though. "Don't worry, Spyder. When I overheard their conversation, I explained to my mate and daughter how important it was to keep that information quiet. What someone does in their private life is just that."

"I appreciate that. But I didn't see her. As a matter of fact, I haven't seen her there since."

"She went with her best friend, Tamara. Jackie didn't want Tamara going alone, so she tagged along. Kind of like Wynter did with Charlotte."

"Tamara… Tamara… Tall redhead?"

118

"That's her, but please don't tell me she's one of your... what do you call them? Subs? Bottoms? If she's into bondage, that's her business, but she's also like a daughter to me, and I sure as hell don't want to know what she gets up to in her private life."

"I would never betray her trust that way, but I can say she isn't into bondage." Jude didn't elaborate because Kayos offered what that female liked, and that was not an image Zander needed about someone he considered a daughter.

It didn't take long to reach Elise's home. There were no cars in the driveway, but there was a detached garage with a breezeway connecting it to the house. Zander parked in front of the garage and cut the motor. The two males exited the SUV. While Jude walked toward the front door, Zander strode to the side of the garage and looked in the window.

"No car in the garage," he said.

Jude rang the doorbell, but he knew in his gut no one was home. He reached out with his Gryphon senses and didn't hear anyone inside. Zander peered through the window at the end of the porch.

"Looks like she's moving."

After peering in the window for himself, Jude walked around the house, looking in each window that wasn't covered by blinds. In all the rooms he could see into, there were boxes stacked up.

"Hey. Get away from there!" The undeniable cocking of a shotgun sounded as Jude turned around, hands in the air. He was surprised to find an old woman standing at the edge of Elise's yard.

"We don't want any trouble, ma'am. We're looking for Elise. Her cousin is worried about her."

The woman narrowed her eyes, and she hugged the gun higher against her shoulder. "Which cousin?"

"Charlotte."

"I haven't seen that girl in months. But you can tell her Elise went on vacation. Her and that nice boyfriend of hers."

"You've met Roger?" Jude asked.

"Roger? Her boyfriend's name is Roland. He fixed my water heater last week. Saved me a bunch of money."

"Do you know where they went on vacation?" Zander asked.

"Some type of cruise. I didn't ask a lot of questions because I'm not one of those nosy types."

The woman finally lowered the shotgun, and Jude breathed a little easier. Gryphons didn't have impenetrable skin like male Gargoyles. Still, Jude kept his eyes on the gun. "Do you know if she's planning on moving? There are a lot of boxes inside."

"Wouldn't surprise me if she was. That Roland's a real catch. Handsome, handy, and dotes on Elise like she hung the moon."

Zander scoffed under his breath before asking, "You wouldn't happen to know Roland's last name, would you?"

"If Elise mentioned it, I don't remember. Anyway, I'll tell Elise her cousin's worried about her when she gets back."

"That would be appreciated. But one more question. Do you know Elise's new phone number?"

"New number? She didn't say anything about that."

Jude had a feeling Elise didn't mention what was

going on because she didn't want the woman to worry. "Okay, well, thank you for your time." He started toward the SUV, and Zander followed.

"Boxes packed, disconnected phone, and she goes on vacation? I'm not buying that," Zander said once they were on the road.

"Me neither." Jude didn't want to bother Charlotte while she was getting the order ready for delivery, so he decided to wait until after she returned to the shop to fill her in.

Something about the older woman niggled at Jude's gut. He knew not everyone aged the same way, but the way she carried herself, the ease with which she held the gun, didn't scream old woman. Neither did her voice. "There's something off about that woman."

"I noticed it too." Zander tapped his fingers on the steering wheel. "She didn't act like an older person, did she?"

"No, she didn't. Her skin wasn't wrinkled, and her voice..." Jude sent a text to Bishop asking him to identify the owner of the house next to Elise's.

"Perhaps she has a really good dermatologist and uses whatever popular serum is on the market to keep her face looking young."

"Yeah, maybe." Jude didn't think so, though. His phone pinged with a text.

Bishop: *House belongs to Barbara Thacker. Husband Tony deceased as of five years ago. He had a substantial life insurance policy, so Barbara is set. One daughter – Marla – has been in and out of jail for misdemeanors, mostly drugs. Last known location New Jersey. Can search further if needed.*

121

Jude: *That's enough for now. Thanks.*

Marla. That name sounded familiar, but Jude had met many females in his life. Instead of dwelling on it, he read Bishop's text aloud. Another message followed. It included a photo of Mrs. Thacker. When they stopped at a red light, Jude showed the photo to Zander.

Zander used his fingers to enlarge the picture. The light turned green, and the Hound returned his eyes to the road. As he accelerated, Zander said, "And the plot thickens."

CHAPTER TEN

Charlotte

ZEDRA STOOD SENTRY as Charlotte and Kristoff loaded the flowers into the van. Ace was nowhere to be seen, but as Jude explained, that was the point of having experienced security. They were close enough to help if needed, but hidden so they weren't obvious. He and Ripper were now trading off watching the shop since Zander had taken over the security cameras.

"Thanks, Sugar Bear." Charlotte hugged Kristoff after he closed the back door to the delivery van. Normally, he or Margie rode with Charlotte, but this particular wedding was small. Charlotte would drop off the bouquets and boutonnières at the church before taking the arrangements to the small inn where the reception was being held. It might be smaller, but it was no less important, especially considering the bride was the mayor of New Albany's daughter. When the woman introduced herself during their initial consultation, Charlotte expected an elaborate setting, but Carrie Ann Drysdale surprised her. They were keeping things low-key – family and a few close friends only. Wynter was the wedding coordinator,

123

and Charlotte didn't want any trouble.

After she and Zedra were on the road, Charlotte told the woman as much. "I know you're here to protect me, but this is our livelihood."

"Don't worry, Charlie. I promise I won't antagonize Wynter. Hell, I won't speak to her if that's what you think is best. I'm here to keep you safe, not cause more trouble."

"Thank you, Zed. I spoke to Wynter earlier when I gave her the code to my new alarm. She was dropping Gibby off at my apartment on her way to the church, and I reminded her you'd be with me."

"Did she explain how we met?" Zedra asked.

"No, and I didn't ask. It's none of my business. You were right that we all have secrets, and if she needs to keep this one, I can respect that." Charlotte was practically an open book when it came to her best friend. She lived life to the fullest with no regrets, but not everyone did. Too many people held themselves back because they were afraid of societal recrimination. Too afraid of what their families would think about their choices. Elise used to be the same way, but one tragic afternoon changed her cousin.

"Can I ask you a personal question?" Zedra rubbed her hands down her jeans as though she were nervous.

"You can, but I reserve the right not to answer. You know, secrets and all that."

Zedra snorted. "Fair enough. I know you met Spyder at Dominion. Is that something you're interested in? The kink?"

It was odd to hear Jude referred to by his biker name. "The lighter parts of it, like what Jude does with his ropes, definitely. I'm not into pain, but I think I

124

might like to be spanked or have one of the softer floggers used on my ass. I'm looking forward to when he and I can have a night alone so he can show me what it feels like to be bound." Charlotte glanced over at Zedra and found the woman smiling. "What?"

"I like you, Charlie, and I think you're just the female Spyder needs in his life."

"I guess we'll see." Charlotte was smitten with Jude Sterling. When Zedra explained how the Hounds of Zeus weren't like other bikers, Charlotte had been skeptical. All she knew of motorcycle clubs came from movies and television shows. But having met several of the members and seeing how respectful they were, Charlotte believed what Zedra had shared. Jude said his MC, as well as his family, was all about rescuing people, and Zedra had reiterated that fact. Seeing them drop everything to watch over Charlotte and figure out who was after her made her a believer.

"Here we are." Charlotte pulled in the parking lot of the church and drove around back until she found the door Wynter mentioned. Zedra had already asked Charlotte to wait in the van until Zed cleared the area, whatever that meant. The woman didn't carry a gun. She didn't look imposing, but looks could be deceiving. After less than a minute, Zedra opened Charlotte's door for her.

"All clear." They walked to the back of the van together, and Zedra helped carry the boxes. The back door was unlocked, and Zedra insisted on entering the church first. "You can never be too careful." Charlotte wasn't a security expert, but she was more afraid of someone sneaking up from behind than attacking from inside a church. She looked over her shoulder, but the parking lot was empty save a few cars, including Wynter's.

"Good morning, Zedra," Wynter said cordially as soon as they stepped inside. "Please, follow me." Charlotte's bestie was in professional mode. She had greeted Zedra with the same smile she would anyone, and Charlotte's worry dissipated. Wynter led them to a classroom the bride and her attendants were using as a dressing room.

"Charlotte!" Carrie Ann exclaimed as soon as she entered the room. "Oh, my gosh! They're perfect. Tracy, look!" The bride grabbed her maid of honor by the elbow, dragging her over to see the bouquets. "Didn't I tell you Charlotte was the best?" Tracy oohed and awed as expected, and she wasn't merely paying lip service. She was genuinely impressed with the flowers. Carrie Ann had wanted simple yet elegant, and that's what Charlotte provided.

"The boutonnières and corsages are still in the van. I'll go—"

"You stay here. I'll get them," Zedra offered.

"Thank you." Charlotte turned to Wynter. "How was Gibby?"

"He was happy to be home, but he had to sniff everything before he settled down. He knows there have been strangers in his space." Wynter tapped her smart watch and read a message. "That was Carlton. He said there was a wreck on Vine Street, so you'll need to go in the back way."

"Good to know." Charlotte allotted plenty of time in case of such things, but having a heads-up was nice. Zedra returned from the van carrying the last two boxes.

126

"Here, I'll take those," Wynter offered. "The flowers are gorgeous, Charlie. You outdid yourself again."

"Thanks, Boo. We'll leave you to it." Charlotte kissed Wynter on the cheek before turning to Carrie Ann. "Good luck today. I know it'll be a stunning wedding."

"Thank you again, Charlotte." The bride cradled her bouquet, inhaling the fragrant flowers.

"It was my pleasure." And Charlotte meant that with all her heart. She had always loved flowers, but it wasn't until one of her girlfriends couldn't afford a florist for her wedding that the idea hit. Charlotte had gone to the craft store and put together a colorful bouquet for her friend and boutonnière for the groom. She had always loved helping Ellen with her flowerbeds in the summer, and helping her friend gave Charlotte the idea of opening her own business. She had started small, making arrangements in her apartment and selling them at the farmer's market. It didn't take long before she was getting requests for weddings, and Charlotte, with Wynter's help, learned about wholesale warehouses, business licenses, advertising, and everything that went into owning her own shop. Ten years later, and Charlotte was one of the most successful florists in the New Albany area.

The drive to the inn took longer than normal because of the wreck Wynter had warned her about, but Charlotte was familiar enough with the area she was able to navigate the back roads and arrive on time. No, the wedding hadn't even started, but the reception needed to be set up and ready to go ahead of time so that when the wedding party arrived, everything was in place. Charlotte had a few close calls in her early days and had learned from those experiences. Once again, Zedra helped transport the arrangements inside. Charlotte had met with Carlton once Carrie Ann signed the contract, and she knew how the venue was being set up. She directed Zed to the back of the dining room where together they placed the arrangements in their appropriate spots.

Carlton rushed into the room more flustered than Charlotte had ever seen. "Sorry I didn't meet you at the door. The mayor called with some last-minute changes."

"No problem. We put everything where we previously discussed, and here is the throw-away bouquet for the cake table." Charlotte took the bag of blush rose petals from Zedra. "And here are the petals for the cake. These need to go in the cooler."

"Got it. Thank you for your punctuality, Charlotte. It makes my day easier."

"No problem. Anything we can do to help?"

Carlton shook his head. "No, but thank you. Mayor Drysdale added four people to the guest list, and space is already tight. I'll figure it out."

"Okay. We'll get out of your hair. See you next time."

Carlton rushed off, waving over his shoulder.

"I'm impressed." Zedra strapped on her seatbelt, smiling. "You have this down to a science."

"I've been doing weddings for a while now. Working with Wynter helps though. We meet several times before the day of the event to know where everything goes. Winter weddings – the season, not the woman – are the hardest. Sometimes it takes a minute to source certain flowers if the bride requests something off the wall, but for the most part, I have good suppliers."

"It's also something you enjoy. I can tell by watching you like working with plants. Not everyone can take several different flowers and put them together the way you do."

"What about you? Do you like working security? I can't imagine it's an easy job." Charlotte couldn't see putting herself in front of someone to protect them even if she were trained.

"Most of the time I'm in the office, so it's not as glamourous as you may be thinking. I do enjoy it for the most part. Sometimes I get men who don't want a female protecting them. They don't think I'm strong enough or smart enough." Zedra glanced in the sideview mirror, and then turned to look out the back. "Charlie, I need you to take the next exit."

"What? Why?" Charlotte flipped on her turn signal and sped up to merge into the outer lane. "Zed—"

"Don't panic, but we have a tail. Black truck, three vehicles back."

Charlotte gripped the steering wheel tighter. She waited until the last second to take the exit, but when she glanced in the rearview mirror, the truck was closing in on them. "Shit, hang on." Charlotte took the right at the bottom of the offramp faster than she should, barely missing a car merging into her lane. When the other driver laid on their horn, Charlotte muttered, "Sorry." The van wasn't made for speed, but she pushed it to its limit. The truck, however, was powerful. Traffic was thick on the four-lane, but Charlotte wove in and out of the cars like a pro.

"Where's a cop when you need one?" Charlotte blew through a yellow light with the truck on her ass. "Seriously?"

"Charlie, you can't outrun them. We need to find somewhere to—" The truck tagged the van's bumper, and both women were pushed forward, their seat belts digging into their chests. "Sonofamotherfucker! Crazy fucking pig licker!" Zedra braced her hand on the dashboard as Charlotte changed lanes before slamming on the brakes. "What are you doing?"

Charlotte made a U-turn in front of oncoming traffic. Cars braked hard and horns blared as cars scrambled to stop or get out of her way. Charlotte didn't let up though. She punched the gas and took off in the opposite direction. "Get Jude on the phone. Tell him what's going on. We need a divers—" A loud pop sounded, and the van careened hard to the right. "Fucker shot my tire!"

"Charlie, look out!" Zedra shouted, like Charlotte couldn't see the light pole they were headed for. Charlotte pulled hard on the steering wheel, but it was no use. She closed her eyes, let go of the wheel, and braced for impact. The airbags did their job, but the seat belt still cut into Charlotte's chest and stomach. The cab filled with the nasty, ashy substance from the airbags deploying, and Charlotte started coughing while waving her hands.

Sirens rent the air, but they weren't close enough for Charlotte's peace of mind. Zedra, still cursing the driver of the truck, released her seat belt. Before Charlotte knew what was happening, an animalistic growl filled her ears as Zedra crawled across the console. Were those fangs? And holy shitballs! Zedra's long hair was no longer auburn. A fur-covered head that looked scarily like a lion smothered Charlotte's face. She couldn't see, but the roar that left her guardian was deafening. Okay, so she'd hit her head and had passed out, because if she'd been conscious, she wouldn't have a lapful of wild animal. That, or she was dead, and this was her version of Hell. Charlotte didn't think she warranted Hell. She'd lived a good life.

"Shit, shit, shit." Zedra lunged backward onto her side of the van. Bloody claws retracted, and Charlotte started laughing. Not in a humorous, this-is-funny laugh but a hysterical, I've-lost-my-mind, high-pitched chortle. "Fuck, I'm so sorry." Zedra wiped her hands on her jeans, but the blood wasn't coming off.

"What the fuck are you?" Charlotte managed to ask after her wheezing stopped. Before Zed could answer, Charlotte's door was wrenched open. Charlotte screamed as she tried to back away from the door, but her seat belt kept her in place. She grabbed at the buckle, and when Zedra reached over to help, Charlotte smacked at her hand.

"Ma'am, please calm down." The man's voice was soothing, not threatening. When a quick peek at his chest revealed a paramedic's uniform, not someone out to kill her, Charlotte relaxed.

"You ladies okay?" Charlotte nodded, but the movement made her dizzy. She released her seat belt, leaned over, and threw up all over his shoes. "I'll take that as a no."

Charlotte remained quiet as the first responders got her out of the van and into a waiting ambulance. The one Charlotte had tossed her cookies on was

131

arguing with Zedra for refusing medical treatment. "Worry about her. I'm fine."

"But you have blood on your hands. Where did that come from?"

"I cut myself on a vase earlier. Seriously, I don't need stitches. Can I ride with her?"

Charlotte wasn't sure she wanted the woman in the ambulance with her. What in the ever-loving hell was that back in the van? As badly as her head throbbed, Charlotte knew she had to have imagined a lion on her lap, because Zedra was not an animal. The police arrived and started questioning her as she lay on the gurney. Another officer questioned Zedra a few feet away.

Closing her eyes against the pain, Charlotte said, "Someone in a large, black truck began following us on the freeway. I tried to get away from him, but he shot out my tire, causing me to hit the pole."

"Do you know why someone would try to kill you?" Officer Blake asked.

That shocked Charlotte. Had the man been trying to kill her or just scare her? "I had a couple things happen at home and at my business. Break-ins."

"Did you call the police?"

"Yes. Officer Sims came to my shop."

"I don't recognize that name."

"My shop, The Blooming Boutique, is in New Latham. I had just dropped off flowers for a wedding and was on my way back."

"Did you get a look at the driver?"

"No. But Zedra might have. She leaned over me, and..." Charlotte clamped her mouth shut. She couldn't admit what she thought she saw.

"And?" the officer urged.

"And I must have blacked out. That's all I remember." Charlotte's stomach threatened to heave again. She looked at the paramedic. "I don't feel so well."

"I need to get her on the bus," he said to the cop. That was enough for the officer to let her go with no further interrogation. The gurney was lifted, and the shuffling didn't help Charlotte's stomach. The paramedic grabbed a plastic bowl and held it beside her head. Charlotte breathed through the nausea, squelching the need to puke. The back doors closed as Zedra was yelling, "Wait!"

It was stupid, but Charlotte was glad for a little distance from the other woman. She needed to wrap her head around what she thought she saw and heard.

"I'm starting an IV. I'll give you something for nausea and pain." The man was efficient. Charlotte barely registered the prick of the needle going in her arm. Needle? Was that the technical term?

"What's that thing you're sticking in my arm?"

"I just explained how I'm starting an IV." His eyebrows dipped as though he was worried about her mental state.

"No, I mean the needle thing. Is it called a needle?" Charlotte needed to know. It was imperative to keep her mind off Zed.

"Oh. It's called a catheter."

"I thought that was what you put in someone to help them pee."

"Same terminology, different use. Can you tell me your name?"

"Charlotte Fanning. What's yours?" Charlotte

closed her eyes, but the memory of the wreck assaulted her senses, so she opened them to stare at the handsome Black man tending to her. He was chuckling.

"I'm Rob, and Cassie is driving. Do you know what day it is, Charlotte?"

"Saturday. Carrie Ann's wedding."

"Very good. Did your friend really cut her hands on a vase?" Rob was busy cleaning Charlotte's face, so he didn't notice when she blanched. "Because I didn't see any glass."

"I don't know. I was trying not to wreck. It was all a blur really." Charlotte was lying, but she wasn't going to tell this man anything that might get Zedra in trouble. Not until she talked to the woman and got some answers.

Zedra

"Look, I need to get to the hospital and check on my friend." What Zedra really needed was to get away from the cops and wash her fucking hands

"What you need to do is calm down and answer the questions. Your friend is being cared for. Tell me again about the blood on your hands." Officer Perez would have been checking off all Zedra's boxes had he not been on the wrong end of this interrogation.

"I already told you I threw a vase out the window

134

trying to distract the driver of the truck. I missed." Yes, that sounded as irrational to her as it did the cop, but there was no way she was telling him her Lion came forth and clawed the driver as he approached Charlotte's window. She couldn't ask him to check local hospitals for a man being treated for gashes down his face. What a clusterfuck. "Look, there's a man out there who just tried to kill my friend. He's the one you should be going after, not me. If you call Officer Sims in New Latham, he'll tell you Charlotte called in a report of her shop being broken into."

It took thirty more minutes of back and forth before he let Zedra go. Thirty minutes for Charlotte to spill her guts to the paramedics about what really happened. When she was cleared to grab their things from the van, Zedra first ordered a ride, then she sent a text to Zander instead of calling. She didn't want the cops to overhear any part of their conversation. She also didn't want to hear her brother yelling at her. She had one job – to keep Charlotte safe. She'd failed.

Her phone rang within seconds of sending the text. "I'll call you back." Zedra hung up. She knew she'd catch hell, especially since Spyder was losing his mind in the background. Her car arrived, and Zedra slid into the back seat. The driver greeted her, and Zedra responded with a grunt. She dialed her brother.

"Zedra! What the actual fuck?"

"I couldn't talk freely. Long story short, we delivered the flowers to the inn and on our way back we got a tail. Four-wheel-drive, black Ford. Charlotte tried to lose him, but he shot out one of the van's tires. She lost control, and we hit a pole. The driver approached the window, but he met with my ferocious

135

side before he could get his hands on her. She's in an ambulance on her way to Mercer. I just got turned loose from the cops. Physically, she'll be fine."

"And mentally? You said the driver met your Gryphon. How fully did you shift?"

The rideshare driver kept glancing in the rearview, so Charlotte spoke in code. "Bushy hair. A mouthful of teeth. Nails needed a trim. Sounded pretty fierce."

"Fuck, Zed. We're going to have to wipe her mind. You better hope nobody had their cell phone out recording."

"I know. It all happened so fast. My first instinct was to keep her safe."

"Shit, yeah. I get it. It's not the first time our animals have popped out to save someone, and it won't be the last. Did you kill him?"

"No, I scratched his face before he took off."

"Did the cops see the blood?"

"Yep."

"Okay, I get it. You can't speak freely. We're on our way to the hospital. We'll meet you there."

"Ten-four." Zedra disconnected, then leaned her head back and closed her eyes. The male who attacked wouldn't be hard to recognize with slashes across his cheek. It would take months for him to heal from those types of wounds, so they hopefully had a reprieve and time to figure out who he was and what he wanted with Charlotte. One thing was certain – the man who attacked was not Roger Smith.

CHAPTER ELEVEN

Spyder

SPYDER CLENCHED HIS fists and closed his eyes as Zedra explained what happened. His claws dug into his palms, and it took all his willpower to push the Gryphon back. He couldn't hear what Zedra was saying because his beast was too fucking loud.

Shut the fuck up and stand down!

But she's hurt!

I know this. Fuck, I know, okay? But you trying to take over isn't helping.

Fucking *finally* the shifter inside backed down. His claws retracted, leaving Jude with blood on his hands. The gashes took their sweet time closing. Zander pointed to the glove box, and Jude opened the compartment. Inside were napkins from a fast-food restaurant. He grabbed a couple to wipe the blood from his palms. Now that he could hold his phone, he called Bishop.

"Bishop, Charlotte and Zed were in a wreck. They were attacked by a male in a black, four-wheel-drive Ford. He shot out their tire, and they hit a pole. I need you to hack into the local cameras and find that fucking truck! No, I don't have a location, shit!" Jude was losing his mind. He handed over the phone when Zander held his hand out.

"Bishop, Zander. Track Zedra's phone. She just left the scene. Thanks." Zander handed the phone back. "You need to pull yourself together before we get to the hospital. You also need to decide how to deal with the fact that Zed partially shifted into her Lion."

"I'll tell Charlotte the truth. She was going to find out anyway."

"Are you sure that's wise this early?"

"I'm sure. Not that I'm testing her, because I'm not, but if she can't handle the truth, I'd rather find out now than farther down the road when I've fallen harder." Jude wouldn't let anyone try to convince him he wasn't halfway in love with Charlotte already. The female was under his skin, and he wanted her to stay there. But one thing was clear – he wouldn't allow anyone else to guard her. He didn't blame Zed. She'd done the best she could under the circumstances, but Charlie had still been injured.

Jude remained calm until they reached the hospital. As soon as Zander had the SUV in park, Jude was out the door, rushing toward the entrance to the ER. Zed was waiting for them outside.

"How is she?"

"I don't know. They won't tell me anything since I'm not family."

Fuck that noise. Jude strode into the building and up to the desk. Using his Gryphon voice, he instructed the woman behind the desk to tell him where Charlotte was. She did, and then she pushed the button to open the door allowing him to enter the back. When he found her, Charlotte was lying on a bed hooked to an

IV. Her face had a few minor cuts, and her lip was swollen. Jude thanked Zeus she hadn't been injured worse, but he hated she was hurt at all. He stepped to the side of the bed and picked up her hand.

"I'm so sorry," Jude apologized for failing to keep her safe and blinked away the tears.

"It's not your fault. And I'm okay." Charlotte's voice was firm, but the frown told a different story.

"You're in the hospital hooked up to an IV. That's not okay." Jude took a deep breath, trying to calm himself.

Charlotte had yet to smile. "It's medicine for nausea. I threw up on the paramedic. I have a fat lip." Charlotte pursed her lips and looked down. "Air bags suck."

"Those air bags probably saved your life. What did the doctor say?"

"Haven't seen a doctor. Nurse said I need a scan to check my brain. Paramedic looked real worried, but I feel fine now."

"Better let them check you out just to be on the safe side. Sometimes injuries take a while to crop up."

"All right, here we— Who are you?" a nurse asked as she entered the area with a wheelchair.

"Jude Sterling, and I'm allowed to be back here," he answered, allowing his Gryphon voice to wash over the woman.

"Charlotte, let's get you down for your CT scan. I'm going to remove the IV first."

"Is that wise? What if she's still sick?" Jude asked.

"That's what the medicine was for." The nurse didn't hesitate to remove the needle from Charlotte's arm. She was quick and efficient, and in less than a minute, she had Charlie in the wheelchair. Charlie waved to him as she was rolled out into the hallway. Jude couldn't follow. Well, he could, but using his voice again would be wrong, so he leaned against the wall and typed out a text to Zander.

Time dragged on, and Jude was tempted to go in search of his female. A different nurse rolled Charlotte back into the bay. "Here you are. Wait here, and the doctor will be in shortly." The nurse didn't help Charlie out of the chair. As soon as Charlotte stood, the nurse was gone. Charlotte sat on the edge of the bed, poking at her lip.

"Charlie?" Jude was worried. The normally effervescent female had been replaced with a quiet mouse.

"Huh?" She looked up at him, lowering her hands to her lap.

"What's wrong? Aside from your injuries. Is something troubling you?" Jude shouldn't broach the subject of Zed's Lion in the hospital, but Charlotte's demeanor bothered him.

"Someone tried to kill me, Jude," Charlotte whispered. "Me. Why would someone want me dead? Is knowing about Roger's kink enough for him to want me out of the picture? I don't get it."

"Knock, knock. I'm Doctor Hardaway." A young male in a white lab coat entered the bay carrying a metal clipboard, interrupting their conversation. The guy looked twelve. "Can you tell me your name?"

"Charlotte Fanning."

"Do you know what day it is?"

"Saturday."

"Very good. Your scan came back clear. No

140

concussion or other head injuries. If you continue to have bouts of confusion, I'd like you to follow up with your primary physician. I'll prescribe something to help with your bruising from the seatbelt, and you can take over-the-counter pain relief as needed. Any questions?" Charlotte shook her head. "I take it this man is your ride home?"

Charlie glanced at Jude and gave him a brief smile that didn't meet her eyes. "Yes."

"The nurse will be back with your discharge papers. Take a few days to rest up, and again, if your pain gets worse instead of better, don't hesitate to see your usual doctor." With that, the young doctor was on to the next patient.

Charlotte was quiet as they waited for the nurse. Jude didn't know how to help other than get her home and settled.

When the nurse returned, she asked Charlie what pharmacy she used and once she had the information, she promised to call the prescription in so they could pick it up on their way home. Unlike when a patient was released from an overnight stay, Charlie was allowed to walk out. Jude held his hand out, and Charlotte clasped it tightly. When they reached the lobby, Charlotte blanched when she noticed Zander and Zedra.

Zander rushed off to get the SUV, and Charlotte ignored Zedra's presence. "I have to get back to the shop."

"You need to relax. Do you not trust your employees to handle the business for one afternoon?"

Charlotte glared at him. "You know I do."

"Then please let me take you home so you can rest

141

at least for today." Jude didn't want to use his voice, but he would if she pushed him.

Charlotte reluctantly agreed. She was quiet on the ride back to her apartment, and Jude used that time to call Margie and let her know Charlie wouldn't be returning to work and why. He then called Ace to fill him and Ripper in. Ace promised to keep an eye on Charlie's employees. Charlotte tried to protest, saying she had too many orders to fill, but Jude reminded her she needed to rest. She stared out the side window, chewing on her thumb. Zedra had tried to apologize, but Charlotte waved her off before climbing into the back seat. Jude sat next to her, but his female was closed off. The silence was uncomfortable. Jude was thankful when his phone rang.

"Bishop?"

"The truck was stolen. It was ditched a couple miles away from the wreck. I don't have eyes on the driver, but I am scanning all hospitals for someone coming in with facial injuries. I doubt he goes somewhere public though. Those types of gashes will be hard to miss and harder to explain."

"He had to either follow Charlotte or somehow know her schedule. This wasn't random."

"I've been thinking about that. What if whoever broke into the shop got her schedule from the computer? Perhaps that's why nothing was taken; they got what they were after."

"If that's the case…"

"They're aware of every wedding Charlotte has scheduled."

"Damnit. Okay, I'll have to talk to Zander about added security until we find this guy."

"And I'll keep looking. We will figure this out, Spyder."

Jude thanked Bishop and disconnected. Charlotte was still staring out the window, but Zander was glancing at him through the rearview mirror. With his shifter hearing, Zander didn't have to ask any questions. Neither did Zedra. When they arrived at Charlotte's apartment, she didn't wait on the others. She walked silently to the door and unlocked it without looking back. She grabbed Gibby before he could escape and took the cat to the sofa and sat down. Jude followed behind and turned off the alarm since Charlotte had forgotten. When he went to close the door, he paused. Zedra was hanging back by the car, and Zander was on his phone.

Jude closed the door behind him and walked back to the SUV. He wanted to be alone with Charlie, so he approached Zedra to let her know his plans. "I've got her for now if you want to grab your things and go home for a while."

"I'm sorry, Spyder." Zedra's eyes were red, but she was keeping the tears at bay.

"Nothing to apologize for. You kept her as safe as you could, but I think she and I need to talk about what she saw. I have a feeling that's what's bothering her more than her injuries. Also, you should have your own protection."

"We haven't had the opportunity to discuss what happened, but one thing I can tell you is it wasn't Roger Smith. The man who attacked was mid-thirties, shoulder-length brown hair, brown eyes. I had to lie to the cops. If there's video out there of the wreck, it will show him coming over to the van, then him running off after I slashed his face. I'm sorry if that puts us all in jeopardy, but my Lion sensed the man was going to attack Charlie. Spyder, he had murder in his eyes. I told the officer the man approached the van, but when he saw we were alive, he took off. Here." Zedra pulled a business card out of her back pocket. "This is the officer's info who took my statement. Charlie will need to get a copy of the police report for her insurance agent."

"Like I said, you need your own protection, especially after what you did to him."

Zander put his arm around his sister. "I've got her covered. Zed, go inside and get your things."

Zedra nodded, and Jude led the way. When the three of them entered the apartment, Charlie hadn't moved. She sat frozen save for the hand rubbing over her cat's fur. Gibby was draped across her lap, offering what comfort he could.

When Zedra got closer, Charlotte stared at the female, her eyes following Zed as she walked through the living area and down the hall. Zedra packed her duffel quickly, and when she returned to the living room, she stopped in front of Charlotte. "I hope to see you again soon, Charlie. I really like you and want to be friends." Zed didn't wait for a response before walking out the door.

Zander clapped Jude on the shoulder. "I'll get your bike and Charlie's car brought here so you don't have to worry about not having wheels."

"Wait." Charlotte dug in her purse and held out a set of keys. "You'll need these. Thank you, Zander."

"You're welcome. We're only a phone call away." Zander inclined his head and walked out of the apartment, leaving Jude alone with Charlie.

Jude wasn't sure how to broach the topic, but Charlotte beat him to it. "Have you ever seen something crazy, but you didn't know how to explain it?" She kept her eyes on Gibby as she spoke. "But the more you think about it, the more you convince yourself it wasn't real? I mean, I have a busted lip from the airbag, so it would make sense my head took a hit and bungled my brain for a few seconds."

Jude crossed the room and took a seat on the coffee table. Charlie finally looked up at him, and the tears in her eyes was his undoing. He lowered to his knees and removed her hands from Gibby's fur. "Charlie..." This wasn't the first time he'd told a human about Gryphons, but it was the first time he wanted the human to not need their memories wiped because of it. "You're not crazy."

"You don't know what I saw. Or what I thought I did." Her voice was barely a whisper.

"Yes, I do, and I promise you aren't crazy. Zedra is special. It's why I wanted her to watch over you. Remember when I told you about the Hounds of Zeus? Not the MC but the ones the god chose to protect humans? They're real. The name is misleading because instead of hounds they are Gryphons. Do you know what that is?"

Charlotte pulled her hands back. "What the hell are you going on about? I didn't have some mythological bird on my lap, Jude. Zedra turned into a lion. I had a large freaking cat on my lap, and she roared."

"Gryphons are half Eagle, half Lion, but the Hounds can call on either of their animals whenever

145

needed. I know this because I'm also a Gryphon."

Charlotte's eyes widened, then just as quickly she narrowed them, scoffing. "Yeah, right. I don't know what you're playing at or why you're lying, but I need you to leave."

"I'm not leaving you unprotected. I can prove what I'm saying is the truth, but before I do, you have to promise you won't freak out."

"I'm already freaked out. This has been the worst day of my life, and considering I've lost both my mom and my aunt who was like my mom, that's saying a lot."

"Okay." Jude held up his hands. "What would you rather see? My Lion or my Eagle? Your apartment isn't large enough for my Gryphon. But if you choose Lion, Gibby is probably going to be pissed. Hmm, I'm amazed he's been so calm around us. Animals normally sense the beast inside us and take issue."

"Because he's a smart cat and knows what you're saying is bullshit?" Charlie rolled her eyes, but at least she'd stopped crying.

"Then let's test that theory." Jude called on his Lion and rumbled deep in his chest. Gibby's head popped up. Jude then let out a growl. He didn't put any heat behind it because he didn't want to scare the cat. Gibby sat up and swiped a paw playfully in Jude's direction. "Incredible." Jude partially shifted, keeping his lower half human. He shook out his long mane and batted at Gibby with his own larger paw. Gibby lunged at Jude, landing on his lap. He stretched up and rubbed his smaller head against the Lion's chin. Jude laughed when the smaller cat began making dough on Jude's thighs. Well, as much as a Lion could laugh. He pushed

146

his animal back, and with human hands, he stroked the Maine Coon's lush coat. "Such a good boy, Gibby. Your cat's pretty chill."

"You... you're..." Charlotte had moved to the other end of the sofa and was squatting on the cushions. "That's not possible."

"I would show you my Eagle, but I'm not sure Gibby would be as amenable. I wonder..." Jude placed the cat on the sofa, moved around the other side of the coffee table where he had more room, and began undressing.

"What are you doing?" Charlotte squeaked.

"I'm going to fully shift, but I don't have any more clothes here, and I don't want to shred these. You can avert your eyes if you aren't comfortable seeing me naked. And remember, even though you'll be looking at a large cat, it's still me. I won't hurt you."

Jude didn't give Charlotte the opportunity to object. Within seconds he was naked and shifting. He sat back on his haunches and waited. Gibby jumped off the sofa and walked right up to Jude, winding between his legs. The smaller cat began purring as he rubbed all over Jude's chest. He'd never seen anything like it. Jude stretched out so he was lying down, doing his best to be as unassuming as a lion could. He chuffed at Charlotte, trying to get her to come closer. She was now sitting on the back of the sofa, her feet on the cushions. Gibby bumped Jude's chin again with his head before curling up between his front legs.

Jude loved being in his Lion form. When he was home alone, he often shifted and lay in front of the fire. He could imagine Gibby doing the same thing. He was amazed the Maine Coon had taken to his larger cat.

147

Jude figured he'd get hissed at, not cuddled with. Jude chuffed at Charlotte again. She slowly lowered herself to the floor and stepped around the coffee table. She reached her hand out, but she wasn't close enough to touch him. Jude remained perfectly still as his pretty florist crept forward, one slow step at a time. Jude dipped his head in a silent request, and Charlotte didn't disappoint. She ran her fingers through his mane and down his back, the same way she stroked Gibby.

"Is this real?" Charlotte knelt at his side and continued the slow glide of her fingers across his back. Jude swished his tail, and she laughed. He licked a stripe up her face, and Charlotte fell backward onto her butt, giggling. Her eyes met his, and she shook her head. "Okay, I'm convinced. Will you shift back so we can talk?"

Jude nudged Gibby with his nose, but the smaller feline didn't move. Charlotte took the hint and picked her pet up, cradling him to her chest. Jude stood then shifted, stretching his arms overhead, allowing Charlotte to get an eyeful of his naked body. He was proud of his physique. He didn't have the height most of his fellow Hounds did, but he was ripped.

"Uh..." Charlotte cleared her throat. "Can you put some clothes on, please? Not that I don't like what I see, because I do. I really do. But if we're going to talk... Yeah. Whooh." Charlotte plopped down onto the sofa and fanned her face.

Turning his back to her, Jude bent over and grabbed his jeans first. "So, what do you think?"

"I think I need a cold shower," she muttered.

Jude looked over his shoulder as he buttoned his

jeans and caught her staring at his ass. Charlotte let her eyes wander down his legs before dragging them back up slowly. When she finally looked at his face, Jude winked. "I was referring to my Lion." He tugged his T-shirt over his head, leaving his kutte on the arm of the side chair.

"Oh, uh. It was magnificent if a little scary."

Jude sat on the sofa, leaving plenty of room between them. Gibby crawled across the cushions and settled on Jude's lap. "I have to say I'm really surprised at Gibby's reaction." Jude caressed the other animal as he studied Charlotte's face. "Surprised at yours, too, if I'm being honest. I half expected you to either run screaming or pass out."

Charlotte shrugged with one shoulder. "I figured if Gibby trusted you enough to curl up between your legs, then I could too. Trust you, not curl up..." Charlotte waved her hand as though it would wipe away her babbling. "I just can't believe shifters are real. Are there other kinds, like werewolves?"

Jude hated this question because he didn't want to lie to her. "I would imagine so, but like the Hounds, they would want to keep their existence a secret. If word got out there were shifters living among humans, it would be chaos. The government would try to step in, and we'd be treated differently."

"So Zedra's like you. And her brother? Are all siblings shifters? Do you have any brothers or sisters?"

Her question was innocent, but it still felt like a knife stabbing through his heart. He turned his gaze to Gibby so Charlotte wouldn't see the pain reflected in his eyes. "Yes, Zander is a Gryphon, and if both parents are shifters, then their kids will be too. If one of

149

the parents is human, the child has a fifty-fifty shot."

"There are children running around shifting? Isn't that dangerous?"

"No. We don't come into our Gryphon until puberty. By that time, the child has been taught what it means for them. How their body will change and how they must keep the secret."

"But you said some parents are human. And you told me the truth. Isn't that risky?"

"It can be, but we're pretty good about choosing who we can trust." Jude stretched his arm across the back of the sofa, tugging on one of her curls. "And I trust you."

CHAPTER TWELVE

Charlotte

CHARLOTTE STILL WASN'T certain this all was real. People shifting into lions? And eagles? Jude hadn't shown her his bird, but she didn't think she was up for any more reveals. Twice in one day was enough. Okay, seeing his lion had been crazy, but she could go for some more show-and-tell if it involved his human form. Dayum! The man was ripped. And his dick? That was a work of art like the rest of him. If she wasn't hurting from the wreck, she would probably ask him to shift again just so she could get him naked.

"What are you thinking about?" Jude tugged on her hair again.

"About you trusting me with the truth," she lied.

"If you betrayed my trust, what do you think whoever you told would say?" Jude arched one bushy eyebrow. Even that was sexy as fuck.

"That I'd hit my head harder than I thought, and I needed to be relegated to the psych ward?" Wasn't that what the young doctor had alluded to? Having more delusions? Had she slipped up and said something she shouldn't have?

"Exactly. Unless you had photographic evidence, whoever you told would think you're cuckoo. All I can pray is no one had their camera phone out when Zed turned furry on your attacker."

"That's another thing I don't understand. She said it wasn't Roger. If not him, then who? Wait. You were going to check on Elise. With everything that happened, I forgot. Did you speak to her?"

Jude tapped his fingers on the back of the sofa. "She wasn't home. There were a bunch of boxes stacked up like she'd been packing. An older neighbor threatened us with a shotgun. Interrogated us. Then she told us Elise had gone on vacation with her boyfriend, Roland. What do you know about her, Barbara Thacker?"

"The interrogation rings true, but the shotgun? That doesn't sound like Barbara. She used to watch me sometimes when Ellen had to work late. She'd make me cookies, and we'd watch soap operas together. Sweetest little woman ever after Aunt Ellen."

"When's the last time you saw her?"

Charlotte curled her leg beneath her, and Gibby resettled on her lap. "It's been a minute. Last I knew, her granddaughter was staying with her to help around the house. Barbara is getting on in age. Her short-term memory has been slipping. She's had several surgeries, and her recovery hasn't been easy on her. She uses a wheelchair most of the time, so you saying she held a shotgun on you sounds off. But like I said, it's been a while, so it's possible she's had some type of physical therapy that's helped with her mobility."

"Maybe. Do you know her granddaughter's

name?"

"Vickie. Not sure of her last name. From what Elise tells me, Vickie has been in and out of jail. Her mom isn't much better. She goes through husbands like some women go through shoes trying to find someone to keep her in the lifestyle to which she's accustomed. And by that, I mean drugs. It surprised me when Elise said the woman had moved in to help Barbara, but if she was between jail sentences, she would need somewhere to crash. She's thirty-something and acts like she's still a kid with no responsibilities."

"What about Vickie? Have you seen her lately?"

Charlotte was curious as to why Jude was so interested in Barbara and Vickie. "The day of Ellen's funeral. Barbara came over afterward to help Elise with all the food. That was before the wheelchair. I walked her to the door, and Vickie was standing on the back patio smoking a cigarette. When I was younger, if she was there when Barbara was watching me, Vickie treated me like a pariah and hid out in the bedroom, so when she saw me that day, she tossed her cigarette and returned inside. Why are you so interested in them?"

Jude released his hair from its band then regathered it into a neater ponytail. Charlotte wanted to run her fingers through his long locks. Wanted to know if it was soft or coarse. Wanted it skimming her face while he held himself aloft as his body moved on top of hers. It had been too long since Charlotte had been with a man, and Jude Sterling was too tempting.

"What are you thinking?" His blue eyes were darker than usual. She chalked that up to the animal inside.

"Nothing I want to say out loud."

153

"What if I want you to tell me?" Jude scooted closer and cupped her cheek.

"I don't think now is the right time for that conversation. I'm in pain, and the things going through my mind would require I be one hundred percent."

"Fuck, Charlie." Jude slid his hand behind her head, threading his fingers through her curls.

"Exactly. I want you to fuck Charlie, but I'm about five seconds away from needing a pain pill and a few hours' sleep."

"Shit, Sweetness, why didn't you say something?" Jude jumped up and rushed to the kitchen. He returned with a glass of water and a bottle of over-the-counter pills. "How many do you want?"

"Four. The ache is getting worse, and I want to knock it out so I can sleep."

Jude tapped out four tablets and handed them over. Charlotte tossed them in her mouth and downed half the water. She handed the glass back, and Jude set it on the end table. "Come on. Let's get you to bed." He held out his hand and gently pulled Charlotte to her feet. She wanted a shower but didn't feel up to taking one, but she was adamant about ditching the clothes she was wearing. Charlotte wasn't shy about her body. She knew she didn't have Wynter's curves, but if Jude was going to be in her life, he would eventually see her naked. Hopefully. When they got to her bedroom, she kicked off her shoes and stripped down to her underwear.

Jude turned the covers down, and Charlotte slipped under them and curled up on her side. Jude walked over to the window and closed the blinds, helping to darken the room. It was still daylight, and

Charlotte never was able to sleep unless it was dark, but she figured she might be able to rest a bit. Gibby jumped onto the bed and curled up at her feet. Jude leaned over and pushed her curls off her face, then pressed his lips to her forehead.

"Get some rest. I'll be in the living room if you need me."

Oh, she needed him, but her body wasn't ready for what she wanted. Having seen Jude naked, Charlotte couldn't wait to explore. To touch. Tease. Lick and suck. She smiled and closed her eyes instead of asking him to lie down with her. Charlotte had a feeling Jude would be the man to ruin her for all others. Except he wasn't exactly a man. He was also an animal. Gryphon. Charlotte imagined Jude shifting into the half eagle, half lion. He said her apartment wasn't large enough to accommodate him. She wondered just how big his Gryphon was?

It wasn't until the door snicked closed that she realized he hadn't left the room. Had he been standing there watching her? Charlotte shivered. What did he see when he looked at her? And why her? He could have any woman he wanted. She hadn't missed the looks he got from the other women at Dominion. How many of them had he played with at the club? How many had he tied up in his ropes? Taken home afterward? Who else had he offered to protect? Probably more women than she wanted to know about. Charlotte liked sex. She had it as often as time allowed, which wasn't much. She couldn't imagine Jude was any different, so was she just another knot in his ropes?

Her body heated thinking about Jude tying her up.

155

She wanted his deft hands on her as he wrapped the jute around her torso, binding her so she couldn't move. What would he do with her then? She'd never been tied up before. Sex with other men hadn't been strictly vanilla. She had been with adventurous men who liked to explore. Would Jude allow her to peg him? Would he like having his prostate massaged while she sucked him off? And god, she couldn't wait to get her mouth on that fine dick of his. Couldn't wait to have it filling her core. Charlotte imagined having her hands filled with his muscular ass as he pumped in and out. Shit. She needed to think about something else, or she'd never get any rest.

Switching gears, Charlotte thought about Barbara. The sweet old woman had been like a grandmother to her. Charlotte felt bad that she hadn't see her in so long. When Charlotte moved out then opened her shop, she didn't visit Ellen as often as she should have. She talked to her aunt on the phone several times a week, but Charlotte had been focused on building her own life, something Ellen encouraged. Ellen had raised Charlotte to be a strong woman capable of standing on her own two feet. She taught her to cook and clean. How to save money out of every paycheck she earned as a teen working retail at the mall. She taught both Charlotte and Elise that faith was something each person had to define for themselves. Ellen raised them in church, but she didn't push her own religion down their throats. She encouraged them to find their own path in both reality and spirituality. When Elise's world was turned upside down at the hands of her boyfriend, she dived headfirst into church, searching for what Charlotte figured was redemption. Elise had become a completely different person than the girl Charlotte admired growing up.

And now Elise was god knew where with a man she didn't truly know. Charlotte didn't need a man to complete her. She was successful and happy. That didn't mean she wanted to be single forever. She dreamed of having a husband to share her ambitions with. Spend her nights with. But she wasn't like Elise, going from one relationship to another just so she wouldn't be alone. Elise had a great job as a nurse, but she was one of those women who needed a man in her life. And now she had another one who wasn't who Elise thought he was. It could be desperation that attracted the wrong sort of guy to her cousin. If Jude had seen packing boxes, that meant Elise had fallen prey to whatever it was Roland was offering. If Elise was planning on moving, then she more than likely planned on selling the house. Charlotte prayed Elise wouldn't be dumb enough to hand over the proceeds to Roland, then have nothing to fall back on when the relationship ended. Because it would end when Elise found out what Roland got up to when he was away from her.

Charlotte needed to find her cousin. She needed to get to Elise before she made the biggest mistake of her life. Biggest since trusting Greg Parker, the man who had ended up being a psycho and sending Elise spiraling. Jude and his friends weren't having any luck finding Roland, so maybe Charlotte could do some digging of her own. She had a key to the house, and if Elise was on vacation, Charlotte could let herself in and do some snooping. She could also stop next door and check on Barbara. Make sure Vickie wasn't taking

157

advantage of her grandmother.

Before she could do any of that, she needed to rest up. Her body ached, but Charlotte had too much to do. She wouldn't let a little pain derail her from helping Elise or from going back to the shop. She had worked too hard to make BBs a success. She had to get the police report so she could send it to the insurance company and purchase a new van. Margie and Kristoff could handle the Valentine's orders, but Charlotte had two more weddings to prepare for. Kristoff was capable of following her designs with direction, but she couldn't put two large orders on his shoulders. The next wedding wasn't one Wynter was coordinating, and that was something Charlotte needed to handle herself.

Thinking of her bestie, Charlotte needed to call Wynter. Her friend would be worried as well as pissed off when she found out Charlotte had been targeted again. Charlotte opened her eyes to check the time. The reception would be over, and Wynter would be on her way home. Charlotte's phone was in the kitchen, so she'd call her later. Closing her eyes again, Charlotte willed her body to sleep, but her mind wouldn't let her. There was too much shit swirling around for her to settle. Knowing it was useless, she threw back the covers and eased her legs over the side of the bed. Charlotte padded into her en suite and took stock of herself in the mirror. Her lip was swollen, her face had several cuts, and her stomach was red from the seat belt doing its job. Her hair was a riot of messy curls. There was nothing she could do about her face and stomach, but she could tame her hair.

After pulling her curls up in a clip, Charlotte

brushed her teeth. As she sipped water to rinse her mouth, her stomach rumbled. She hadn't eaten since that morning, and she wasn't one to skip meals. Charlotte pulled on some sweats and an oversized hoodie, then made her way to the living room. Charlotte stopped short when she found an irate Wynter facing off with Jude.

"Charlie!" Wynter rushed past the man, knocking her shoulder into his in her effort to get to Charlotte. "Oh my god! Your face!" Wynter dragged Charlotte into a bear hug. Charlotte winced, and Jude growled. Why did she find that so sexy?

Wynter turned loose, whirling around to see where the noise came from. "What the fuck was that?"

Jude stalked to Charlotte and gently cupped her face while glaring at Wynter. "That was me warning you to be careful. She doesn't need to be mauled with her injuries."

"Listen, Mr. Long Hair, that's my best friend you're warning me away from. I would never hurt her."

"But you did. I told you her stomach and chest have bruises from the seat belt, yet you still hugged her too tightly." Jude turned his troubled eyes to Charlotte. "Why aren't you resting?"

"My mind wouldn't shut off, and I'm hungry."

"Come sit down. I've got chicken warming in the wok. I just need to add the veggies. It'll be ready in a few minutes." Jude led Charlotte to the sofa and got her settled with a blanket over her legs. Gibby, who had been twirling through their legs, jumped onto her lap. Jude brushed his hands through the cat's fur. "Do you want milk with your supper?"

159

"Yes, please." Charlotte couldn't help but smile at her Gryphon. *He's not yours.* But she wanted him to be. No man had ever cared for her the way Jude was. It didn't matter that he was a shifter or that they hadn't been on a date or had sex yet. She wanted the gorgeous biker in her life. She wanted to get past being a target and see what it was like to date. To ride on his Harley. To spend lazy Sundays together. To make love. To fuck like bunnies. To be wrapped in his ropes.

When Jude turned to Wynter, Charlotte expected him to growl again, but instead, he asked, "Would you like a glass of wine?"

Wynter's mouth gaped. She hadn't expected the question any more than Charlotte had. "Uh, yeah. Yes. Please. Would you like help with supper?"

"I got it. You visit with Charlotte. Gently."

Wynter sat on the other end of the sofa, lowering herself slowly. Charlotte curled her lips inward to keep from laughing. Master J had spoken, and Whirlwind Wynter had listened. Jude returned with a glass of wine. After handing it off to Wynter, he walked between the sofa and coffee table, running a finger down Charlotte's face on the way past. Wynter's eyes were wide, her glass halfway to her mouth.

Charlotte smiled as she rested her head on the back of the couch. No doubt Wynter had questions. Hell, Charlotte had plenty of her own.

"How was the wedding?" Charlotte couldn't speak freely about Jude with the man in the room. Having an open-concept apartment didn't allow for privacy.

Wynter finally took a sip of what looked like Riesling. "The flower girl ran down the aisle and dumped all the rose petals at the groom's feet. The ring bearer loudly announced he had to poop when he walked by his grandmother. The father of the bride threatened the groom about hurting his little girl before handing her off. Then at the reception, the groom's nephew decided he wanted cake 'now!' and ran his hand through the frosting."

"So, perfect?"

"Pretty much. Your throw-away bouquet was torn apart by two of the single ladies, and one of the single guys dove through the air for the garter. And when I say dove, I mean an Olympic ten through the air with no splash upon entry. He had been flirting with the woman who ended up wrenching the bouquet free, and I guess he believes the superstition about them being the next power couple. It would have been cute if she wasn't a good ten years older than him."

"What's wrong with that?" Jude asked from the kitchen.

"Normally nothing, except the guy is sixteen." Wynter rolled her eyes and took another sip of wine. She set it on the end table when Jude approached with two plates. "This smells delicious. Thank you."

"You're welcome." Jude returned with Charlotte's milk and made sure both women had everything they needed. What he didn't do was eat with them. Instead, he started cleaning the kitchen. Wynter pointed her fork his direction and raised her eyebrows. Charlotte shrugged and dug into her meal. It was as tasty as it smelled.

Wynter waited until they had finished eating to ask, "Will you tell me what happened?"

Charlotte explained all about the truck and the wreck. She lied about Zedra's part, only saying she

161

scared the man off.

"And you have no idea who it was? Zedra's sure it wasn't Roland?"

"She's sure, and no. I'm hoping Jude's hacker friend will figure it out, but as for Roland..." Charlotte turned to Jude. "I want to go to Elise's and do some snooping. If she really is on vacation, I can go in and take a look around. See if there's anything there alluding to his true identity. I also want to check on Barbara."

Jude sat down on the coffee table. "We can do that tomorrow."

"I'll be at work tomorrow. We should go tonight."

"Charlie—"

"No, Jude. I know what you're going to say, but I have several big orders I need to work on. I trust Margie and Kristoff to take care of the everyday orders, but I always do the wedding arrangements. I'm surprised they didn't stop by here to check on me."

Jude crossed his arms over his chest. "They called while you were in your bedroom. I told them you were resting and that you'd call tomorrow. Charlie, please..." Jude slid to his knees and took her hand in his. "Please give yourself one more day."

Charlotte couldn't think straight when he gave her those big blue eyes. "How about a compromise? We go to Elise's tonight, then I'll work half a day tomorrow."

"Or we go to Elise's in the morning and if you feel up to it, you work half a day."

Wynter piped in, "I'm with Mr. Long Hair on this one, Charlie. Please wait until tomorrow, and I'll go to the shop and help. I'll answer the phone so Margie and Kristoff can focus on helping you."

162

Charlotte sighed. "Only if you agree to stay here tonight. I don't like the idea of you going home alone."

"Who says I'll be alone?" Wynter winked. "I have my own Master bodyguard, thank you very much."

"Where is Roman?" Charlotte had forgotten all about the other biker.

"He went home to shower and grab a bag. I told him he could shower at my place, but he turned me down." Wynter pouted, and Charlotte laughed.

"Okay, tomorrow then. But I want to call Margie and Kristoff. We still need to be careful with my stalker out there. I'd rather open later when we're all together than put them at risk."

"Ace and Ripper have them covered. I promise your employees are safe." Jude's eyes flashed golden, and Charlotte got the message. The two men were more than just bikers; they were Gryphons, and they would keep Margie and Kristoff safe.

CHAPTER THIRTEEN

Spyder

WHEN SPYDER CALLED Hawk and told him what happened with Charlie, they decided Hawk should stop tailing Wynter from a distance and guard her more closely. Hawk waited until the wedding was over to tell Wynter about her best friend being in a wreck. She didn't give him time to explain everything. She asked where Charlie was, and as soon as the words were out of his mouth, Wynter jumped in her car and made a beeline for Charlotte's apartment with Hawk following. Jude was glad Hawk had been there when Wynter arrived to act as a buffer. Wynter wanted to barge into Charlie's room, but he insisted Charlie needed her rest. Hawk had been the one to convince Wynter to wait a while.

Hawk had also used his Gryphon voice on the female when she began getting upset. Their special brand of coercion wasn't to be used for monetary gain, nor were they supposed to influence someone into anything personal. Hawk hadn't abused his power, but Wynter still felt the pull to the male. She relaxed and listened to Roman, and for that, Jude was grateful. When Hawk offered to watch over Wynter that night, she agreed quickly. All the Hounds were used to females flirting, wanting their fifteen minutes with a bad boy. Hawk was already attracted to Wynter, so being her bodyguard wouldn't be a hardship. If they ended up together? That would be a plus as far as Jude was concerned. Having mates who were best friends would be great in the long run. If not, well, Jude wouldn't think that far ahead.

Having Hawk watch over Wynter allowed Jude to be alone with Charlie. As much as he wanted to get her naked and do all sorts of kinky things to the female, he wouldn't risk it until she was healed. He would use their time together to show her his softer, more nurturing side.

Jude allowed his Lion's eyes to come forth, and Charlotte's own eyes widened a fraction. The side of her mouth twitched, and she reached out a hand. Jude took it, rubbing his thumb over her knuckles. He took the gesture as her way of saying she accepted him and the others as shifters. Or maybe she just wanted to hold hands. He didn't mind touching her. Jude might be into kink, but he also enjoyed the simpler aspects of being with someone like holding hands. Snuggling on the sofa. Taking care of their needs if they weren't able, like throwing together a simple stir fry. To him, being in a relationship was a partnership. He might be dominant in the bedroom or the club, but in other facets of life, he wanted there to be a mutual give and take.

Charlotte was successful. She'd grown her business from the ground up. That took strength, smarts, and determination. She might not be a badass like Maveryck's mate, Natalia, but Charlotte was strong in her own ways. He had only known her a couple days, but Jude already admired the female and wanted to see where things between them progressed.

Someone knocked, and Charlie's hand tightened in his. Jude brought her knuckles to his mouth and kissed them. "That's probably Hawk."

Wynter jumped up. "I'll get it."

Jude shook his head. "Hang on, Wynter." The female froze, looking over her shoulder at him. "Just to be on the safe side, let me get it."

"Where's your gun? As a bodyguard, shouldn't you be carrying?"

Wynter had no idea how her words would affect Jude, and for a few seconds, he was the one frozen. The memory of that day rifled through his brain faster than the bullet that had taken out his sister.

"Jude?" Charlie moved to get off the sofa, and Jude snapped out of it.

"I'm good," he lied. "Just—" Pounding again, this time louder.

"Spyder, it's me." Hawk had no idea the maelstrom going on within Jude, but the male did know he would be reluctant to open up. Jude motioned for Wynter to proceed now that they knew who it was. The female flounced across the floor and opened it with a flourish. The shy woman from Dominion was gone. Perhaps it had been the setting that kept her from being her true self. Or maybe Hawk had worked some kind of magic, bringing her out of her shell.

"You ready to go?" Hawk asked Wynter as soon as he stepped inside.

"Yes, Sir." Wynter gave a mock salute with her sassy tone.

166

Hawk's eyebrows nearly hit his hairline. "Naughty girls get spankings."

Wynter squeaked, and Hawk's eyes darkened. Those two needed to get the fuck out of there.

"Charlie wants to run by Elise's in the morning and look around before going into work. We're meeting Margie and Kristoff at nine, so you can drop Wynter off around then."

"Sounds good. Charlotte, is it okay to leave Wynter's car here? I don't want us traveling separately."

"That's fine. My neighbor only uses one of their parking spaces."

"Excellent. Let's go, Trouble." Hawk motioned toward the door, and Wynter bypassed the male to walk over to Charlotte so she could hug her friend.

"I'll see you in the morning."

"Have fun," Charlotte teased, and Wynter winked at her. Yep, Hawk magic.

Jude was a little envious thinking about the other couple going to Wynter's and getting their freak on. Hawk inclined his head to Jude as he ushered Wynter out of the apartment. Jude locked the door behind them and set the alarm. "Let's get you back in bed."

"I like that idea." Charlotte's gaze was heated.

"Charlie..."

Charlotte place Gibby on the floor, then flipped the blanket off her legs and stood. When she looked at him again, her disappointment was clear. "You can take the guest room. Goodnight." She didn't wait for him to respond. She slipped down the hallway, and her door closed with a loud thud.

Gibby let out a disgruntled *"mrawr."*

"Yeah, I hear you, buddy. Fuck." Spyder ran his hands down his face. He could give her something without hurting her. He didn't want Charlie thinking he didn't want her. Mind made up, he turned off the lights and stalked after her. He knocked once and opened the door without more warning. Charlotte's hair was no longer piled on top of her head, and she had already removed the sweats and hoodie and was unclasping her bra.

"Do you mind?" she snapped.

"Not at all. As a matter of fact..." Jude closed the door to keep the cat from disturbing them, then crossed the small room and took over. He pushed the straps down her arms, gliding his fingertips across her skin. Goose bumps popped up along her arms, and Charlotte shivered. He dropped the bra and stepped up behind her, his hands resting on her hips just above her panties. "I want you, Charlie, I just don't want to hurt you." Jude pressed open-mouth kisses to her bare shoulder, his fingers teasing the lace band stretched across her hips. Jude nuzzled her neck, sucking gently at the skin there. "I won't fuck you tonight, but I will show you how much I want you." Jude slid one hand beneath the lace, pleased to find soft curls there. He hated when women shaved their pussy. He skimmed the other hand up her stomach, careful to avoid putting pressure on the bruise. He cupped one breast and kneaded the mound. Charlie leaned her head back against his shoulder, her breaths coming faster.

"Jude..."

"Shh. I've got you, Sweetness." And he did have her. In both his hands. He used one to twist and tug her nipple while the other delved lower to find her already wet. Jude curled his fingers, getting them slick with her juices, and swirled his middle finger around her clit. He alternated between rubbing her nub and sinking his fingers inside. "That feel good?" he husked against her ear.

"Uh huh."

"I can't wait to see you trussed up in my ropes, your gorgeous tits on display. I'll spread you apart and keep you there where I can do more of this." Jude pushed two fingers inside her pussy, rubbing that spot that would make her squirt if he focused long enough.

"Jude, please."

"What do you want, my sweet Charlotte? You want to ride my fingers? Want me to finger-fuck you? Or do you want my mouth on that beautiful pussy? Tongue-fucking you until your sweet release coats my beard?"

"Yes." Charlotte turned her face toward his, her breath a mixture of teriyaki, milk, and her. It shouldn't have been a good combination, but it was intoxicating. Jude added his breath to hers as he kissed her, their tongues tangling in a slow, seductive rhythm matching his fingers thrusting inside her slick heat. Charlotte wrapped her hand behind his head, holding him in place. She arched her back, grinding her ass against his hard dick. With her free hand, she tried to undo his jeans, but the angle was awkward.

He released her nipple and unfastened his button before lowering his zipper. This was supposed to be about her, but fuck if he didn't want her hands on him. He pushed his jeans down his hips, and his cock sprang free. Jude pushed his dick down and rubbed it against the satin covering her ass. Zeus, how he wanted his dick to replace his fingers. Charlotte spread her legs, allowing his erection to slip between them.

"Fuck, you make me want to do bad things to you."

"Then do them. I want you." Charlotte licked his lips before crashing their mouths together in a brutal kiss. She sucked his tongue hard, and fuck if that didn't shoot straight to his dick.

"Godsdamn, woman."

Charlotte bent over the bed, resting on her forearms while pushing her ass against his erection. "Come on, Jude. I won't break."

"Fuck it." Jude released a claw and sliced through her panties, giving him access to where he ached to be. He fisted his dick and rubbed the tip against her opening. Charlotte, in her impatience, thrust back, and he was in fucking heaven. "Fuck!" Jude's beast was close to the surface, demanding he bite her and claim her. "Hold on," he warned before setting up a brutal pace. He had intended to be gentle with her, taking care not to hurt her, but his female was too tempting. And yes, she was his.

Charlotte grabbed onto the comforter, but she didn't just lie there and take his dick. She met him thrust for thrust. Her pussy was slick and tight. The perfect combination to have him ready to bust a nut within seconds. But he had more control than that.

"God, yes! Give it to me, Jude. Fuck me harder. I want to walk funny for days."

"That mouth... Fuck, Sweetness..." Jude slapped her right ass cheek, testing the waters.

"You can't do that," she complained. His hips faltered until she uttered her next words. "You have to get the other side. Make it even." Jude chuckled and spanked her left cheek.

"Why is that so hot? Fuck, do it again," Charlotte begged. Who was he to deny the female what she wanted? Jude alternated sides, smacking her pale skin until both cheeks were red with his handprints. What a fucking sight to behold. Charlotte lowered a hand between her legs, her fingers spread so she could feel his dick shuttling in and out her pussy. They disappeared from around him, but her hand remained between her legs as she teased her clit. Jude wished she were on her back so he could watch her please herself. See her tits shaking with each thrust. Next time.

"Get yourself there, Love. I'm ready to fill you up."

Charlotte gasped. Jude didn't know if it was from the L-word or his dick. He forgot about it as more of her gasps and grunts filled the air along with a few flattering words about how big his cock was and how she'd never felt anything like it. If Jude got his way, she would never be with another man as long as she lived.

"Jude, fuck..." Charlotte's pussy clamped down on his dick, her inner walls pulsing with her orgasm. Jude let go, coming with her. He emptied his seed deep inside her core. He hadn't asked about birth control because he didn't give a single fuck if she got pregnant. Charlotte fell onto the bed, her heavy breathing escaping her smile. "Holy shit, that was..." Charlotte blew out a breath.

Jude pulled out, his jizz leaking down her legs. If she wasn't hurt, he would scoop it up and press it back inside and around her clit until she came again. Instead, he tucked his dick back inside his jeans and zipped up. Jude sat down on the bed and pushed

Charlotte's hair off her face. "Yeah, it was. Do you want me to run you a bath, or would you rather shower?"

"I'm not sure I can walk that far," she said, grinning.

"Then I'll carry you." Jude leaned down and brushed a kiss across her temple. He always tried to be an attentive lover, but with Charlotte, he needed to take care of her. A few years back, one of his bottoms had called him Daddy, but he shut that shit right down. He was a caregiver, yes, but he didn't want to make someone else's decisions for them. He preferred a partner who was strong, someone like Charlotte who was in control of her own life and choices. "Fuck, you're perfect," he whispered against her skin.

"Perfectly useless." Charlotte rolled to her side and propped up on her elbow. "I knew sex with you would be good, but whew!" She blew a strand of hair off her forehead, grinning. "This is going to be fun."

Jude chuckled at her enthusiasm. It was refreshing to have a female who enjoyed sex and wasn't afraid to show it. Society had long ago tried to make women feel bad for having the same urges as males, which was stupid. They had the same desires and needs. He hated the double standard.

"So, bath or shower? I need to get you cleaned up so you can get some sleep."

"Shower. I only take baths when I have the time to add bubbles and relax a while."

Jude kissed her again, then stood and walked to her bathroom to get the water heating. When he returned, Charlotte was on her back with her arms spread. A sated grin adorned her freckled, scraped-up

172

face. Her lip had to be throbbing after their harsh kisses. He grabbed her hands and pulled her to her feet.

"Are you joining me?"

"No, ma'am. You are too tempting. I'll use the hall bathroom to clean up." Jude patted her still pinkened ass and made a hasty retreat. As soon as he opened the bedroom door, Gibby rushed in and jumped on the bed. Jude stepped across the hall to the full bath. He stripped and reluctantly washed Charlotte's scent and their mixed release off his dick. He snooped in the drawers and found a new toothbrush along with some toothpaste beside a stick of women's deodorant. Jude figured they belonged to Wynter. He'd replace the toothbrush the next time he went to the store.

Since he didn't have a change of clothes, Jude grabbed up his things and gathered Charlotte's darks from her hamper. He took them to the closet where the washing machine was located. After starting a load, he carried his boots to her bedroom and placed them on the floor by the bed. He was still there as Charlotte's guardian, even if things had changed between them. At least for him they had. Maybe for her he was just a good time.

Jude tossed her shredded panties in the garbage before turning down the bed. Steam billowed out of the bathroom when Charlotte opened the door and strode naked to her dresser. She pulled on a fresh pair of panties and sleep shirt before looking around. "Where are my clothes?"

"In the washer. I needed to do mine since I didn't bring a bag with me, so I added yours."

Charlotte got a funny look on her face, one Jude

173

couldn't decipher. Was she mad he washed her clothes? Was she treating their sex as a one-and-done? Did she still expect him to sleep in the guest room? Jude's gut rolled. He'd never been the one on this side of the equation before. He was the one to choose how long he hung around. Whether he spent the night or went home right after getting his rocks off.

"I'll just..." When he turned toward the door, Charlotte caught his wrist.

"Where do you think you're going?"

"To check on the clothes," he lied so she wouldn't see his insecurity.

"Oh, okay." She leaned up and kissed his cheek. "I'll be waiting."

Jude pressed a kiss to her forehead. He had no choice but to leave the room since he lied about the laundry. *Dumbass*. He should have trusted her to want the same things he did. Jude leaned against the kitchen counter, giving himself a few minutes to stall. Noticing the pain relievers, he dumped a couple pills out, then poured Charlotte some water. The washing machine was almost finished, so after swapping the clothes to the dryer, Jude took the medicine to the bedroom. Gibby was still curled up at the foot of the bed. Charlotte was on her side, her hands tucked between her cheek and pillow. Her curls were spread out behind her, and she was eyeing his bare body. She was adorable, even with her heated gaze.

"I brought you some pain meds."

"Thank you." Charlotte sat up and held out her hand, and Jude dropped the pills onto her waiting palm. She took a few sips of the water before handing it back. When she laid back down, she pulled the

174

covers back and patted the space next to her. Jude turned out the overhead light and slid in beside her. Charlotte rested her cheek on his arm and wrapped hers around his middle. "This okay?" she asked.

"It's perfect." Jude kissed her curls and relaxed. It had been months since he slept beside a female. He had shared a bed with Emberlynn, the waitress he met in New Roseville, but the sex had been lacking. If he hadn't been hiding out from Josiah Talbert's men, he never would have spent one night with the female. Jude didn't like to lead women on, but her home had been a safe haven if nothing else.

Jude hadn't thought about the cult leader in a while. Talbert had escaped, but at least Rhiannon was free from the compound and her father. Where Ryker was in charge of all things mercenary, his father, Sutton, oversaw the Hounds' mission to take down The Ministry. Jude was glad to not have either responsibility. He was happy to help however he could with both aspects without having to make the tough calls. Jude wondered what Charlotte would think about his mercenary work. Knowing he was getting evil humans off the street was one thing, but would she approve how he went about it? Some people didn't understand cold-blooded murder even if the victim didn't deserve to breathe. It was a discussion they would have to have if they progressed further with a relationship. He would rather know her opinions before he fell any harder.

Keeping his other senses open, Jude closed his eyes and enjoyed the contentment of holding Charlotte while she slept. A little while later, the dryer buzzed indicating the cycle was finished, so Jude slipped his

175

arm from beneath Charlie's cheek. He had helped with laundry growing up. Indigo insisted he learn how to cook, do laundry, and clean so that when he got out on his own, he would be prepared. The same as their father had taught Michelle how to change a tire, check the oil in the car, and other things typically thought to be a male's job. Jude couldn't wait until it was his turn to teach his own children. Being around Mayhem's twins made Jude want kids more than ever before. Those two little boys were such a joy. Major was boisterous and funny, whereas Marshall was quiet, but just as much fun. They had their own personalities the same way Mav and War did.

After pulling on his briefs, Jude folded the clothes. He took Charlotte's to the bedroom where he hung up her pants and tops. He quietly opened drawers until he found where she kept her panties and sweats. Her bras he had left hanging above the washer to air dry just in case. It was how his mom did hers. Jude couldn't wait to introduce Charlotte to Indigo. His mother was a good judge of character, and if the two females got along, that would further cement Jude's notion that Charlie was the female he'd waited his whole life for. Some males didn't need or want their parents' approval of their mate, but it was important to Jude that the two most important females in his life get along. He would never want to have to choose between the two.

Jude slipped back into bed, settling his chest against Charlotte's back from where she had turned over in her sleep. Trusting the alarm system Zander installed to do its job, Jude closed his eyes. Even with the threat to Charlotte hanging over their heads, he had never felt as at peace as he did lying there with this female in his arms. He silently vowed to protect her and figure out who was responsible. He would make the male pay, and then he and Charlotte would move forward together.

"HOLY FUCK, SWEETNESS." Jude opened his eyes. There was no way he was missing what was happening between his legs. Strawberry-blonde curls sheltered his view of Charlie going to town on his dick. She was lying on her stomach with her feet crossed in the air behind her as she bobbed up and down. He worried about her bruises, but they obviously didn't bother her, or she wouldn't be lying on them. Jude reached down and pushed her hair back so he could see her mouth stretched over his erection. He hated to think about how she was so good at giving head, but he wouldn't lie and say he wasn't glad for her previous experience if this was the end result. Fuck, her mouth was talented. And her gag reflex? Nonexistent.

She smiled around his length, winked at him, and went back to sucking. He released her hair and fell back against the pillow. Jude closed his eyes and enjoyed everything she was doing. Charlotte tugged on his balls, teased his perineum, then focused on his balls again. Jude was no stranger to prostate play, and if his pretty florist wanted to explore his ass? He was all for it. Not wanting to wear her mouth out, Jude didn't hold back his release. When he felt the tingle in his spine, he warned her.

"I'm coming, Sweetness."

Charlotte didn't change her rhythm. She kept the same steady pace, and soon, he was shooting down her throat. She swallowed every spurt like a champ, and when she was finished, she pressed a sweet kiss to his tip. "Good morning." Charlotte crawled up his chest and pecked a kiss to his cheek.

"Nuh uh. None of that." He thrust his tongue in her mouth and relished cum and morning breath combined. "It is a good morning. Damn, woman. I could get addicted to you."

Charlotte rested her chin on his chest. "Yeah?"

"Yeah." Jude glanced at the clock. "Let me grab a quick shower, and then I'll make us some breakfast."

"Or you take a quick shower, and I'll cook for you."

"Deal." Jude kissed her again before heading to her en suite. He was getting ahead of himself, but he could see the two of them together every morning getting ready for their days. His Gryphon purred saying they were on the same page.

CHAPTER FOURTEEN

Charlotte

CHARLOTTE STOOD IN Elise's living room and stared. It looked nothing like the house Charlotte had grown up in. Gone were all signs of Ellen and Charlotte having been there at all. It hadn't been that long – a couple months – since Charlotte had visited her cousin, but in those eight or so weeks, Elise had been busy. Charlotte had a few photos at the apartment of Ellen, but the ones she cherished most were the ones Elise had sitting around her home. Now they were gone. Forgetting finding clues of who Roland was, Charlotte began tearing open boxes.

"What's wrong?" Jude asked.

"Ellen's photos, they're all gone. Elise might have already packed them, but something feels off."

"What do you mean?"

Charlotte threw her arm out wide, gesturing to the room as a whole. "Nothing's the same. Everything from my past is gone. I was here a couple months ago, and it didn't look like this. It's like Elise is trying to erase her mom from her life."

"If she's planning on moving, she probably started

packing the smaller stuff first. She could be planning on hiring someone to pack the less important things, but she wanted to make sure the photos were packed with care."

"Maybe." Charlotte didn't think so. She wasn't psychic, but something felt off. "Help me look. Please."

Jude did as she asked, and together, they checked each box. It didn't take long since there weren't that many, but none of the photos were anywhere to be found. "This doesn't make sense." Charlotte fell back onto the sofa as she studied the living room. They had gone through the whole house and came up short. "I don't understand. The furniture is the same, but there's nothing left... nothing here to indicate Ellen ever lived here." Charlotte hopped up and strode to the bedroom she'd used. When she opened the door, she froze. It was empty. Elise had always left that room alone in case Charlotte ever wanted to spend the night. Granted, Charlotte never had, so maybe Elise decided the furniture wasn't needed any longer, but she would have asked Charlotte if she wanted the furniture. At least the old Elise would.

Finding her feet, Charlotte made her way to Elise's bedroom. It hadn't changed. The walls were still decorated with all things "Jesus." Crosses in varying styles littered the walls along with framed prayers and Bible quotes. Charlotte took a good look around, searching for anything that would show Roland had been there. With Elise being reformed, as she called it, Charlotte couldn't imagine her cousin letting the man into her bedroom. But, like Zedra had said, everyone had their secrets. Charlotte knew going through Elise's things broke a trust she likely wouldn't get back if Elise found out, but Charlotte did it anyway. She was searching for photos of Ellen as much as she was looking for clues about Roland.

Charlotte was about to give up when she noticed a lone shoebox on the top shelf of the closet. Pulling it down, Charlotte held her breath as she tugged the lid off. Inside were old photos and newspaper clippings. The pictures weren't of Ellen, though. They were of Elise when she was younger. Before her boyfriend had tried to kill her. Charlotte had been young when it all went down, but she knew the story. Replacing the lid, she put the box back where she found it. Charlotte couldn't think of that version of her cousin without crying. The cousin she missed almost as much as she missed her aunt.

"Find anything?" Jude asked from the bedroom door.

"No." At least nothing that helped them find Roland. Charlotte walked over to the nightstand and picked up Elise's Bible. She opened it where a bookmark poked through. Elise had highlighted a verse in the book of James about knowing the right thing to do. It wasn't the only passage highlighted, but it seemed to be the last one Elise had focused on. Charlotte closed the Bible and put it back where she found it. She then opened the top drawer and rifled through the detritus. There was nothing out of the ordinary from markers, pens, notepads, and skin cream. No sex toys like Charlotte had at home.

She had saved Ellen's bedroom for last. Elise had turned it into an office/craft room. Jude followed silently as Charlotte crossed the hall. She half expected it to be empty as well, but when she opened the door, it was just as she remembered. Charlotte walked to the desk and sat down. First, she searched the drawers and the various papers stacked on the corner of the desk. Finding nothing but bills and bulletins pertaining to the church, Charlotte opened the laptop and turned it on. As she waited on it to boot up, someone knocked on the front door.

"I'll go see who it is," Jude offered. Charlotte nodded and returned her focus to the computer. It was an older model, so Charlotte was still waiting when Jude called for her. "Charlie? Can you come in here?"

Charlotte expected Barbara or possibly Vickie. She didn't expect the New Latham police. "Officer Sims? What's going on?"

"That's what we're here to find out. A neighbor called and said someone was breaking in over here." The same officer who had come to the shop on the morning of the break-in had his hand on the grip of his pistol, while his partner had his weapon drawn, pointing at the floor.

Charlotte was getting tired of talking to cops. She'd never been in trouble in her life, and now she couldn't get away from them, even if she wasn't doing anything wrong. "No break-in. I have a key. This is my cousin's house, the house I grew up in. I haven't been able to get her on the phone, so I stopped by to check on her."

"Is your cousin here?" Officer Sims asked.

"No. I was worried about her when I called the hospital where she worked and her supervisor said Elise quit her job. Like I said, she wasn't answering, so I got worried. I was in her office looking for any clue as to where she might be. You know, like vacation brochures or something like that."

182

Officer Sims pointed to the boxes. "Looks like she's getting ready to move."

Charlotte wrapped her arms around her middle. Jude remained quiet, and Charlotte wasn't sure how much to say. "Maybe. Or maybe she's feeling charitable. Elise is big on giving."

"Are you and your cousin close?" the other officer, Biggs according to his name badge, asked.

"We talk on the phone about once a week, so closer than some cousins, not as close as others."

Officer Biggs holstered his gun. "Do you think your cousin is missing?"

"I honestly don't know at this point. It's possible she could have gone away with the man she's been seeing, but that doesn't explain why she wouldn't answer her phone."

"Unless she went on a cruise," Jude said, leaving out the part that Barbara had mentioned that to him. "My mom didn't have reception when she went on one."

"Who are you?" Officer Biggs asked Jude.

"Jude Sterling, Charlotte's boyfriend." Jude held his hand out, and Officer Biggs shook it.

"Hounds of Zeus. I've seen your MC around. Heard you all are some of the good ones."

"We do our part." Jude was dressed in his usual jeans, white tee, and black vest. Now she knew why he never needed a jacket in the cold. He was part animal. Or was the animal part human?

"Unless you want to file a missing persons' report, there's nothing else for us to do here," Officer Sims said.

Charlotte didn't know what to do. They had come

183

to Elise's to snoop, not find her. It would look odd if she didn't. "I'm really worried about her. I'd like to file a report."

"Come by the station, and we'll get it taken care of," Officer Biggs said, his face softer now that he didn't think they were intruders.

"I heard about your wreck. Officer Blake called me from New Albany and asked about the break-in at your business. Do you think it's possible whoever is after you might have taken Elise?"

"Oh, god. I didn't think about that." Charlotte turned to Jude, and he pulled her into his arms.

"Let's not jump to conclusions, Sweetness. For all we know, Elise is with Roger, and she's enjoying some time away."

Charlotte nodded against Jude's chest. He took over the conversation with the cops, and Officer Sims said they'd be expecting her down at the station later.

Jude showed them out the door, and when he closed it, he leaned back against it. "Fucking nosy neighbors. You know your cousin. Do you think she's in trouble?"

"I don't know what to think. But the computer should be booted up by now." Charlotte returned to Elise's office and sat back down. Unfortunately, the laptop required a password. After trying several times with no luck, Charlotte gave up and leaned back in the desk chair. Jude leaned against the doorframe, watching her.

"What do you want to do?"

"Go to work. If I don't hear from Elise in the next day or two, I'll file the report. I'd rather be safe than sorry."

184

"You're going to have to tell them about Roger."

Charlotte stood and crossed the room, placing her hands on Jude's hips. "I know. Hopefully, they can figure out who he is."

"Maybe." Jude kissed Charlotte's forehead. "Are you ready to go?"

"Yes. I want to run next door and say hi to Barbara while we're here."

Jude led Charlotte out of the house, locking the door behind them. He held her hand as they walked across the driveway, through Barbara's yard, and up the steps. Before they got to the door, Vickie flung it open.

"What do you want?" The woman couldn't have put any more venom in her tone if she tried.

"I wanted to check on Barbara." Charlotte forced herself to smile.

"Well, she ain't here. She's gone to get her hair done, so you can just fuck right off and take that piece of shit with you." Vickie slammed the door. Charlotte raised her fist to knock, but Jude caught her arm.

"Let me handle this."

Charlotte stepped back, and Jude banged on the door. When Vickie opened it, Jude calmly said, "You will let us in the house, and you will keep your mouth shut." Charlotte felt a change in the air and wondered if his shifter was coming out to play.

Vickie took a step back allowing them to step inside. Charlotte entered the house she knew as well as Elise's and headed straight for Barbara's bedroom when she didn't see the older woman in the living room or kitchen. After searching the house, Charlotte looked at Jude and shook her head.

185

"Where is Barbara?" Jude asked. There it was again, that shift in the air. Charlotte shivered.

"She's at Marla's. Mom came and got her a few weeks ago."

Charlotte found that strange. Barbara washed her hands of her daughter years ago. "Why is she there?"

"I'm not telling you shit. You need to get out of my house."

"This isn't your house. It's your grandmother's."

Jude took a step toward Vickie. "Why is your grandmother with Marla?"

"Mom said she's going to convince Grandma to sell the house and move in with her. She needs the money."

Charlotte wanted to throttle Vickie, then go find her mother and do the same. Fucking leeches.

"What do you know about Elise and Roger?" Jude asked.

"I don't know no Roger. Elise's man's name is Roland, and he said they were going on a cruise."

"Do you know Roland's last name?"

"Nope. Not my business."

Jude got right up in Vickie's face. "You will treat your grandmother with respect. You will not take advantage of her. You will not call the cops if you see anyone next door. You get me?"

"Yes." Vickie bobbed her head up and down. Hell, Charlotte wanted to agree with him, and he wasn't speaking to her.

"When you see Elise, tell her to call me," Charlotte said.

When Vickie opened her mouth to spout some shit, Jude stared at Vickie, and she glared at him.

"Fine." As soon as they were across the threshold, Vickie slammed the door.

Charlotte waited until they were in the car before asking, "How'd you do that?"

"Gryphons have the ability to 'voice' humans. We can coerce them into telling the truth as well as forgetting something they shouldn't know. Say we find someone we want as our mate, but that person can't handle being with a shifter for whatever reason; we can erase the knowledge of Gryphons from their mind."

Charlotte was glad she wasn't driving, or she'd probably have wrecked. "That's fucking scary. Mind control. Everyone's your puppet." Charlotte didn't like it. Not one little bit. How many times had he used his voice on her?

"Charlie, I can feel your trepidation. We don't use it randomly. It goes against everything we are to force someone to do something against their will unless we feel someone is in danger. I only voiced Vickie to get the truth about Barbara. I would never use it on you unless you decided you didn't want me in your life, and then I would only remove the knowledge that the Hounds and I are Gryphons. You would remember everything else that happened between us." Jude grabbed her hand and threaded their fingers. "I hope that never happens."

"You keep saying mate. Explain that."

"That's what we call our significant other. Gryphons don't have fated mates, one being chosen for them by the fates. We can choose who we want to spend our lives with, but when we do find our one being, whether they're another Gryphon or a human, we complete a bond, and it's for life. There is no

187

divorce. No running away when the going gets tough."

"But you just said if the human decides they can't handle it, their mind is erased."

"That's only if the bond hasn't been completed. I've never known a bonded mate to want out of the relationship."

"What happens if one of you dies? Does that break the bond?"

"It does. I have some friends who have found a second mate years after their first mate died, but I will say it wasn't easy for them. But Gryphons live longer than humans, so going without a mate for a hundred years isn't easy."

"How long do you live? How old are you?"

"A Gryphon can live a couple hundred years. I'm forty-seven. My mom is one hundred three, but she doesn't look any older than I do. We stop aging around the forty-year mark. Some earlier. When you meet my mom, you'll see what I mean."

"You want to introduce me to your mother?" That surprised Charlotte. She didn't think they were anywhere near that point in their relationship.

"I do. She's the most important person in my life, and I want her to meet you."

"Wait. She had you when she was in her fifties? How is that possible? I mean, I know how, but isn't that dangerous?"

"Shifters are different than humans. I've heard of some having offspring even later. But that's with a Gryphon female. Human mates bear children when they're younger."

"Do you want kids?" Charlotte hadn't been around many children in her life, but she liked them in principle.

"I do. I want to carry on the Sterling legacy." Jude's voice was soft, and Charlotte figured there was a story there, but they had pulled into the parking lot at BBs, and he changed the subject. "How are you feeling?"

"Good. Stomach's still a little tender, but my headache is gone."

"That's great, but I still don't want you to overdo it today."

"I won't. I promise."

Jude brought their hands to his mouth and kissed her knuckles. "Wait there." He got out of the car and walked around to her side, opening the door for her. He helped her to her feet and kept her hand in his. Ace appeared from behind the building.

"Spyder, Charlotte. All's quiet, except for Kristoff. Kid's been singing pop songs at the top of his lungs for the last couple hours." Ace was grinning, and Charlotte knew why. Kristoff couldn't carry a tune to save his life.

"Oh, lord. I better get in there and save him from Margie. She can only take so much before she's ready to put duct tape over his mouth." Charlotte tried to pull away from Jude, but he dragged her back into his chest, kissing her deeply. Jude's tongue was a weapon all its own. He kissed the way he fucked – all in. When he finally released her, Charlotte's head was dizzy, and she swayed a bit. Jude smiled smugly, knowing what he did to her. "Not fair," she muttered, and he smiled wider. Jude Sterling was stunning, but when he flashed those pearly whites? It did things to her stomach, like made her want to give him all the babies. Yep, he was dangerous.

189

Wynter stood behind the counter on the phone with Hawk sitting on a stool behind her. She smiled when Charlotte walked through the door. Margie rushed over and hugged her gently. The music in the back wasn't loud, but Kristoff was.

"Thank god you're here." Margie turned loose and pointed to the workroom.

"I'm on it." Charlotte entered the back room and grinned at the sight of Kristoff shaking his ass while using a white rose as a microphone. Instead of turning the radio down, Charlotte sang the next line with him. Kristoff turned quickly, his smile falling.

"Charlie! Oh my god. Let me look at you." He dropped the flower and rushed to her side. Kristoff reached out and gently brushed her cheek, tears forming. "I was so worried. You need to tell Hunky McHunkerson that he can't keep you holed up in your apartment if you're hurt. I wanted to see you with my own eyes."

Charlotte laughed and hugged her friend, patting him on the back. He was like a little brother to her, and if he had been the one in a wreck, she'd have been just as frantic. He and Margie were more than employees; they were family.

"I'm okay, Sugar Bear, I promise, but I'll be sure to pass along your message." Charlotte untangled herself and walked over to turn the radio down. "Let's see where you are with the order." And just like that, they moved to the table and fell into their normal rhythm. Jude slipped silently into the room and took a seat in the corner. Kristoff returned to his usual effervescent self, singing to the radio and flirting shamelessly with Jude. Jude took it in stride, winking back when Kristoff said something outrageous. It warmed Charlotte's heart to see Jude playing along.

Jude's phone rang, and his face lit up. He excused himself to take the call, and Charlotte wondered who was on the other end. Who brought *her* smile to his face? They may have met only a few days ago, but Charlotte knew she wanted a relationship with Jude. For that to happen, they needed to talk.

CHAPTER FIFTEEN

Spyder

JUDE KEPT AN eye on Charlotte, making sure she didn't overdo it. Ace kept watch over the outside of the shop, giving Jude the opportunity to hang out inside. He sat quietly in the corner of Charlotte's workroom. She and Kristoff had a system in place. They worked while they chatted and sang along to the radio. Kristoff was a funny young man who seemed to love life and Charlotte as well. He joked and flirted with Jude. Jude didn't take the man seriously because he learned quickly that was the male's personality. Kristoff had a boyfriend he cared for a great deal. Flirting was just part of Kristoff's personality.

Wynter was in good spirits, and Jude attributed that to her spending the night with Hawk. Hawk wasn't one to dish about his conquests, but he had a shit-eating grin on his face when Jude asked how his night went. That said it all. Jude's own smile was probably as big. If their sex the night before was any indication, Charlotte was perfect for him. He hadn't been kidding when he told Charlotte he wanted her to meet Indigo. It would be the one thing that could make or break a relationship with the female. He prayed to

Zeus the two females got along, because he wanted Charlotte in his life.

It was almost quitting time when Jude's phone vibrated. Seeing his mom's name on the display, he stepped outside to talk to her. "Hey, Mom."

"I have great news. I've decided to take the house close to Rory."

"That is great news. What can I do to help?"

"I'm planning on downsizing, so I need you to come by and let me know if there are things you want for your house." Indigo never spoke of Jude's place as home. He'd bought the house many years before, but without a mate and kids, he slept there but not much more. He never asked fellow Hounds over for cookouts or poker night. He did have his playroom, but he rarely brought anyone there for Shibari. He had never taken a date home for sex or to spend the night. When he tried to imagine Charlotte and Gibby there with him, he couldn't imagine it. It wasn't a home. Charlotte's apartment was nice, but it wasn't large enough for the family he could envision the two of them having.

"Jude? Are you still there?"

"Yeah, I'm here. I was just thinking. I've met someone, and I want to introduce her to you."

"Really? You didn't mention someone when you stopped by last week."

Jude knew if anyone looked at him, they'd see a goofy grin. "That's because I've only known her a few days. It's been a little wild really." Jude explained how someone was after Charlotte. He left out how they'd met at Dominion. He and Indigo were close, but there were certain things a mother didn't need to know about her child.

193

"Oh, that poor girl. "

"She has no idea who it could be. She's swears there are no jilted ex-boyfriends or disgruntled customers."

"What about her cousin? You said Elise has a history of choosing the wrong males. What if one of them is trying to get back at Elise through Charlotte?"

Fuck. Jude didn't want to get into the whole Roger thing because that would mean mentioning Dominion. "That is possible. The man Elise is seeing now isn't who he says, so I have Bishop digging into his past."

"Rory mentioned Bishop spending time with Lucy in New Atlanta. She's happy Bishop is going to take on more of the computer responsibilities now that…"

"Now that what? Mom, what's going on?"

"Dammit. I'm not supposed to say anything, but I know you can keep a secret. Lucy's pregnant."

"Wow, that's great. Can you imagine what that child will turn out to be?"

"Right? She could be either Gryphon or Gargoyle, or a hybrid of the two."

"She? They know it's a girl already? How far along is Lucy?" Jude wondered if War was aware he was going to be a grandfather.

"Oh, that's another story. You've heard of Connor?"

"Yes, he's Tamian's cousin's son. The one with the gift of visions."

"Connor drew a picture of Lucy holding a baby girl. Lucy didn't even know she was pregnant at that point. That little boy will grow up to change the world. You mark my words. Anyway, is there anything you want before I start sorting through what I'm keeping or donating?"

"I got everything I wanted last time you moved, so go ahead and get rid of whatever you don't want to keep."

"Sounds good. I look forward to meeting your mate. Let me know when to expect the two of you for dinner."

"I didn't say—"

"You didn't have to. You've never wanted to introduce me to anyone you dated until Charlotte. That tells me how special she is."

"She really is, Mom. I'll talk to her about dinner and get back to you."

"Don't wait too long. I don't want to try and cook when my dishes are packed up."

"I won't. Love you, and I'll call you soon."

"Love you too, Son."

Jude disconnected and tilted his head back. The air was cold, but the sun was warm on his face. If it weren't for the threat hovering over Charlotte, Jude would say his life was perfect. There had to be someone from her past she hadn't thought of. All this could be happening because of Elise, as his mom had said, but why would they target Charlotte and not her cousin? Why take photos of Charlotte unless the person wanted her to know they were watching? They knew her schedule, and Jude planned to be with Charlotte from now on wherever she went. Nothing about this made any sense.

His phone rang, and Jude's heart sped up seeing Bishop's name.

"Bishop? Please tell me you have something."

"I do. It's not much, but I have a photo. I've

cleaned it up as best I can. It's the male who was driving the truck. Sending it to you now."

Jude opened the message, but nothing about the male seemed familiar, not that it should. "Do you have a name?

"No. I'm still working on that. I wanted to get the photo to you to see if Charlotte recognizes him."

"I'll go ask her now and let you know." Jude thanked Bishop and hung up. As he walked back inside, Benny pulled into the parking lot. He waived at Jude but didn't get out of the car. When Jude entered the shop, Margie was waiting on a customer. Jude didn't want to interrupt, so he continued on to the workroom. Charlotte and Kristoff were cleaning off their tables while Wynter stood off to the side playing on her phone.

"Charlie, I need you to look at something." He held his phone out, showing her the photo. "Do you recognize this man?"

Charlotte studied the pictured, her forehead wrinkling. Wynter walked over and looked over Charlotte's shoulder. Charlotte shook her head. "I can't say I do. Who is he?"

"You know who reminds me of?" Wynter asked. "Corey Sizemore."

"From high school?"

"Yeah. I mean his hair's longer, but look at his face. He has that same scowl like he's pissed at the world."

"Huh, you're right. But I haven't seen Corey since we graduated." Charlotte turned to Jude. "Is this the guy who tried to kill me?"

"Yes. Are you sure you haven't seen this Corey guy since high school? Think hard, Charlie. It's important."

"I'm positive. We didn't run in the same circles. We weren't friends, and we certainly never dated. Why the hell would he want to hurt me?"

"If this is him, at least we have a name. I'll let Bishop know so he can start running a check on the guy." After texting the name to Bishop, Jude noticed Charlotte staring off into space. "Charlie?"

"Sorry. Just trying to think back. Wynter, didn't Corey have an older brother?"

"Yes, but I think they might have been stepbrothers, because if I recall correctly, they had different last names."

"Do you think that's important?" Jude would take any clue they had at this point.

"I'm not sure. There's something tugging at my brain, but I..." Charlotte squeezed her eyes closed, and Jude waited patiently. "Crap. Maybe it'll come to me later. Let's finish getting closed up. Margie and Benny are going to dinner for their anniversary, and I could use a good meal myself." Charlotte went back to straightening the area. Jude wanted to push her to think, but he knew when your brain wasn't cooperating, that only led to frustration.

Hawk stood beside Wynter when she asked everyone, "How about dinner at my place?"

"That's a great idea. I need to take my bike home and get my SUV. Charlie, how about you ride with them, and I'll meet you there?" Jude loved driving Charlie's Camaro, but it wasn't as safe as his vehicle.

"Can I go with you instead? I've never been on a bike." Charlotte was cute when she was excited, but he only had the one helmet. Her pout was just as cute when he told her maybe next time. In fact, it was so cute they begged off supper with Wynter and ended up at the local Harley shop to get her a helmet. And boots. And a leather jacket and riding gloves. The salesclerk tossed in a balaclava for free. When Charlotte tried to pay, Jude hip-checked her out of the way and slid his credit card into the reader.

Charlotte vibrated with excitement once they reached her apartment. She stopped long enough to give Gibby some rubs, then ran to her bedroom to change clothes. Jude turned off the alarm when Charlotte forgot and scooped the cat up in his arms. The feline baffled Jude. "Why are you not scared of me?" he asked aloud. Gibby responded with a purr and nudged Jude under his chin. Jude sat on the sofa with Gibby curled up on his lap. He thought he'd have to wait a while, but Charlotte returned in less than ten minutes, decked out in her new gear. She looked like a biker's wet dream.

"I'm ready." Charlotte twirled around in her new clothes.

"I'd say you are." Jude placed the cat on the sofa and stood. "You should wear leather more often."

Charlotte had bundled up under the leather jacket like he suggested. Being Gryphon, the cold didn't bother him, but for a human, riding in the winter in Upstate New York could be uncomfortable. Jude reached down and scratched Gibby behind the ears. "We'll be back in a little bit, buddy."

Jude reset the alarm before ushering Charlotte outside to his bike. He had explained how to ride on the way to her apartment. He helped her with her helmet, strapped his own on, then straddled the leather seat. When he had the bike upright, he gestured for her to climb on. Charlotte set her left foot on the peg, slung her right leg over the seat, and settled against his back, wrapping her arms around his waist. At his suggestion, she had chosen a helmet with a removable face shield. She would need the barrier in the colder months, but during the summer, it would allow her to feel the wind on her face if she removed it.

If the weather had been nicer, Jude would have taken the long way to his house, but he didn't want her first ride to be miserable. Jude wanted Charlotte to enjoy herself enough she would ride with him often. His larger body shielded a lot of the wind, but he couldn't keep all of her warm. She took to the curves like a pro, not trying to lean more than necessary, and if she was uncomfortable, she didn't show it.

Jude kept his eyes peeled, making sure they weren't being followed. That was another reason he took the most direct route home. Being on the bike put them at greater risk. If whoever was after her decided to run them off the road with another stolen truck, they wouldn't have the cage to protect them

When they arrived at his house, Charlotte climbed off the bike with a huge grin. At least he thought she was smiling. The balaclava covered her face from the nose down. She lowered the fabric. Yep. She was grinning like a kid who'd just gotten off a roller coaster. "That was the shit! When can we go again?"

"It wasn't too cold?" he asked, helping her out of her helmet.

"Nope. It was invigorating. I know we didn't ride that long, but *whoo!*" Charlotte pumped her fist in the air and wiggled her ass. "What a rush!"

Jude couldn't stop himself from grabbing the front of her jacket and pulling her to him. He kissed her hard, and Charlotte returned the kiss with equal fervor.

"Let's take this inside." Jude grabbed her gloved hand and led her to the side door. "Don't expect too much. I bought this house about twenty years ago, but really, it's somewhere to lay my head at night."

"I'm sure it's fine." Once inside, Charlotte looked around as she removed her jacket and gloves. She walked around the living room, tapping her finger against her lips. "Is that your vest?" She pointed to his father's kutte.

"No, it belonged to my dad. The technical term is kutte, not vest."

Charlotte smiled at his correction. "I like that you have it there. Your house is nice, Jude. It has a lot of potential. Just needs a few plants." She winked at him. Of course the florist would mention the lack of greenery.

"I would need a professional to help keep them alive. You know someone who could help with that?"

"I happen to know a really good friend. Loves working with plants."

"While you scope out the best places for your *friend* to help, I'll get started on supper. You want something to drink? I don't have any milk."

"Whatever you're having is fine." Charlotte removed a couple layers she'd put on for the ride. He turned the heat on so she wouldn't freeze, then grabbed two beers out of the fridge, handing one to her. Jude kept the thermostat set on low since he rarely had company. When he did, whoever visited was usually a Gryphon, and the colder temperature didn't

200

bother them either.

"Thanks." Charlotte tipped her bottle at him before taking a sip. He had given her one of the ciders left over from when Indigo had visited a few months back.

Charlotte remained quiet as she made herself at home, walking through his house. He removed a couple steaks from the fridge and seasoned them while the air fryer preheated. He had been skeptical when his mom told him about cooking meat in the appliance, but it did an amazing job. It was quick, and it didn't dry the meat out.

"Holy shit. That's a lot of ropes." Ah, she had found his playroom. He had several mannequins he practiced his technique on. His wall was lined with all colors of silk rope he used for demonstrations. He preferred natural rope when he played with a partner, and he had both jute and hemp varieties. He also had a frame he could suspend a partner from, but it had been many years since he used it. After getting the steaks into the air fryer, Jude joined Charlotte.

"Is that for suspension?" Charlotte pointed at the wooden frame Jude had built himself.

"It is. Do you think that's something you might like to try?"

"Probably. First, I want you to tie me up the way you did Mistress M so I can see how it feels."

"I can do that. We'll need to talk first. Set expectations."

"I remember. I might have been ogling your ass in those leather pants, but I *was* listening." Charlotte took a sip of cider, her eyes crinkling at the corners. This female was trouble, and Jude loved it.

"Come on. We'll talk while we eat." Jude gestured

toward the door, and Charlotte glanced at the frame again before walking out of the room. He could envision Charlotte hanging suspended while he plowed into her pussy from behind. It would take time to build up to that though. Binding someone took trust on the bottom's part. He would start out small, wrapping her chest and arms to make sure it was something she was comfortable with. If she enjoyed a chest harness, he could add in binding her legs to her arms, letting her get a feel for being completely at his mercy.

The timer on the air fryer beeped. Jude flipped the steaks before washing a couple potatoes and wrapping them in paper towels to nuke in the microwave. He preferred to bake them in the oven, but he was short on time. "I don't have salad fixings, but I can sauté some asparagus if you want something green."

Charlotte held her bottle aloft in front of her lips, frowning. "You eat that stuff?"

Jude laughed at the look on her face. "I take it you're not a fan?"

"Hell, no. I mean, I'd eat it if I were starving, but it's not something I eat on purpose. Besides, it makes your pee smell funny. I wonder..."

"What?" Jude prodded. When Charlotte blushed, he guessed where her mind had gone. "You wonder if it makes cum taste funny too?"

Charlotte chugged the rest of her cider, then wiped her mouth with the back of her hand. "Well, yeah. I've heard that pineapple makes it taste sweet, so it would only make sense asparagus has the opposite effect."

"Pineapple juice is a myth, but I wouldn't put money on asparagus not making jizz more bitter."

"How about we don't test that theory? Now what can I do to help?"

"You can grab the sour cream and cheese for the potatoes and another cider if you want one. Indigo left those last time she visited." Jude pulled a couple plates from the cabinet and placed them on the counter.

"Who's Indigo?" Charlotte asked with her head in the refrigerator.

"My mom. It's a thing with Gryphons. As we get older, we become more like friends with our parents. I do call her Mom when I'm around her, but when talking about her to others, I generally use her name."

"Indigo, I like that. It's unique."

"So is she. I think you'll like her." Jude prayed she did anyway.

He plated the steaks and unwrapped the potatoes. They sat together at his kitchen table. Jude's house didn't have a separate dining room. He had turned the larger of the two spare bedrooms into his playroom, so he had to remember to lock that door when his mother stopped by. They may be friends, but he still didn't need her knowing about his kink.

"This is delicious. I never would have thought to cook steak in an air fryer." Charlotte licked her lips, and Jude's cock took notice. Knowing what it felt like to be balls-deep in the female had Jude ready to skip supper and take her to bed.

"Indigo hates grilling, so she has spent time figuring out alternative methods of cooking. Popping single-serving items into an air fryer is easier for her."

"That makes sense. I may need to invest in one."

"We could take mine to your apartment. That way I can use it to cook supper for us after you get off work."

Charlotte stirred her potato, mixing the butter and cheese. "You plan on cooking for me every night?"

"For as long as you let me." Jude took a sip of beer and covered a belch with his fist, apologizing. "I really think there's something here, Charlie. I want to pursue a relationship with you. I'll be honest. I am looking for my mate. Unlike human marriages, there is no divorce. Once a Gryphon completes the bond, it's for life. That's why it is imperative to be sure both parties are completely onboard. I know we just met, but you called to me and my Gryphon when we laid eyes on you at Dominion." Jude set his beer down. "I thought I found my mate many years ago, but she chose someone else. In hindsight, I'm glad she did, or I wouldn't have met you."

Charlotte laid her fork on her plate and put her hands in her lap. "I won't lie and say I don't feel the connection, but I don't know you. Not really. Say we pursue this thing between us. What does that mean for you going to Dominion? Will you continue playing with other women? And what about your job? I only know you work security. I'd like for you to tell me about that. Tell me about your life growing up. About being in a motorcycle club. I need to know who Jude Sterling is."

CHAPTER SIXTEEN

Charlotte

CHARLOTTE COULDN'T BELIEVE Jude was seriously talking about being mates. Earth-shattering sex wasn't a good enough basis for that type of commitment. They had known each other less than a week, but they didn't *know* each other. She had done a lot of crazy shit in her life, but jumping into a life-long relationship with this gorgeous creature would not be added to the list. Not yet.

"Let's finish eating, and then we can either sit on the sofa or go back to your place." Jude stabbed a piece of steak and put it in his mouth. The man even made chewing look sexy.

Charlotte dug back into her potato. She had to admit having someone cook for her every night sounded wonderful. She loved to cook but only on her days off. They finished their meal in companionable silence, and afterward, they cleaned up the dishes together.

"Would you like another cider?" Jude asked as he put away the sour cream.

"No thanks. I'm good." Charlotte wanted to keep

her wits about her in case they did play with the ropes.

When they sat down on the sofa, Jude laced their fingers together. "Do you want my life's history first, or would you rather talk about expectations in the playroom?"

"Since we're here, let's go over expectations. We can get into the other stuff later." Charlotte wanted to know about Jude, but she wanted to be tied up more.

"Okay. Before we dive into what you want from the experience, let's address one of your earlier questions. You asked if we had a relationship would I continue to play at Dominion. The short answer is no. I would never disrespect you that way. That doesn't mean I won't continue to give demonstrations because I'm currently the only Shibari Master Silas has. But if you enjoy the ropes, you could always be the bottom during the demo. If you don't feel comfortable doing so bare, you can either keep your bra on or wear a bodysuit. If you decide it isn't for you, I would then ask whoever is the bottom to cover up if them being bare-chested makes you uncomfortable. Shibari doesn't have to be sexual. In most cases, it isn't. For me, it's about the art and the trust the bottom gives me in wrapping them up so they can let go of stress." Jude lifted their hands and kissed Charlotte's knuckles.

"I'm not saying it can't be sexual for you and me. I already know seeing you wrapped up will turn me on, but if you want to be bound to give up control, to have your mind taken to a calm place, I'll control my urges."

Charlotte wasn't sure if she wanted it to be sexual or not. "How did you get into Shibari? And what do you get out of tying people up?"

"You already know Hawk is a Master, and one of

206

the other Masters is also in our MC. My mentor, an older Hound, invited us to Dominion the first time. I watched his Shibari demonstration, and I was hooked. As for what I get out of it, control mostly. I like knowing I have total control over someone's body and mind. Not to take advantage, but to offer them a release they don't get elsewhere. Plus, I love the artistic value. My buddy, Hayden, he builds bikes from the ground up. He also does these amazing sculptures using things like chains and sprockets. When I told him I admired his artistic talent, he said he admired mine too. It was then I realized my rope work is an art form. I realized it on some level before, but until he said it... I guess it had been more about the kink. About the control factor. I like taking care of people, and Shibari allows me to do that."

"What about the other kind. Kin-something or other?"

"Kinbaku. The only difference between it and Shibari, as far as I'm concerned, is the intent. Shibari is more relaxing. Freeing. With Kinbaku, the intent is to turn the bottom on. The ropes are tighter, and the placement more intense, not allowing the bottom any movement whatsoever. There are many who would say there is no difference between the two forms. I could bore you with the studies, but I won't."

"Have you ever been the bottom?" Charlotte would love to see Jude tied up.

"I have. You can't become a Master without knowing what feelings you're invoking. Working on mannequins or volunteers as you learn placement and different forms is well and good for the technical aspects. But it's about more than the art form. My mentor spent the first part of our sessions teaching me the rope work, then the second part he used what I learned on me so I experienced what each one invoked. It was never sexual, considering he was a male. So that leads back to what you want out of it."

"I want the release. To give up control to you and forget about being attacked. I want to let go of being in charge all day every day. I love what I do at my shop, but most days, the business part of it pulls me away from the joy of creating. I want to forget about what's going on with Elise. I trust you to do that for me."

"Would you like to try it tonight? Or would you rather continue talking? Getting to know more about me?"

Charlotte was torn. She was afraid if he got her in his ropes, she would forget about wanting to ask more questions, but she really wanted to know what it felt like to be the bottom to his top and not in a sexual way. Charlotte hadn't lied when she said she wanted to forget for a while.

"I'd like to try since we're here and you have everything you need."

Jude stood and held out his hand. "Why don't you go pee if you need to, then grab some water and bring it to the playroom? While you do that, I'll go set up."

"Okay." Charlotte was happy to take a few minutes beforehand to get her mind in the right space. She had to remember this wasn't about sex. When she walked into the room a few minutes later, Jude had removed both green and pink rope from the hooks on the wall, and he was unwrapping them. Ambient music played low, transforming the otherwise sterile room into a spa-like atmosphere.

"I'm using silk for your first time. The material is softer, plus I think these colors will look stunning against your skin. Put the water on the table and strip down to your underwear please." Charlotte did as asked, thankful Jude had cranked the heat up in the house. He pointed to a large pillow on the floor. "Please kneel here." Charlotte lowered herself to the cushion, placing her hands on her thighs. "We'll go with the stoplight system for safe words. Not that I think you'll need them, but just in case you feel uncomfortable, you'll have them." Jude placed a pair of scissors next to the glass of water. "Being a Master, I know how to tie the ropes in such a way I can get you out of them quickly. I'm not doing anything elaborate for your first time, but the scissors are there for your peace of mind."

Jude stood in front of Charlotte and brushed her curls off her face. "Close your eyes. Take a deep breath and think about pushing all the negative in your life out as you exhale. As you inhale, take in the positive I'm sending through my fingers." Jude's hands were on Charlotte's shoulders, his touch light. She inhaled his scent, letting it wash over her, and as she exhaled, she did her best to push all the bad shit out. One of his hands disappeared. When it returned, it held one of the ropes. Jude draped the silk across her shoulder where his hand had been. "Keep breathing."

Charlotte kept her eyes closed, allowing her other senses to take over. Jude began wrapping the rope around her chest. She envisioned what she had seen him do at Dominion, transposing it from Mistress M's body to her own. Jude's fingers brushed her bare skin as he wound the rope around not only her body but within the rope itself. The tighter the rope became, the more stress escaped from her pores.

"How are you doing, Sweetness?"

"Green. So green."

Jude chuckled but didn't say anything else. Gently, he gripped her right wrist and brought her arm behind her back. He replaced his grip with rope before doing the same to the other arm, then he secured them together. Jude trailed his fingertips up her arms to her shoulders, where he allowed them to rest with the barest of pressure. Charlotte liked that he kept them connected.

After what felt like hours, Jude asked, "What do you think?"

"I'm supposed to think?" Charlotte teased. "This is bliss. Other than my thighs burning a little, I would like to stay this way for hours."

"Why didn't you tell me your legs were hurting? Fuck, I'm so sorry. I should have checked in more than I did."

Charlotte finally opened her eyes when she felt Jude come to stand in front of her. "I wasn't thinking about my legs. I wasn't thinking at all. I have never felt so at peace."

"Here, let me help you up." Jude gripped her under her armpits and lifted her to her feet. Charlotte wobbled a fraction, but he was there to steady her. Charlotte had no doubt her face held a goofy smile, like she'd had too much to drink. "Better?" Jude asked, his brow furrowed.

"I'm perfect." Or she would be when her legs stopped tingling. "I have to say the way you explained it doesn't come close to the experience."

Jude brushed her hair back from her face and pressed his lips to her forehead, leaving them there longer than usual. With his body close to hers, Jude reached around and tugged at one of the ropes. Within seconds, her arms were no longer bound behind her back. Taking advantage of the freedom, she snaked her hands behind his head and pulled him down for a proper kiss.

When they came up for air, Jude stepped behind Charlotte. "Wait. Before you untie me the rest of the way, can I see it?"

Jude turned Charlotte so she faced a full-length mirror. "Oh wow." Charlotte trailed her fingers across the rope between her breasts. She wondered how it would look on her without a bra.

Jude stood at her back, staring at her reflection. "You are stunning."

Charlotte had never felt prettier. "Next time, I want to try it while naked," she admitted.

"Yeah?" Jude ran a finger along the top of the lace edge.

Charlotte watched his hand in the mirror as goose bumps rose on her skin. If he didn't stop, she was going to beg him to fuck her. As appealing as that sounded, she needed them to slow down and talk.

Jude must have noticed the change in her mood because he took a step back and unwound the ropes. Charlotte continued staring at her reflection. With the rope removed, the impressions left were just as intriguing.

"Here." Jude offered her the glass of water. "Drink up, but don't chug." Charlotte sipped the refreshing liquid. The ice had melted, but the water was still cold.

While she drank, he caressed her body, trailing his fingertips down her arms and across her chest, following the lines where the ropes had been. Jude was tender, and Charlotte basked in his attention. After several, peaceful minutes, he kissed the side of her neck before grabbing the ropes. He folded them carefully before hanging them on the wall.

"Next time, I'd like to take your picture before I untie you."

"Okay." Charlotte was flattered he would want a reminder.

"Let's get you dressed and back home." Jude took the empty glass and left Charlotte alone. She missed his presence as soon as he walked out of the room. She wondered if that was an aftereffect of playing or if it was something else. She couldn't deny their connection. Being around the man constantly had her twisted. She felt deep down Jude was good, but she still wanted to know more about him.

After dressing, she made her way to the kitchen where he was leaning against the counter staring at his phone. "Everything okay?"

Jude pocketed his phone. "Oh, yeah. I was checking to see if I had any messages." Jude picked up her new jacket and held it out. She slipped her arms in, then pulled the front together, hugging herself.

"Did I thank you for my new things?"

Jude grabbed a small duffel before leading her to the side door. "You did. Did I tell you how badass you look in leather? I like having you on my bike. I can't wait to take you on a longer ride. We do group rides, too, where the mates and kids come with us. I think you'll enjoy getting to meet everyone." Jude opened

212

the passenger door on his large SUV. Once she was seated, he tossed the bag in the back seat, then got in. "You ever been camping?" he asked as he started the ignition.

"I have. Believe it or not, that's something I used to do with Wynter and her parents when we were growing up. While I preferred to sit around the fire, Wynter would tromp through the woods. As a matter of fact, she still goes with her folks at least once a year. Is that something you like to do?"

"It is. Last time we went, the twins kept us entertained for hours."

"The twins?"

"Yeah, Marshall and Major are the cutest four-year-olds on the planet. Maveryck, their dad, is the VP of the Hounds. He lived with a female for a while, and one day, she took off. Four years later, she pops up with twins and drops them off, saying she can't deal with them anymore. All while this is going on, Mav was out on a job. He got the surprise of his life when he got home. I guess now would be a good time to tell you some of us are mercenaries."

"Like, you go out and kill people for a living?"

"Yes. But those we take out are the vilest people alive. Rapists. Sex traffickers. Pedophiles. People in power who are never brought to justice because of who they are or who they can pay off. People who don't deserve to breathe. When we're given a mark, we do our own due diligence. Study the person and make sure the information we have is the truth. We never take out an innocent. Is that something you can live with?"

"What about sending them to jail? Is that not an

option?"

"Some of them have already been to jail, but when they get out, they go back to doing whatever got them put there in the first place. And like I said, some have the means to get away with their crimes and never even get arrested. These are people who harm little kids. Sell other humans as sex slaves."

"Then yes, I'm okay with it. How often do you go out on these jobs? Isn't it dangerous?"

"There are enough of us that we only go out about once a month. Sometimes not that often. It can be dangerous. Hayden and I did a job down in South Texas last year where the marks were a drug trafficker and his wife. Turns out, the wife was innocent. Hayden had a gut feeling about the female, and he was right. She had been traded by her father to pay off a debt to the drug lord. She and Hayden are now living happily together with Mercedes's son, Mateo. There were guns involved, but in the end, we saved the girl and her son. I'm not a fan of guns, so I don't usually take a job where they're needed. I prefer to use my claws."

"You mentioned your MC protected humans. Is that what you meant?"

"That, plus Mav's father, Sutton, who used to be the club's President, goes after cults. You've heard of The Ministry?"

"Yes. We learned about them in school."

"Sutton handed over the MC to Mav's oldest brother, Ryker, so Sutton could focus on shutting down the cult. When we aren't taking merc jobs, we're searching for compounds run by The Ministry. It's amazing how many people choose to live off the grid away from society. Like with our mercenary work, we make sure these groups are the ones keeping people against their will. Ryker's mate, Rhiannon, was one of those. Her father took her to live with The Ministry after her mom passed away. She managed to get away after living there about ten years. The leader, Josiah Talbert, took off, but the compound is still running without him. Rhiannon is someone I want you to meet. She loves working with plants. Has what you'd call a gift. I think the two of you would get along great." After slowing for a stop sign, Jude turned right onto her street.

"There are others in their family who were taken by the cult as well, but those are stories for another day. Sutton and his mate, Rory, offer anyone who is there against their will a safe place to stay until they can get back on their feet. I'm telling you all this so you'll know the Hounds spend their lives trying to make the world a better place. If you and I make a go of things, you'll become part of the Hounds family."

Jude pulled into the parking lot of Charlotte's apartment, waved at the guard who was now accustomed to seeing them together, and continued to her door. When he parked, he shut off the engine. "Let's continue this inside." Jude reached into the back seat for the duffel bag, then came around to open Charlotte's door. He swiveled his head as they walked up the sidewalk. She appreciated him being on the lookout. If she didn't have him watching out for her, she'd probably never leave her apartment.

Once inside, Charlotte picked up Gibby while Jude set the alarm. Instead of placing the bag by the door, he carried it to her bedroom. Charlotte dropped down on the sofa, snuggling her cat to her chest. Gibby put up with it longer than usual before jumping down. He met Jude at the end of the hallway and wound his way between Jude's legs.

"Hey, furball." Jude picked Gibby up and got a few of his own snuggles in. When he walked over to sit next to Charlotte, Gibby curled up on Jude's lap, closing his eyes.

"Traitor," Charlotte muttered. "I think he likes you better than me. Do you think he recognizes your Lion?"

"Maybe. Or maybe he just has good taste." Jude winked at her, taking the sting out of his remark. He stretched his arm across the back of the sofa and tugged on one of Charlotte's curls. "What else do you want to know?"

Charlotte was pretty much on information overload with the mercenary surprise. She told him she was good with it, but it still shocked her that he came right out and admitted he killed people for a living. "I think I'm good for now, so why don't you tell me more about these twins."

Jude gushed about the two little boys who had been a surprise to their dad. He had her laughing with stories about things they said and did. How Major called Jude Spiderman. How they called their dad's mate Lolly-Tolly Lollipop. How they had their own sidecar and loved to ride as much as the adults. Charlotte could hear the love and admiration in Jude's words. The way his eyes crinkled at the edges when he smiled at something they did. He would make a fantastic father to his own kids. Charlotte wasn't a woman whose biological clock was ticking. She wanted children, but she didn't feel the need to have them soon just because she was in her thirties. If she were to get pregnant, it would happen when it was supposed to.

Then she thought about Jude's job and how dangerous it was. She likened it to being a cop. Would she be okay knowing every time he left for a job he might not return? Thinking about her own brush with death, she realized that wasn't fair to Jude. Death didn't only happen for those who put their lives on the line. Death didn't discriminate with regards to age or jobs. Good people got cancer and died way too young. Others were victims of wrecks and drive-by shootings and basically being in the wrong place at the wrong time. In other words, worrying about Jude, who was a shapeshifter, was pointless and unnecessary. If it was his time to go, he would. It could be on a job or riding his bike. Then again, he could live to be two hundred.

"Why would you want to mate with a human when you could possibly live twice as long?"

"Because if you love someone, the time you get to spend with them is worth any amount of pain after they're gone. Would you give up the time you spent with your mom or your aunt if you knew you would lose them early on in your life?"

Charlotte shook her head. "No. No I wouldn't. But that's different."

Jude slid his hand beneath Charlotte's and twined their fingers. "Is it really? None of us are promised tomorrow. I would rather take the chance at loving someone with the possibility of spending decades with them rather than losing out because I was scared. Not everyone needs or wants a partner in their life, and that's okay if that's how they feel. But I want someone I can come home to at the end of the day and share

217

everything with. I want what my parents had before my dad was taken away. I want to have children with my mate and teach them the way my parents taught me. I've lived a life of solitude for almost fifty years. I'm ready to know what it feels like to not be alone."

Something inside Charlotte broke wide open. This strong male – this Gryphon – wasn't any different than everyone else where matters of the heart were concerned. He wanted love. A future. A forever. His vulnerability was painful yet beautiful. In that moment, Charlotte knew she would do anything in her power to be everything he needed.

CHAPTER SEVENTEEN

Spyder

JUDE HAD NEVER felt so vulnerable in his life. After seeing the way the other Hounds found their mates and came together quickly, he began to doubt himself. He knew Charlotte was the one for him, but what if he wasn't it for her? He set Gibby on the sofa between them, then stood and headed to the kitchen for a glass of water.

"Jude," Charlotte said, right behind him. He stopped walking but didn't turn around. "Jude, look at me." He sighed, his shoulders dropping. Jude looked over his shoulder, and the worry on her face made him feel like a fool. Charlotte stepped in front of him and pressed her palms to his cheeks, rubbing her thumbs gently under his eyes. "Thank you for opening up to me. I like you. A lot. Nothing you said makes me want to run. In fact, it did the opposite. I told you I feel a connection. I do, and that scares the shit out of me. My life has been all about having the best floral shop in the area. I've worked hard to build my business. Yes, I've dated, but not often. Not for a while." Charlotte wrapped her arms around his neck, settling her hands under his ponytail.

Smiling up at him, she continued. "Being with you these last few days made me realize what I was missing. I've never put much stock in things like destiny or fate, but I'm starting to think there could be something to that. If Elise hadn't met Roland, I wouldn't have followed him. If I hadn't followed him, I wouldn't have stepped foot inside Dominion. Without going to the club, I never would have met you. If you're not opposed to a future with a human, I want us to be together. The only thing that I see as a possible issue is you working at Dominion, but that's my own hang up. If you tell me you can do your demonstrations without it being sexual, I'll have to trust you mean it. I don't share, Jude. If you and I have a relationship, it has to be monogamous, or it won't work for me."

Jude pressed his forehead to hers. "We'll have to work on getting you to trust me enough so you're my demo partner. Until then, I will insist my partners are covered. I promise you there is nothing sexual when I do a demonstration. When I'm standing in front of a group explaining what I'm doing, it's clinical. As for being monogamous, I feel the same way. I have waited my whole life for you, so there's no way I would do anything to screw this up. At least nothing like cheating. I can't say I won't fuck up in other ways because I'm not perfect. But I will never do anything on purpose to hurt you or to sabotage what I hope we can build together. We'll take things as slow as you need, but know this; I'd move us in together tonight if you allowed it. We're spending every second together right now because of the threat against you. It's spoiling me."

Jude pressed a soft kiss to her lips, tightening his grip on Charlotte's hips. "When the threat is over, things will even out. I'll go off on jobs. You'll work without me hovering. It's going to be hard to not see you as often, but I'm hoping we'll get to a point soon where we at least spend every night together. If and when you decide it's time to live together, I want to look at houses in this area. Your apartment is nice, but I want a place that's ours. My house is too small for growth."

"Growth." Charlotte arched a perfectly shaped eyebrow over her pretty, seafoam eye. "You mean like a bigger playroom?"

"I mean a different kind of playroom. One filled with toys not of the kinky kind. I want a large backyard. A covered patio where we can have cookouts in the summer and snuggle up by a fire pit in the winter. I want a state-of-the-art kitchen where I can cook for you every night. A dining room with a large table to accommodate our friends and family. And yes, I want a playroom for the two of us that stays locked to keep prying eyes away from our private business."

"That sounds wonderful, but I don't have a lot of money saved up. I put everything back into my shop."

"Oh, Sweetness. My house is paid off. I make good money doing what I do. I've been saving for a long time, and I can pay cash for the next house I buy, even if you decide you want to live in a mansion. You want a new Camaro? It's yours. You want a bigger building for your business? Done. If you want to sell your business and travel? We can do that too. I'm not bragging; I'm letting you know money isn't anything you'll ever have to worry about."

"I love my business. I love taking individual flowers and putting them together to make something extraordinary. Maybe someday I'll be ready to leave that behind, but not any time soon. Is that a problem for you?"

"Not at all." Jude swayed with Charlotte as though there were a slow song playing on the radio. They were talking about a future together. Communication was key, at least that's what his father taught him. So was compromise. It wasn't always fifty-fifty. Sometimes the scales were balanced in favor of the male. Sometimes it leaned toward what the female wanted. "I want you to be happy. I know I'm getting way ahead of myself here, but if this works out, I see a child or ten in our future." Charlotte jerked back, her eyes wide. Jude laughed and kissed her nose. "Just saying. But I have no problem being a stay-at-home dad. I take merc jobs because I feel it's my duty to rid the earth of scum so our future children live in a better world, but I would stop taking assignments if I needed to. I have no issue with you continuing to work as long as it's what you want to do."

Charlotte started them swaying again. "It amazes me that you're still single. Everything you've said sounds absolutely perfect. So how is it no one else has captured you?"

"Because I haven't found the perfect one for me. Until you."

"What makes me the one? Surely there are other women who have been what you're looking for. I mean, I'm nothing special. I'm pretty enough. I've built a good business. I'm kind if not a little crazy at times. I can cook, and I do keep a clean home. But none of those things make me any better than someone else."

"You're wrong about not being special. You're more than pretty enough. To me, you're the most beautiful woman in the world. You're strong. Determined to succeed. You're smart and adventurous. You, Charlotte Fanning, are the whole package. I mentioned before I thought I had found my mate many years ago. It was a blow to the ego when she left me; I won't lie. But she had nothing on you. I'm glad she chose someone else. As perfect as you think I am, I'm not. I have issues like anyone else. I guess those issues were too much for her. That's why I offered to take things slow with you. To give you time to see the male I am, faults and all."

"And what happens when you finally see my faults? Because I have them too."

"Then we'll be faulty together. I have never witnessed a perfect relationship. My parents came close, but even they disagreed. My father would forget to take off his muddy boots. My mother would burn dinner because she got lost in a book. They would get upset, but they never fought. They would apologize and talk things out. I never once heard either of them raise their voice to the other even if they were angry. They talked it out, kissed, and got back to being head-over-heels. My father always said communication is key, and I believe him. Whatever there is we don't agree on, if there are little things that drive us crazy about the other, we talk it out. We never go to bed angry, even if we spend all night working through whatever it is we're upset about. Relationships take work, and I'm willing to do the job."

"Speaking of jobs, I need to get some sleep. Would

you like to shower with me?"

"I would love to."

Charlotte led Jude to her bathroom where they stripped each other and got under the hot spray. As Jude shampooed her hair, Charlotte said, "Thank you for sharing with me. For letting me know more about you and what you want."

After rinsing the suds from her hair, Jude ran conditioner through her curls. "You're welcome. I want you to always feel like you can talk to me. I want to share everything with you, Charlie. The good and bad. I want to be the one you count on to keep you safe. To make your dreams come true."

"You really are something else, Jude Sterling. I wish Ellen were still alive to meet you. All she ever wanted for me and Elise was our happiness. I don't know that my cousin will ever find hers, but I think I've found mine with you."

Zeus, Jude prayed that was true. As much as it hurt when Belinda chose someone else, Jude was now glad she had, or else he wouldn't have met Charlotte. He hadn't lied when he said he thought she was perfect. He still wanted to introduce her to Indigo, but in that moment, he knew his mom's opinion no longer carried as much weight. He loved his mother beyond measure, but she wasn't his future. Charlotte was. He knew it in his soul.

After drying off, they took turns drying their hair. When they climbed into Charlotte's bed, Jude wrapped her in his arms. Gibby made himself comfortable at their feet, and Jude enjoyed the rightness of it all.

Charlotte brushed her fingers through his beard before kissing him softly. "Goodnight."

"Goodnight, my sweet Charlotte."

As Jude lay there with his face buried in his female's curls, he savored the smell of her conditioner and the softness of her skin. He vowed silently to be the best male possible so she would agree to be his mate.

THE NEXT DAY was quiet. Jude watched over BBs, giving Ace and Ripper a break from guard duty. He and Charlotte met up with Hawk and Wynter for supper at Wynter's home, and it was clear the other couple had gotten close. While the females were talking about an upcoming wedding, Jude cooked, and Hawk stood close by drinking a beer.

"Things look cozy with you and Wynter." When Hawk didn't say anything, Jude glanced at his friend, noting the faraway look. It wasn't one of contentment or happiness. "Or not?"

Hawk rubbed his temples with his free hand. "I don't know, Spyder. On the surface, everything's wonderful. She's funny and outgoing one minute. Shy and reserved the next. She's intelligent, like sometimes I can't comprehend how smart she is. During the day, things are perfect. But at night when it's the two of us, she's nothing like the prudish female we met at Dominion. That woman doesn't have a submissive bone in her body. On one hand, it's hot as fuck. On the other, how do I make that work when I'm a Dom? I've never been with someone who fights me for control. And don't get me started on my Gryphon. More than once, it's tried to come out and show her who's boss. I want her, but how can that work when everything she is goes against everything I am?"

"Does she refuse to give up control all the time? Or is it something you can compromise on? Being a Dom doesn't mean you can't also be submissive if your partner is perfect otherwise."

Hawk cleared his throat as the females entered the kitchen.

"Do you need any help?" Charlotte sidled up to Jude, looking in the skillet.

"You can grab plates. The biscuits need about five more minutes." Jude had opted to make breakfast. He was a big fan of biscuits and gravy, but with Charlotte going in so early, they ate something quick most mornings.

Wynter poured milk for Charlotte and juice for the rest of them while Charlotte got plates out of the cabinet. When the biscuits were ready, Jude placed them in a basket Wynter had set out and carried them to the table along with a bowl of gravy, scrambled eggs, and a platter of bacon and sausage. The two couples dug in, and other than moans of appreciation, talk was minimal while they ate.

Charlotte

"THAT WAS DELICIOUS. Thank you." Charlotte patted Jude's leg.

"You're welcome. Listen, since the shop is closed tomorrow, what do you say about going with me to see Indigo?"

Charlotte still felt it was too soon to meet his mom, but she wanted to make Jude happy. "I'd like that."

"Who is Indigo?" Wynter asked.

"My mom. I've told her all about Charlotte, and she wants to meet her." Jude slid his chair back and began gathering dishes.

"You cooked. I'll clean." Wynter stood and grabbed the empty bowls. "You call your mother by her first name?"

Jude stacked the plates by the sink. "Usually. At this point in my life, she's one of my best friends."

Charlotte used her hip to move Jude out of the way so she could help Wynter. "I think it's great you have such a good relationship with her still. From what you told me, she's a special lady."

"She really is." Jude pressed a kiss to Charlotte's temple before he and Hawk left them to it.

"Meeting the parents already?" Wynter whispered.

Charlotte rinsed the plates, then stacked them in the dishwasher. "Just the one, but yeah. She's important to Jude, and I have a feeling her opinion carries a lot of weight with him. I really hope she likes me."

"Why wouldn't she? You're one of the best people I know."

"Aw, thanks, Boo."

"I have to say, the way you and Jude are with each other? If I didn't know better, I'd think you had been together years, not days. I worried at first, but the two of you fit."

"It's too soon to tell for certain, but I think you're right. He's such a good guy."

"He's not hard to look at either, although I prefer the 'tall, dark, and handsome' type myself."

"Yeah? How's that going?"

Wynter dropped a soap tablet in the slot, pressed the settings, and closed the dishwasher door. "Girl, that man is fire, but he's also a little intense. I guess that comes from being a Dom. Has Jude tied you up yet?"

Charlotte dried her hands before turning to lean against the counter. "Yes, and let me tell you, I've never encountered anything like it. You would think being bound would be restricting, and in a sense, it is, but it's also freeing. It's like being wrapped in a warm embrace where you can just give over control and let your mind be free of all the daily stress. He has a frame he built that allows him to suspend the bottom. I can't wait to try that."

"He has this in his house?"

"Yep. He turned one of the spare bedrooms into a rope room." Charlotte glanced toward the living room where the males were watching television. "I really like him, and I want to see where this goes. I think he could be it for me, and if that's the case, I don't want him having other women as his demo partners."

Wynter's eyes were huge. "You're going to let him tie you up naked in front of all those people?"

"He said I could wear a bra or bodysuit if I didn't

want to assist him bare. I kept my underwear on when he worked on me, and the effect was still striking. And who knows? Maybe one day I'll feel brave enough to try it naked." Charlotte wiggled her eyebrows, and Wynter laughed. Her best friend knew she was full of shit.

MEETING INDIGO WAS more nerve-wracking than thinking about being naked at Dominion. Charlotte had never dated anyone long enough to meet their family. Not that she and Jude had been together long. Hell, she wouldn't call what was between them dating. She didn't know if a Gryphon would want to be called boyfriend. But they weren't mates. They were definitely lovers, but that wasn't an appropriate way to introduce your significant other. There was no one in her life other than Elise who didn't know about Jude, so Charlotte really didn't need to worry about what label to use.

"Is your mom's house the one you grew up in?" Charlotte asked when they got close.

"No. She moved from our original home after we lost my sister."

Jude had already told her how his father died, but this was the first she learned he had a sibling. "I'm so sorry."

"It was a long time ago." Jude didn't elaborate, so Charlotte didn't push. She knew the pain of talking

229

about loved ones who had passed on. "Mom wanted me to apologize in advance for the house being in disarray. She's getting ready to move, so her house is full of boxes."

"I'll keep that in mind." Charlotte tapped her thigh to the beat of the song playing. It was nice knowing they had similar taste in music. When Cyanide Sweetness came on, Jude turned it up, and Charlotte bobbed her head. When they first set out that morning, Jude talked about the Hounds. Not the MC, but the shifters. He explained how War's daughter, Lucy, was mated to a male named Tamian. He confided in Charlotte that Tamian was a Gargoyle shifter, and another Gargoyle of their Clan was father to the lead singer of Cyanide Sweetness. Jude also explained about the formula Lucy and Jonas Montague were working on. It blew her mind that the scientist who cloned the first human baby was connected to Jude's Gryphon family.

If Lucy and Jonas were successful, they would be able to prolong human life. It was a slippery slope, playing God. Jude's words. He explained that on one hand, he was all for the formula working. Gryphons would no longer outlive their human mates. On the other hand, if word got out about the formula, it would cause chaos. Charlotte considered the possibility of living for two hundred years or longer. The serum would include Gargoyle DNA, and according to Jude, those shifters could live to be over one thousand. Knowing there were two types of shifters had her asking, "Are there other types of shifters running around appearing human?"

Jude hesitated before saying, "Probably."

Charlotte had a feeling his reluctance to answer said more than that one word, but she realized the importance of secrecy when it came to the truth. As with the formula Lucy was working on, if word got out there were shifters, that, too, would cause chaos.

When they pulled in the driveway, butterflies danced in Charlotte's stomach. Jude brought her hand to his mouth and kissed it.

"Don't worry. She's going to love you." He came around to her side of the SUV and helped her out. The front door opened, and Charlotte froze. It couldn't be. Charlotte stared at the woman. She couldn't help it. This was Jude's mother, not Elise's friend who...

"Are you okay?" Jude squeezed her hand. Charlotte nodded, swallowing hard.

Jude led Charlotte up the steps. If he hadn't warned her ahead of time, Charlotte would never have believed the young-looking woman standing on the porch was his mother. Indigo Sterling was stunning and didn't look a day over forty. The fact that she was the spitting image of someone else played havoc with her head.

Indigo's smile was as brilliant as her son's. "Hi, honey." She kissed Jude on the cheek. "Charlotte, it's so good to meet you. Please come in. I hope Jude told you I'm packing. Please excuse the mess."

"It's my pleasure, and he did. Please don't worry about it." Charlotte had never seen a neater mess in her life. If it weren't for the boxes stacked at the edge of the room, she wouldn't have known Indigo was moving. The walls were bare of photos and artwork, but the house was still furnished nicely.

"Come on into the kitchen. The lasagna only needs

231

a few more minutes, but everything else is ready. Jude, be a dear and fix Charlotte something to drink. I have tea, lemonade, milk, beer, and wine. Wait, Jude said you don't like wine. I have some cider if you prefer that instead."

"Lemonade would be great. I haven't had any since I was a kid. My aunt used to keep some in the refrigerator."

Jude pulled out a stool at the island for Charlotte before fixing her a glass. "Mom, what do you want?"

"I'll have lemonade since you have it out. Charlotte, I took a look at your website. I have to say you are extremely talented. How did you get into flowers, if you don't mind me asking?"

"I don't mind. I don't know if Jude told you, but my mother passed away when I was young, and her sister took me in. My cousin, who is fifteen years older, moved out a couple years after I moved in, so that left Ellen and me. I helped her in her flowerbeds and found I had a knack for growing things. I got my love of flowers from her, and being a florist is a way to keep those memories alive."

"I'm sorry for your loss."

"Thank you. I had a lot of good years with her. She taught me about gardening. How to cook and take care of a house and pay bills. All the things I needed to know when I moved out on my own."

"It sounds like you have wonderful memories of the time you had with your aunt. When our loved ones pass on, it's those memories that keep us going. Remembering the good instead of dwelling on the bad."

Charlotte's heart thudded against her ribs. She

wouldn't ask. She couldn't. It had to be a coincidence. Unless Jude knew who Charlotte was and he somehow blamed her. If he was the one... No. He was good. He wouldn't hurt her.

"Charlie?" Jude stroked a hand down her arm.

"I'm sorry if speaking of your past brought you pain." Indigo's eyes were shining, and Charlotte felt bad.

"No, it didn't. I was thinking of something else. It's been a rough week."

Indigo's face switched from remorseful to pissed off. "Jude, please tell me you're closer to finding this bastard."

Jude sighed and sat down next to Charlotte. "We have a photo, but Bishop is still trying to figure out who the male is. Wynter, Charlie's best friend, mentioned he looks like a guy they went to high school with, but neither one has seen the male since they graduated. If it is the same man, they can't figure out why he would want to harm Charlie."

"Sometimes people don't have a good reason." Indigo removed the casserole dish from the oven. "Come on and fix your plates."

Charlotte no longer felt like eating. Her mind swirled, and her stomach rumbled but not from hunger. Still, she put a small portion of vegetable lasagna on her plate and sat down, forcing herself to eat. After a few minutes, Charlotte could no longer hold it in. "I can't do this," she blurted. If she didn't address the truth, the probability of throwing up was great. Setting her fork down, Charlotte drank a big gulp of lemonade.

"Do what? Charlie, what's wrong?" Indigo placed

her hand atop Charlotte's, but Charlotte pulled back.

"You look just like her." Charlotte brushed a tear off her face.

"Who?"

"Michelle. That's your daughter's name, right? And your sister?" Charlotte asked, looking at Jude.

Jude shoved his chair back so hard, it tipped over. "How the fuck do you know that?"

Indigo gripped Charlotte's hand again, only this time she clung tightly and wouldn't turn loose. "Charlie, how do you know Michelle?"

The tears fell like rain down her cheeks, but Charlotte didn't try to brush them off. It would do no good. "Because she came to visit Ellen with Elise. Back before..."

"Charlotte." Jude slammed his hands on the table. Silverware jumped, and their glasses sloshed liquid over the sides. "Back before what?" His face reddened, and the vein at his temple pulsed.

"Before Elise's boyfriend shot her."

CHAPTER EIGHTEEN

Spyder

JUDE WAS GOING to throw up.

"Elise… Elise is Elizabeth?" Indigo asked.

Charlotte nodded. She was no longer looking at Jude, and it was a good thing. He didn't want her to look at him. Didn't want her to speak to him. Fuck, he had to get out of the house. He pushed off the table and stormed out the back door. He didn't go far though. He couldn't. He needed to hear whatever shitty explanation Charlotte gave for barging into his life. Oh, fuck. Had she known who he was? Had she come to Dominion seeking him out? Jude slid down the wall outside the door, landing hard on his ass.

"Talk to me, Charlie," Indigo pled.

"After… after what happened, Elizabeth changed. Her name, her personality, her address. Everything. She couldn't handle what happened to Michelle. Said it was her fault for choosing the wrong man. For allowing Greg into her life. She had broken up with him because she felt something was off. She didn't tell me this, because I was still a kid to her, but I overheard her telling Aunt Ellen everything. Ellen tried to convince her it wasn't her fault. That she wasn't the one who... Ellen convinced Elise to see a therapist. It didn't help. Nothing did. That's when she started going to church seeking redemption. I think she still is."

"No wonder you looked like you saw a ghost when you got out of the car. Because you did. I have to ask. Did you not recognize Jude's name? Did you know who he was?"

"No. I swear it. I'm fifteen years younger than Elise, and by the time she and Michelle became friends, I was hanging out with Wynter all the time. I only met Michelle a couple times when they came to visit Ellen, and I never knew her last name. Or it's possible I heard it afterward, I don't know. Ellen kept me away from the reporters and the police when they came around. She needed to focus on Elise, so she sent me to Wynter's house. I stayed with their family a couple months. I was just a kid, and the adults wouldn't talk about what happened around me. It was impossible not to find out what happened though."

Jude turned his head toward the door at the sound of a chair scooting. "I'm so sorry. If I had known..."

"If you had known?" Indigo prodded.

"I never would have allowed myself to fall..." Charlotte cleared her throat. "It doesn't matter now. There's no way Jude can look at me and not think about his sister. Or you your daughter. I'll always be a painful reminder of what happened. Thank you for lunch. I'm going to call for a ride. I won't cause either of you any more hurt."

As much as he had been shocked to find out Elise was really Elizabeth, hearing Charlotte almost admit she'd fallen in love was even more surprising. And enough to get him moving.

When Jude walked back inside, Indigo was holding onto Charlotte's wrist as she tried to leave the kitchen. "Please sit back down."

"Charlie, please don't go." Jude strode across the room and took her hand away from his mother's. "Please," he begged. The pain in her eyes, the tears still falling, were real. Her words had been the truth. Jude felt like a dick for doubting his mate. Fuck. Charlotte *was* his mate. He'd known it on some level. Had even acknowledged it to some degree. But hearing she would walk out of his life so she wouldn't cause any more pain for him and his mother? That solidified the truth.

Jude cupped her face and used his thumbs to wipe the tears. "I'm sorry I yelled. It was a shock to know you are related to Elizabeth. The pain of losing my sister is still raw after all these years. Sometimes it seems like yesterday. Hearing a handgun still triggers a panic attack." Jude rubbed the back of his neck.

"You were there?"

Jude took a step back and shoved his hands in his pockets. "Yes. Michelle and I were close. She had already told me all about Elizabeth breaking up with Greg. Michelle asked me to keep an eye on him because he had threatened Elizabeth, so I did. For weeks, I watched him. It wasn't hard to do because he never left his house. When he finally did, he returned to work, only when he got there, they fired him for having stayed away without calling in. I was sitting across the street on my bike, but my shifter senses allowed me to hear their heated words. Greg didn't take it well. When he left, he drove straight to

Elizabeth's apartment. He was driving erratically. Blowing through red lights and stop signs. I got caught behind a few cars, giving him the opportunity to put some space between us. He got there a few minutes before I could. I heard shouting, from him, Elizabeth, and Michelle. I ran."

Jude took a deep breath. "Even with my shifter speed, I wasn't fast enough. I burst through the door just as the gun went off. Michelle threw herself at Elizabeth, putting her body between the bullet and her best friend. Greg dropped the gun when he realized what he'd done. If it hadn't been for a neighbor yelling that they'd already called the police, I would have shifted and torn him apart. I did use my voice on him, telling him to sit down and not move. I rushed to Michelle, but there was nothing I could do."

Charlotte closed the distance between them, laying her hands on his chest. "That's why you hate guns."

"Yes. That's the reason I try not to take jobs where I have to carry one." Jude placed his hands on Charlotte's. "Will you please forgive me? I promise to never yell at you again."

"There's nothing to forgive. Neither one of us expected our pasts to be connected. It was a shock to all of us, I think."

"If you two will sit back down, I'll reheat your plates," Indigo offered.

Jude lifted Charlotte's hands and kissed her fingertips. "Do you think you can eat now?"

"Yes. I'd hate to let your mom's hard work go to waste."

Jude pulled Charlotte to his chest and hugged her tightly. He buried his face in her curls, letting the softness calm him further. He so wanted to address her previous admission of falling for him, but he would wait until they were alone to do so. When they were seated, Indigo lightened the mood by talking about her new house. She also asked Charlotte more about being a floral designer. When they finished eating, Jude offered to do the dishes so the two females could talk more.

As they were saying goodbye a few hours later, Indigo pressed a palm to Charlotte's face. "I'm sorry for all the losses in your life. I know I can't replace your mom or your aunt, but I'm here if you ever need someone to talk to. I'm so happy you and Jude have found one another, and I look forward to getting to know you even better." Charlotte thanked her with fresh tears in her eyes.

Jude started his car to let the heater warm up, and by the time he and Charlotte climbed inside, it was toasty. Charlotte adjusted her seat warmer after a few minutes, then leaned her head against the window. After her admission about Elise's identity, Charlotte had spent all her time talking to Indigo. Jude was thankful they got along so well, but he couldn't help but feel as though Charlie had been avoiding him. Now it was even more evident.

"Are you okay?"

"Yeah, it's just been an emotional day." Charlotte didn't look his way when she spoke, and Jude wasn't sure how to proceed.

"Charlie, I'm really sorry."

She did turn to him then. "You've already apologized. I just..." Charlotte crossed her arms over her chest. "I don't know how to process everything. I know I'm not responsible for what happened all those years ago, but I feel there will be times when you resent looking at me. I'll always be a reminder."

"As you saw, my mom looks almost exactly like Michelle did. Do you think I resent her? I can tell you right now, I don't. She's the one who kept me from completely falling apart. Sure, she's a reminder. She would be even if they didn't favor so much. It's the same for her when she looks at me. I'm the spitting image of my father with the exception of my hair. That's one reason I grew it out, so she would see me and not my dad. Michelle and I were close. There's so much in everyday life that reminds me of her. A certain song. Chocolate chip pancakes. Riding my bike. Both Michelle and Indigo loved riding. Mom would ride with Dad, and I'd double Michelle. We'd take off and go wherever the road led us. I miss that. Miss having someone on the back. It thrilled me to no end when you enjoyed riding the other night."

"Do you ever take your mom for rides now?"

"No. I've offered, but that was their thing – hers and Dad's. The bike I ride now was his. Hayden's added a little more chrome to it, but it's still a reminder for her. She's the one who insisted I have it. I let it sit in the garage several years before I decided that wasn't honoring him properly. My dad was the best male I know next to Sutton Lazlo. I'll never fill Dad's boots, but I'm trying."

"If the way your mom brags about you is any indication, I'd say you're succeeding." Charlotte held her hand out, palm up. Jude grabbed hold. Tightly. "I want you in my life. You and Indigo. I enjoyed spending time with her. It felt a little strange, knowing how old she is yet seeing a young face. That'll take some getting used to."

"If Lucy can get the formula figured out, it's possible you'll stop aging too. Is that something you'd be interested in?"

"Spending hundreds of years with you? Definitely."

MONDAYS WERE MARGIE'S day off. With it being Valentine's Day, Wynter was at The Blooming Boutique to help answer phones and work the counter while Charlotte and Kristoff worked in the back. Charlotte called her best friend as soon as they got home and told her everything. Jude had gone to take a shower, giving Charlie a modicum of privacy, but being a shifter, he was able to hear every word she said. He endured the highs and lows right along with his mate. She laughed and cried, but the best part of the call was when she admitted to being in love with him. Wynter must have cautioned her, because Charlotte said she knew it was soon, but she also knew what she felt was real. By the time he was out of the bathroom, Charlotte had hung up and crawled into bed. He slid in next to her, and instead of talking, he made love to her. When they were both sated, he spooned her from behind and fell asleep knowing he was loved.

When noon rolled around, Hawk offered to go pick up lunch, leaving Spyder to watch over Wynter. There was no door leading outside from the workroom. Ace kept an eye on the outside of the building where someone could try and get through the window. Charlotte and Kristoff were secure.

The phone rang again. Being Valentine's Day, it had been nonstop all morning. Wynter answered, and she waved at Spyder, then pointed at the phone. "Yes, she's here. Hold please." Wynter pressed the hold button and replaced the receiver in the cradle. "It's Elise asking for Charlotte."

"I'll tell her." Jude walked to the workroom and picked up the portable handset. "It's Elise."

Charlotte grabbed the phone and stabbed at the buttons, putting it on speaker. "Elise?"

"Charlie, Vickie told me you came by looking for me."

"Oh, thank god. I was worried about you."

"Worried? Why?"

"Uh, maybe because you quit your job and wouldn't answer your phone, then went on vacation with Roland."

"I had my phone shut off for a few days, but I didn't go on vacation. Where did you hear that?"

"From Barbara. When I couldn't get hold of you, a friend of mine stopped by there to make sure you weren't hurt or worse. Barbara came outside and talked to him. I went to the house later to see if I could get any clues to help us find out where Roland lives. The man has been lying to you. When we were leaving, we went to talk to Barbara, only she wasn't home. Vickie was there. She also said you and Roland were on vacation and that Barbara had gone to stay with Marla."

242

"Barbara hasn't been home in weeks. As for Roland, you're mistaken. I may have had my doubts in the beginning, but he's proven to me he's a good man."

"Elise, Roland is lying to you about who he is."

"Roland isn't the one lying. I saw the pictures, Charlie. Of you at that club. How could you subject yourself to that kind of lifestyle? That isn't how Mom raised you."

Charlotte glared at the phone. "You leave Ellen out of this. I visited the club after I followed Roland there. I wanted to know what kind of man he was, and I found out. He's a liar and a cheater. He's leading a double life. When I went in the club to try and get closer to him, he hit on me. He acted in a way unbecoming of a Dom, so the owner put him on suspension. My friend followed to find out more about him, and that's when he saw Roland at his home with his wife and kids."

"This friend must be lying to you. Roland took me to his community. He stayed there the whole time while I checked it out. I belong there, Charlie. I'm important there. They have one doctor, but he doesn't live there full time, so it's like I'm in charge. I even helped this guy who'd been attacked by a wild animal. You should have seen the slashes on his face."

Jude pushed the mute button. "Charlotte..." Elise was still talking about helping the man in the background. "Slashes on his face? The man who tried to kill you?"

"Oh, fuck me sideways." Charlotte's hand trembled as she reached to unmute the phone. "Elise, when did this animal attack him?"

"Why does that matter?"

"Just answer the question. When did it happen?"

243

"A couple days ago."

"And why didn't he go to a hospital?"

"The members of the community are private people. They keep to themselves."

"It's a fucking cult, Elise. It's not a community. It's a compound, and you're their latest victim. That man with the slashes? He tried to kill me. He ran me off the road, and when that didn't work, he came after me in the van, only I had a friend with me."

"You can't know—"

"I can, Elise. He's mid-thirties, shaggy brown hair. Tell me I'm wrong."

"Oh, God. Wh-why would he do that?" Elise's voice trembled.

"Probably to get me out of the way. Did you mention to Roland I'm on the deed to the house?"

"Y-yes, why?"

"He convinced you to sell the house, didn't he? Maybe he sees me as a threat. He wants you to sell everything you own and invest the money, not give me half of the proceeds. Not that I would take it even if you offered. But these people are bad news, Elise."

"But they're not. They're like me, Charlie. They all want to live with others like them. Away from a sinful world."

Jude put his hand on Charlotte's shoulders and squeezed. Wynter, who had entered the room, sat down next to Charlotte and grabbed her hand.

Jude spoke up before Charlotte could respond. "Elise, this is Charlotte's boyfriend. What's the name of the preacher who runs that community?" Jude didn't give his name in case she remembered him.

"Abraham, why?"

244

"Fuck me," Jude muttered. "Abraham Goodman, and his wife's name is Ruth, right?"

"How do you know that? Did you follow me?"

"I know this because Ruth is the grandmother of a friend of mine. She was taken to one of these communities when she was younger. It took her thirteen years, but she managed to escape. She's engaged to one of my best friends. His family has been going after The Ministry for years. The community you found yourself a part of is like Charlotte said – a cult. They lure good people in with promises of a better life, when all they're doing is taking your money to further their cause. I'm surprised they let you leave."

"I had to come home to sell the house and my belongings since they said I wouldn't need them anymore. Oh, God. John really tried to kill Charlie?"

"Yes, he did. These are not good people, Elise. I have no doubt there are some of the members who aren't bad, but men like Abraham aren't doing your God's work. They hide behind that message so they can raise armies. They've been around a long time. They're the ones who took responsibility for the apocalypse."

"But John's face... What caused those marks if not an animal?"

Charlotte looked up at Jude. Wynter wasn't aware of the Gryphons. Neither was Elise. They couldn't know the truth. Jude squeezed her shoulder again. "The woman in the van with Charlotte grabbed a gardening tool. You know those small hand rakes? She slashed his face with it."

"I can't believe this. Any of it. Everyone there is so nice. I fit in. I finally found my place, and..." Elise

245

sounded so defeated, and it broke Charlotte's heart. "Someone's at the door. I need to go see who it is."

"Elise, if it's Roland, don't let him in. He's dangerous. You need to come here. Better yet, let us come get you. Elise? Elise!" A dial tone sounded indicating Elise had already hung up. "Damnit. Jude, we need to—"

"Hello? Anyone here?" a man called out.

Wynter stood. "I'll take care of the customer." She walked toward the front of the shop, leaving a frantic Charlotte behind.

"We need to go." Charlotte removed her apron and tossed it on the table. "Kristoff, I'm—"

"Charlie, stop. I've got things covered here. I can put together a dozen roses in my sleep."

"Thank you, Sugar Bear." Charlotte kissed her friend on the cheek. Jude's Gryphon bristled, but Jude pushed back. There was nothing romantic or sexual between Charlotte and her employee.

Jude placed his hands on Charlotte's biceps. "Sweetness, we need to wait on Hawk to get back. I'm not going to leave Wynter and Kristoff alone with only Ace outside."

Wynter stuck her head in the door. "Charlie, the customer wants to speak to you about a special arrangement. I tried to get him to buy one already made, but he wants something besides roses."

"Okay. I'll be right there."

Jude followed Charlotte to the front where a man dressed in an ill-fitting suit stood waiting, his hands in the pocket of the coat. "Are you Charlotte?" he asked.

"That's me. What can I help you with?"

The man pulled a gun, and Jude's knees threatened to give out. "No!" The next few seconds were a blur. Wynter produced a sound from her chest reminiscent of a dog growling. Jude lunged for Charlie just as the gun went off, and they landed in a heap, his body covering hers. The report from the pistol took him back to the past. *Michelle.* Jude couldn't breathe. *Not now. Fuck!*

CHAPTER NINETEEN

Charlotte

CHARLOTTE WAS DEAD. That or she'd hit her head when Jude tackled her to the ground. There was no way a gray wolf had thrown itself between the shooter and Charlie. A wolf that a few seconds before had been her best friend. Both Hawk and Ace stormed in the front door while Kristoff knelt beside Charlotte's head.

"Charlie?" Kristoff's eyes were wide. "Why is there a wolf in here?" That was an excellent question. One she couldn't answer.

"What the actual fuck?" Charlotte thought it was Ace who asked, but she couldn't be sure. Jude's dead weight on top of her was smothering.

"Oh, god. Jude!" Charlotte tried to push him off so she could see if he'd been shot.

"Spyder, were you hit?" Hawk asked. He squatted next to them. "Charlotte?"

"I'm okay, but he's freaking heavy. I can't breathe."

Hawk rolled Jude off her, and Charlotte looked around. Ace stood close to the wolf, which was balanced on top of the shooter, baring its teeth. Kristoff

248

had backed away and was sitting on his butt, keeping his eyes on the animal. Hawk hovered over Jude, telling him to snap out of it. Oh, shit. Jude hated guns.

"Jude?" Charlotte pushed Hawk out of the way. She pressed her hands to Jude's cheeks. "Jude, look at me. I'm fine." When that didn't work, Charlotte straddled Jude's hips and stroked his face. "Breathe with me, Love. I need you to focus on me and breathe with me." Jude stared at her, matching his breaths with hers.

The shooter continued screaming, and Charlotte couldn't focus. "Someone shut him up!" When the wolf growled, Charlotte pointed. "No. Not you. Ace, do that thing." Charlotte twirled her hand in the air.

"Shut up," Ace commanded. Charlotte felt the power in his words. The wolf moved off the man and flopped down on its side.

"Charlie?" Jude blinked, coming back to himself.

"I'm here, Love. Right here. You saved me." Charlotte pressed a kiss to his lips before helping him to his feet.

"Actually, I think the wolf saved you," Ace said.

"Wolf? Why is there a fucking wolf in here?" Jude repeated Kristoff's question. He took a step in front of Charlotte, but she grabbed his arm.

Hawk rushed over to the animal and dropped to his knees. "Shit, she was hit." He gingerly ran his hands along the wolf's flank, and it growled. "Can you shift back?"

"She? How do you know it's a 'she'? And by shift, do you mean—?"

"We need to do damage control," Hawk said, cutting Ace off. "Jude, you help Kristoff with what he witnessed, and Ace, you need to get answers out of him." Hawk gestured to the shooter.

Jude had begun pacing, his hands in his hair. Charlotte stepped in front of him and pulled his hands down. "Jude, I'm fine. We all are." Charlotte glanced over to where Hawk stroked Wynter's head. How in the hell was Wynter a fucking wolf? Charlotte had so many questions, but they would have to wait until Wynter shifted back to human. "We need to call the cops, but we can't do that until you do your thing." Charlotte tapped the side of her head.

Jude nodded. "Thank you. If you hadn't talked me through my panic attack, I'm not sure I'd have come out of it."

"Yes, you would have. You're strong, Jude Sterling. And right now, you need to help Kristoff."

While Jude was wiping Kristoff's memory and Ace was interrogating the shooter, Charlotte slowly approached Wynter. She knelt beside the wolf's head and carded her fingers through the dense fur. "I am so mad at you." The wolf chuffed, and Charlotte laughed, blinking back tears. "Thank you for saving me," Charlotte whispered.

"This certainly brings things into perspective. Wynter, can you shift back, or do you want me to take you to a vet?"

The wolf snapped her teeth at Hawk. Not hard enough to do damage, but enough to let him know to back off. The change happened much slower this time. Wynter's wolf snout shortened and bones popped as her fur disappeared. Less than thirty seconds passed, and Wynter returned to her human form.

"Getting shot fucking hurts," Wynter seethed, looking down at her hip. She poked at the hole in her jeans. "I need to shift again to try and get the bullet out. If that doesn't work, I'll call my dad." Her dad was a veterinarian. For some reason, that made Charlotte giggle.

"You think this is funny?" Wynter snarled.

"Nope. Not one bit. How is it you can shift with clothes on when—?"

"Charlie!" Jude warned. Shit. Charlotte had nearly outed the Gryphons. "Kristoff isn't feeling well, so he's taking the next couple days off."

Kristoff rubbed his temples, and Charlotte went to him. "You go home and relax, okay? We have enough arrangements, and I can handle any walk-in customers."

"Thank you, Charlie. I'll see you Wednesday."

Once the younger man was gone, Charlotte returned to Wynter's side.

"I'm sorry I couldn't tell you my secret. As for my clothes, it's part of our magic." Wynter looked around the room. "Is it too much to ask all of you to forget what you saw? The truth of our kind isn't exactly common knowledge, and if it gets out there are shifters in the world..."

"Chaos would ensue. Yeah, we'll keep your secret." Hawk brushed Wynter's hair back from her forehead. "So much perspective," he whispered before standing and backing away. Charlotte stared in wonder as Wynter once again shifted to her animal. Charlotte was amazed. Shocked, pissed off. Worried. But mostly, she was amazed that her best friend was a shifter. As she waited for Wynter to change back to

251

human, so many memories flashed through Charlotte's head. Things that now made sense, like whenever they went camping, Wynter would take off through the woods on her own. When she got hurt, Wynter shrugged it off like it was no big deal. She preferred her steaks rare. "Ooh, gross," Charlotte muttered, thinking of her gorgeous bestie eating other animals in her wolf form.

"I'm sorry if I'm weirding you out," Wynter said. "I must say, you're taking this extremely well."

"You aren't weirding me out. I was thinking about... never mind. We can talk about all this later. Did shifting work, or do we need to get you to your dad?"

Wynter bent over and picked up the bullet. "I'll be fine. As much as I want to tear that bastard's head off, we need to figure out what we're going to tell the police though."

"About that." Ace stood. "I think we should handle this ourselves. Warren had some interesting news to share with the class. He gave me the location of the compound he and Roland are part of."

"Elise! Jude, we have to go." Charlotte had forgotten about her cousin.

Jude grabbed her hand when Charlotte headed for the door. "No. Today is Valentine's Day. You don't need to close your shop. I'll send Hawk to check on Elise." He turned to Hawk and explained, "Roland recruited Elise to be a nurse. He took her to the compound where she spent the last few days. She came home to pack her house so she could sell it and all her belongings. She called Charlie right before Warren attacked. Before she hung up, someone knocked on

Elise's door. Charlie had filled her cousin in on Roland's duplicitous nature, so we need to get over there."

"I'm coming with you," Wynter said. Hawk opened his mouth, most likely to protest, but Wynter held up her hand. "Just try and stop me."

Charlotte didn't care who went as long as they left then. "Elise's safety is more important to me than selling flowers, so I'm going with you. But what about him?" she asked, pointing to Warren.

"I'll take care of him," Ace said. "I'll call Sutton and let him know everything Warren told me."

"While you're at it, please call Zander and Bishop. Bishop needs to fix the security feed so it doesn't show Wynter shifting, and Zan needs to be aware Bishop's messing with the feed."

"I can do that. Charlotte, why don't you get in touch with Margie and have her come in to take care of customers? I'll have Zedra and Ripper come back to help. That way you don't have to worry about the shop while you go see about Elise."

"Good idea, and thank you." Charlotte turned to Jude. "Can we go now?"

"Yes." Jude clapped Ace on the shoulder as they walked by. "Thank you, Brother."

As the two couples were walking toward the front door, Wynter stopped in front of Warren and performed a perfect roundhouse kick upside the man's head. "That's for trying to kill my best friend, you fucker."

Hawk grabbed her around the waist and dragged her toward the door. "Come on, Bruce Lee. He'll get what's coming to him."

253

After they were all situated in Jude's SUV, Charlotte turned sideways in her seat so she could look at Wynter. "I am so pissed at you."

"I'm sorry, Charlie. If I could have shared what I am with anyone, it would be you."

"Not for that, you idiot. For jumping in front of a bullet. If anything happened to you, I couldn't bear it."

"Yeah? Well right back at ya."

"So, werewolves are a myth, huh, she-wolf?"

"Yes. As far as I know, they *are* a myth. Then again, who knows? We call ourselves wolf shifters. Unlike the stories about werewolves, we aren't these deranged beasts that only turn at a full moon. We can shift between our two selves whenever we want. The pack my family originated from has been in the Northern Territory for centuries. My grandparents migrated down from Canada about three hundred years ago when my grandfather wanted to live more in his skin than fur. In the old pack, everyone lived together on pack lands. My grandmother was the youngest daughter of the Alpha, and she convinced him to let her and my grandfather leave to start their own pack in the States.

"Instead of continuing with the old ways, my grandfather decided to spend his life as a human, shifting only when he wanted. He didn't buy up a bunch of land where his family would live together. Instead, they kept their wolf half hidden from the world. For all intents and purposes, my grandparents were just another couple starting a new life. They raised my father and his siblings with the knowledge of what they are. They also gave them the choice of returning to Canada to live with the pack if they preferred. None of them did. So, we're not your typical wolf shifters in that sense. But I do have an excellent sense of smell, and my nose tells me there's something different about these two." Wynter pointed at both males.

Charlotte waited for Jude or Hawk to respond. It wasn't her secret to tell. After a moment of silence where Jude and Hawk stared at each other in the rearview mirror, Jude nodded.

"You're right," Hawk said. "It's why I quickly agreed to keep your secret because we have our own. Jude and I are Gryphons. Our animal is half Eagle, half Lion. We can shift into either animal, or we can fully shift into our Gryphon."

Wynter narrowed her eyes at Hawk. "That's why I couldn't tell what any of you were other than something besides human. You smell different. Like Zedra. She's a Gryphon too, right?"

"She is."

Wynter brushed her hair off her face as she looked at Charlotte. "And you knew this. That's why you didn't completely freak out when I shifted."

"Yep. Zed partially shifted into her Lion when John attacked me. I thought I was losing my mind, so once I got home from the hospital, Jude told me the truth and showed me *his* Lion. I'm kind of jealous. All of you are something special."

"Hey." Jude reached out and grabbed Charlotte's hand. "Just because you aren't a shifter doesn't mean you aren't special in your own way." Charlotte's stomach fluttered. No man had ever made her feel the way Jude did. She might not be a shifter, but she could be a mate to one. She had come close to telling him she loved him when they were lying in bed the night before after making love. Charlotte wanted Jude in her life. Wanted Indigo to be a mother figure. She could envision being part of his extended family of bikers, hanging out with the other mates. Having his Gryphon babies.

"What did you do to Kristoff to convince him he didn't feel well?" Wynter asked Jude, interrupting Charlotte's musings of the future.

"Gryphons have the ability to manipulate human minds. We use it to wipe memories, like Kristoff seeing you shift. We also use it to get the truth out of men like Warren. It's a lot less messy than torture."

"I'd like to torture that bastard." Wynter squirmed in her seat as her eyes flashed silver.

"Is your wound bothering you?" Charlotte couldn't believe Wynter had been shot.

"It's still a little tender. Ace said he was calling someone named Sutton with the information he got out of Warren. Who is he?"

"Sutton is like the Alpha of Gryphons in our area. He used to be the president of our MC until he decided to focus all his energy on going after The Ministry. Not all Hounds have regular jobs. Some help Sutton and Rory, his mate, track down The Ministry and rescue individuals who are there against their will. They expose their true intentions. Some cults are nothing more than communities wanting to live off the grid, and we leave them to live in peace. Those like the one who attacked Charlotte and recruited Elise have been lying to the world for decades, and we feel it's our duty to take them out to keep humans safe."

"I can't believe Master R is part of a cult. How does that even work? I thought those people spewed Bible verses left and right."

"They do, but the ones in charge use the Bible to hide their true agenda, which is usually chaos and greed."

"What's our game plan? Roland has already tried twice to have Charlotte killed," Hawk asked Jude, his voice low. Charlotte shivered at the malice.

"I think we should use the neighbor. Have Vickie call and ask him to come help with something so we can draw him away from Elise. I'll take care of Roland while you get Elise out of her house."

Charlotte squeezed Jude's hand. "Elise needs to hear the truth from Roland, or she won't believe he tried to have me taken out."

"I'll voice him once I get him away from Elise. Convince him to tell her the truth."

Wynter leaned forward between the seats. "Then what? Are you turning him over to the cops?"

Jude released Charlotte's hand, then rubbed his beard. "We'll have to. They're already involved in two towns."

Hawk growled. "We don't have to. I say we kill the fuckers and let the cases go cold."

"I like the way you think," Wynter responded.

Charlotte turned to look at her best friend. "Who are you and what have you done with my Wynter?"

Wynter's smile turned from happy to devious. "I'm not as innocent as I pretend."

"I'll say," Hawk muttered, and Wynter snapped her teeth at the male.

Charlotte's mouth fell open. "Oh, my god." She punched Jude's arm. "Are you hearing this?"

Jude grinned. "Yep."

Charlotte settled back against her seat with a huff, and Wynter cackled. Fucking cackled like a crazed old woman. Charlotte didn't know whether to be thrilled or miffed that Wynter wasn't the shy, innocent woman she pretended to be. The more she thought about it, miffed won out. She understood why Wynter couldn't tell Charlotte about being a shifter, but to pretend to be all prudish? That hurt. Charlotte had never been anything but herself with her best friend.

"You okay?" Jude asked quietly.

"Fine." Charlotte was anything but. If Wynter pretended to be a goody two shoes all these years, what else had she hidden? Was Charlotte even her best friend? Pity party of one, Charlotte would take a table in the corner where she could sulk in private. They pulled into Elise's driveway, so figuring out where she truly stood with Wynter would have to wait.

"No cars. I'm going to look in the windows first." Jude got out, and Hawk followed, leaving Charlotte alone with Wynter.

"Charlie?" Wynter scooted forward, leaning between the front seats. "Talk to me."

"What's there to talk about?"

"I know you, Boo. You're pissed at me."

Charlotte turned sideways and sighed. "I'm not pissed. Just... wondering if we're really friends."

"What? How can you doubt that? We've been best friends for years."

"And you know every single thing there is about me. I have never hidden who I am or how I am. You, on the other hand, have always pretended to be this shy, innocent person, yet now, with Hawk, you're like someone completely different. If that part of you was a lie, what else was? I know you and Zedra have a past, yet you won't tell me about that. Are you bisexual? Because if you are, I don't care."

"It's not like that. I am shy, but Roman brings out the inner wolf. I think deep down I knew he was different, and I could let loose with him. I've never been aggressive in the bedroom, until him. It was like my wolf took over." Wynter looked out the window as the two males walked around the house. "In my family, we don't live the same way most wolf shifters do. If it weren't for us going camping once a year, I never would shift. I've always known I'm a shifter, but my parents made it so it's not a big deal. When my grandparents talk about how they were raised, I feel like I'm missing out. I wonder what it would be like to live with others like me who are free to run in their fur whenever they want.

"I have kept the sexual part of myself tamped down out of fear. Afraid my wolf half would somehow take over, and then what? I don't have the ability to control someone's mind the way Jude and Roman can. I wish I did, then I could be myself and not worry about shifting if things get too intense. I came really close the first night Roman and I were together, but somehow, deep down, I knew I could be myself. My true self. As for Zedra, she and I had a weekend together. It was intense, and my wolf did try to take over. That was the first time that happened, and it scared the shit out of me. So much so I told her it had been fun, but I wasn't looking for anything serious. She

259

knew I was lying, and she tried several times to get me to go out with her again. I was too chickenshit."

"Have you dated any women since?"

"No. I've never found another woman I was attracted to. I'm sorry, Boo. So sorry for not confiding in you."

"I get it." Charlotte reached out and touched Wynter's face. "I'm sorry, too, for doubting you."

"Roman's coming back."

Hawk slid into the back seat with Wynter. "Spyder's going next door to talk to the neighbor. Charlie, what kind of car does Elise drive?"

"A Toyota Camry. Why?"

"I need to call Bishop." Roman got back out of the car.

"Who's Bishop?" Wynter asked.

"Remember the picture of the guy who attacked me? Bishop's the one who sent it. He's a hacker. If they're getting him involved, that means they noticed something in the house. I'm really worried about Elise."

"It's possible Elise listened when you told her Roland is bad news and took off. Have you tried calling her again?'

"No. I was too busy dodging bullets and finding out my bestie is a wolf. That still blows my mind. How's your hip?"

"It's fine. Being able to shift helped. It'll be good as new in a few days. Here they come." Charlotte didn't like the look on either man's face.

Jude opened Charlotte's door. "I need you to come inside. There's something you should see." Knowing Wynter wouldn't stay put, Charlotte reached over and turned off the ignition, then handed Jude the keys. She grabbed her own keys from her purse and walked with the others to the front door. Once inside, Jude led her to the kitchen and pointed to a sheet of paper on the island. "I was able to read that using my Eagle's vision." Charlotte picked the paper up and read it.

Charlie,

I talked to Roland, and you had it all wrong. He has a twin brother named Roger. That's who you saw at the club. Roland washed his hands of his twin when he wouldn't turn from his sinful ways. I stand by my decision to be with Roland and the others. They need me. He swears he had nothing to do with trying to kill you, and I believe him. He said he didn't care about the house. He only wanted me to sell it because I won't need it any longer. Since your name is on the deed, you can have it. Keep it. Sell it. I don't care.

I'm tired, Charlie. Tired of being alone. Of not having people in my life who get me. This community does. I love you like a sister, but I need this for me. You have your own life, and I'm proud of you. I know Mom would be too. Please let me have this.

I'll always love you,
Elise

Jude hugged Charlotte from behind, and she leaned her head back against his shoulder. "She's really gone."

CHAPTER TWENTY

Spyder

JUDE DIDN'T WANT to believe Elise could be so naïve as to think Roland was telling the truth, but when he'd gone next door to talk to Vickie, she wasn't there. Barbara was. The older woman looked like hell. Like she had her own issues she was dealing with.

"I spoke to Barbara. She said Elise came over to tell her she was moving. When I asked how Elise looked, she said, 'It's been almost twenty years since I recognized the girl she used to be. Elise seemed serene.' And yes, I voiced her to make sure she was telling the truth."

Charlotte stepped out of his embrace and took a look around the kitchen. She then walked through the house, looking in every room. Jude remained in the kitchen, giving her time to sort through her feelings. She returned, her face a mask of fury.

"She knew. Elise all but admitted to John's guilt, and yet she willingly returned to the compound knowing she would be living with the man who tried to kill me. That's fucked up."

"You're not wrong, Boo." Wynter had read the letter while Charlotte walked through the house. "Now what? We have Warren. We know where John is. Are we going to let them both get away with trying to kill Charlie?"

"Fuck no." While Jude was visiting Barbara, Hawk first called Bishop to see if he could corroborate Roland's claim he had a twin, and then Sutton to tell him Elise planned on returning to the compound. "If Elise wants to live in a cult, there's nothing we can do about that. Yet. But we can do something about the others. Sutton suggested having Warren go to the police and turn himself in. Ace will voice him into admitting who all was involved. As much as I want to go in and kill the motherfuckers, this is one time we need to let the cops handle things. Then maybe if Elise sees John and Roland being arrested, she'll come to her senses. Are you good with that, Sweetness?"

"As long as the three of them go to jail, then yes. I need a minute." Charlotte opened one of the drawers and retrieved a steak knife. She then started going through the boxes Elise had packed. Jude called Ace and told him to proceed with getting Warren to turn himself in. By the time the conversation ended, Charlotte had finished with her mission. Her hands were empty. "I had to search one last time for photos. Can we go now?"

Before Jude could get to her, Wynter strode to Charlie, hugging her best friend. Jude wanted to be the one soothing his mate, but he let the friends have their moment. As they walked out, Charlotte turned back and took one last look.

Instead of going home, Charlotte insisted on returning to her shop. Jude figured she needed to stay busy to keep from thinking about Elise. He would rather keep her busy in other, more personal ways, but they had time for that later.

It was a good thing they returned to The Blooming Boutique. The shop was full of customers when they arrived. Ripper was standing guard outside, and Zander was watching over the females inside. As though they had all worked together for years, Zedra handled the phones, and Wynter rang up customers while Margie and Charlotte filled the orders. Within the time they had left earlier until their return, all the pre-made arrangements had been sold, so Charlotte and Margie were busy nonstop until it was time to close the doors.

"I can't thank you all enough for helping today." Charlotte removed her apron as she spoke. "Margie, I want you to take the next two days off."

"That's not necessary. If you're here, then so am I. Especially with Kristoff being under the weather."

"I appreciate that, but I'm closing the shop tomorrow. Kristoff will be back Wednesday, and things will be much slower. As for the rest of you, I'd love to treat you all to dinner tonight. I couldn't have done this without all of you. I know one meal isn't repayment enough for all the time you put in today, but it's a start. I'll find a way to make it up to all of you."

"Oh, Boo. You know I don't expect payment," Wynter said.

"Neither do I," Zedra added. "But if you insist, how about if I ever get married, you can give me a discount on a bouquet."

Charlotte choked out a laugh through the tears in her eyes. "Deal. Now, where do you all want to eat?"

Zedra and Zander politely turned down her offer, and Jude had a feeling it was because of whatever past Zedra had with Wynter. He hadn't missed the look of longing on Zedra's face at seeing the other female cozied up with Hawk. Margie called Benny and had her husband meet them at Carlotti's. Jude had never eaten at the restaurant, but he knew they would be returning. The food was some of the best Italian he'd ever tasted. With Margie and Benny accompanying them, talk of attempted murder was off the table. Jude didn't want to rehash it anyway. He wanted Charlotte to relax, and when he got her home, he had just the thing.

Ripper thanked Charlie for dinner and promised to see them Wednesday. Jude prayed the cops arrested John and Roland by then, and Ripper's help wouldn't be needed. The rest of them said their goodbyes with each couple going their separate ways. They were almost to Charlotte's apartment when Jude's phone rang.

"Bishop? What do you have?"

"Roland was telling the truth. It took some digging, but he and Roger are brothers. Their last name is Smithson, but it looks like Roger shortened his to Smith about fifteen years ago. He works for an investment firm owned by his wife's father. The father happens to be a deacon in his church."

"And the wife probably has no idea what her husband gets up to when he's out late. Thank you, Bishop."

"Any time."

Jude relayed what Bishop found to Charlotte.

"Master R is a cheating douchebag. I'd really like to tell his wife who she's married to."

"Who says you can't?"

"Really? Isn't it like some bro code to keep secrets or something?"

"Fuck no. Don't get me wrong. If a couple has an open relationship, that's their business, but I hate a cheater. When someone makes a promise to another, they should honor that promise. I'm sure Roger knew the kind of woman he was marrying, and I would lay bets he only married her to stay in his father-in-law's good graces. If that's the case, he doesn't truly love her. He's a selfish prick, and I'd love to see him get what's coming to him. If you want the wife to find out who she's married to, I'll help you devise a plan."

Charlotte smiled, but it didn't meet her eyes. Jude wanted to change that. "We're going to your apartment so you can pack a bag, and we'll take Gibby back to my house. I have just the thing to help take your mind off everything."

"Does it involve ropes?"

"It sure does. How do you feel about that?" Jude held his breath.

"That sounds amazing. Maybe this time you'll show me how your suspension frame works."

"Fuck, Charlie."

"Exactly. I want you to fuck Charlie while I'm hanging in the air."

"Zeus, I… You're perfect." Jude almost told her he loved her, but he wanted to wait. Charlotte needed him to show her how he felt. And as much as he would love to fuck her while suspended, she wasn't ready. "And I promise we will get to that soon, but we need to work up to it. I will suspend you, but it will not be an elaborate enough set-up for sex."

If Charlotte was disappointed, she didn't let on. "I trust you, Jude. You are the Master."

"Remember, Sweetness, communication is essential. You have your safe words, but this is more intense that what we did the first time. If you are uncomfortable in the least, you need to tell me."

"I will. I promise."

Jude had Charlotte take a bath when they arrived at his house. He used that time to center himself. Binding someone safely to be suspended was something he'd done many times. He couldn't wait for the day he could make love to her as she hung from the suspension beam. It would be a new experience for him. Yes, he had fucked bottoms before, but that had been years ago. Back when the grief from Michelle's death had been fresh. Back when he tried to lose himself in any willing body to keep his mind off his pain. This was different. This was Jude and Charlotte – Gryphon and mate. After tonight, he prayed she would agree to the bond.

Jude chose several lengths of hemp and placed them on the ground beside Charlotte. Before he began with the ropes, he pulled her into his arms and cradled her to his chest. "Close your eyes. Try to erase all thoughts and let your senses take over. Let my touch soothe you." Charlotte relaxed against him, and Jude brushed his fingers down her arms. Over her thighs. Along her cheeks. Jude pressed his lips to her skin as he continued exploring with his fingertips. When she completely relaxed, he picked up the first rope and wound it around her torso first. Jude alternated between using his touch and the hemp to embrace his female. The binding wasn't elaborate. This wasn't for show. He used the minimal amount of rope that would safely allow him to suspend her to the rigging and still be comfortable. He would have preferred to spend hours showing her how she looked in several colors, but this was about Charlotte. About what she wanted and needed.

Instead of using a metal ring in the center of her back, Jude used three separate ropes to raise her. They would eventually get to the point where he hogtied her and used the metal ring at her back to lift her off the floor, but they would have to work up to that.

Jude took a step back, letting his eyes take in this amazing creature. Charlotte hadn't uttered a sound during the process, but the serenity on her face was all he needed to know she was comfortable. He left her suspended long enough to snap a picture on his phone before he lowered her to the floor. Jude held Charlotte in his arms, once again caressing her with his fingertips and lips. He unwound the ropes slowly, keeping her in the moment as long as possible. When she was completely bare, Charlotte opened her eyes.

"I love you." Charlotte caressed his face, running her fingers through his beard. "I know it's soon, but I have never felt as complete as I do in this moment. Being in your arms, in your ropes, it's everything I never knew I was missing."

"I love you too. I already consider you my mate, but one day, I hope you agree to the mate bond. I want everything with you, my sweet Charlotte. I want to spend every day showing you how very special you are. I want to love you for the rest of my life."

"I want that too. I'm ready."

Jude brushed Charlotte's hair off her face. "You are?"

"Yes. You've already shown me the type of male you are, and I couldn't ask for anyone better. I figure why wait when I know you're perfect for me? Take me to bed, and make me yours."

Jude cradled Charlotte in his arms, then shifted his legs underneath him so he could stand. He carried her across the hall to his room and gently lowered her to the bed. His pulse raced in anticipation, and his Gryphon pushed against him. Jude pushed back. He wasn't going to rush this experience. He had waited almost fifty years for his mate, and Zeus willing, he'd never have another. Completing the bond was the single most important moment in his life, and Jude wanted it to be special. Not rushed.

Jude removed the leather pants Charlotte had asked him to wear. His cock bounced against his stomach upon release, and he stroked it as he gazed down at his mate. Her eyes moved to his hand, and she licked her lips. He wanted her mouth on him. Wanted the wet heat surrounding his dick. But he wanted to make love to her more. Charlotte spread her legs in invitation as she cupped her breasts and rolled her nipples.

Not willing to wait, Jude put a knee to the bed and settled between her thighs. He gripped his erection and rubbed it through her slick folds a couple times before pressing against her entrance. Charlotte wrapped her feet around his thighs, pulling against him, urging him closer. Jude gave her what she wanted. What they both wanted. Moving slowly, Jude made love to Charlotte.

He held himself aloft on his palms so he could see her face. Love shone in her eyes. He could get lost in their seafoam beauty. Charlotte slid one hand around the back of his neck and tugged his head down. When their lips met, she attacked his mouth. Her tongue danced with his, swirling and teasing. Jude appreciated how Charlotte wasn't afraid to show him what she wanted. The night before had been slow and sweet. By the way she ate at his mouth, she wanted something different right then. He was more than eager to give it to her.

Jude prided himself on being a generous lover. He had stamina for days. Usually. With Charlotte writhing against him, moaning into his mouth, scratching his skin with her nails, knowing he was going to claim her soon, Jude's body raced toward release. Not wanting to come yet, he pulled out and slid lower so he could taste her. Jude licked her clit, circling the nub with his tongue, then sucked it between his lips.

Charlotte grabbed his hair, pulling. "Jude...Oh, god, you're good at that." She placed her feet on the mattress and pushed her core against his mouth. Grinding, using him for her own pleasure. Jude spread her thighs wider and speared her pussy with his tongue, relishing the taste. He let his tongue dip lower to her pucker, testing the waters. Charlotte didn't disappoint. She grabbed the backs of her thighs, opening herself to whatever he wanted to do. Jude dreamed of the day she returned the favor.

His beast pushed against him again, urging him to take her. Bite her. Bind her to him. Jude licked from her tight pucker up to her clit and bit down. Charlotte lowered her feet again and pushed against his mouth.

"Jude, please. I'm... yes... Oh, god."

Jude wanted to feel her release around his cock, so he crawled up her body, sinking his dick inside her slickness with ease. His hair hung down, swinging with each thrust. Charlotte grabbed it, wrapping it around her fists. "God, I love your hair." She pulled enough to sting, and Jude relished the pain. He changed the angle of his dick so it rubbed against her clit. Charlotte's breath hitched, and she tightened her grip. "Jude... Do it."

His shifter vibrated, urging Jude to give her what they both wanted. His eyes flashed as his beast tried to take over.

"Are you sure?" Jude was close to losing control of his shifter and his orgasm.

"Yes, bite me. Make me yours."

Jude couldn't hold back any longer. He fucked her harder, quickening his hips. He allowed his canines to elongate. Charlotte's eyes widened, but instead of shying away, she pulled her hair off her shoulder. Jude surged his hips forward as he lowered his mouth to her neck. He struck fast. Charlotte cried out as her orgasm overtook her. As her pussy tightened around his dick, Jude's own release raced through his body. His Lion roared inside his head. His claws lengthened, ripping the bedding beneath his hands. Jude retracted his fangs and licked Charlotte's skin. The tang of blood had his cock shooting again.

That moment was what he'd waited for his whole life. The connection, the sharing of body and soul with his one perfect being. Jude raised up to find tears seeping from the corner of Charlotte's eyes. When she swiped her thumbs across his cheeks, he realized he, too, was crying.

Smiling, Charlotte whispered, "I feel you. In here." She pressed her hand to her heart. "That was... I don't have the words."

"You don't need them." Jude lowered his body, keeping most of his weight off her by resting on his forearms. Charlotte met his mouth and kissed him softly. As she nibbled on his lips, the smile never left her mouth. After what felt like hours, Jude's dick slid from her body, their mixed release following.

"Is that a one-time deal, or can you bite me again? Because I gotta tell you, I saw stars."

Jude grinned and kissed the tip of her nose. "Nope. I can snack on you whenever you want."

Her smile dimmed, but only a little. "I wish I had fangs so I could bite you back."

"You don't need fangs for that, Sweetness. You have teeth. Feel free to use them anytime. Unless you're blowing me. Not then. That shit's no fun."

Charlotte laughed. "I'll remember that."

And she did. Jude's dick hardened against her thigh, and Charlotte urged him to his back. She winked, then turned so she could suck him off. He grabbed her legs and situated her pussy over his face so he could lick his cum off her thighs. When he had it all, he turned his focus to her clit. As he ate her out, she used her mouth and fist to pull another orgasm from him. After they both got off again, Jude tucked her to his side. He wanted to spend all night buried inside his mate, but he didn't want her to be too sore the next day, so he happily held her close. They were silent after that other than Charlotte humming against his chest.

As he cuddled his mate, Jude thanked Zeus for bringing such an amazing creature to him. He was content. He was in love. And he was now complete.

Charlotte

"DO YOU WANT to stay in bed all day, or would you like to go for a ride?"

"Is that a trick question?" Charlotte felt like it was.

Jude rubbed his beard against her belly, the soft hairs tickling her skin. "Nope. Not a trick. But the weather is supposed to be somewhat mild today, so I thought you might like to ride when it's not freezing." Jude had suggested Charlotte bring her riding gear when she packed the night before. Now, she was glad she'd listened.

"And where would we ride to?" As much as she enjoyed their lovemaking, Charlotte really wanted to be back on the bike.

"I want to introduce you to Rhiannon. And if we're lucky, we can stop off and see the twins. If I call and let them know we're going to visit, I bet Mayhem would put the kids in their sidecar and meet us at Ryker's."

"I'd like that."

"Excellent. Let me make a couple calls, then we'll shower."

Gibby jumped on the bed and stared at her a beat before licking his paw.

"Hey, buddy. You hate Momma, don't you? You know I'm going to leave you alone, and you're pouting."

Jude leaned down and grabbed Gibby, pulling him onto his chest. Gibby began making dough with his claws. "We could get him some little kitty goggles, and I could stuff him in my jacket."

Charlotte rolled to her side and propped her head on her hand. "You're ridiculous."

"What? You've never seen a biker kitty?"

"No, and neither have you."

"I think we should get him a sibling so he's not alone when we're gone. What do you say, Gibby? You want a baby brother or sister?"

Charlotte's smile widened. "Uh, Jude. We can't leave a baby alone with the cat."

"I know that. I was talking about a kitten. But now that you mentioned it, when do you want to start trying for a real baby?"

Charlotte blanked her face, doing her best to look serious. "Hmm, a couple years?"

"What?" Jude sat up, dislodging Gibby. The cat glared at him, then padded over to Charlotte and curled up against her stomach.

"What?" she asked innocently.

Jude pushed Charlotte to her back and straddled her hips, careful not to smush the cat. "Two years? Charlotte. Sweetness. I can't wait that long. My biological clock is ticking. I'm not getting any younger."

"Yes, but you're not getting any older either."

"I most certainly am. In three years, I'll be fifty."

"Haven't you heard? Fifty's the new twenty."

Jude glanced down at Gibby. "Your momma thinks she's funny." He turned back to Charlotte. "You're not funny."

"I'm hilarious."

"You" — he booped her nose — "are cute. Smart. Sexy as fuck. Great in bed. Hilarious, you are not."

Charlotte smacked his chest before gliding her fingers through the hair between his muscled pecs. "Are you naturally fit from being a Gryphon, or do you work out?"

Jude placed his hands on either side of her head and did a few pushups, kissing her each time his mouth came close to hers. "You're all the workout I need."

"Now that we're mated, will you show me your Gryphon?"

"I sure will. Let's go into the playroom. There's more space in there."

Charlotte followed Jude, her heart beating double time at the prospect of getting to see her man fully shifted.

Jude stopped her just inside the door. "Stay right here. I'll shift to my Eagle first, then I'll move on to the big guy. Remember, I will never hurt you." Jude stepped to the middle of the room, and Charlotte admired every inch of his naked body. Within seconds, his human form morphed into the largest Eagle she'd ever seen. He was almost completely white. Jude had explained how the Hounds took on one of the elements, and his white feathers indicated he had an affinity for air. He squawked at her. Okay, squawk might be a stretch. The sound was closer to a giggle. Could birds giggle?

Charlotte mentally braced herself. "I'm ready."

The transformation wasn't as fast, but it didn't take long for the Eagle to change and grow. The most fascinating creature imaginable stood still, his eyes locked on hers. The Eagle's head, wings, and front legs were still there, but his back half was that of his Lion.

"Wow." Charlotte took in the majestic animal. The top of his head grazed the ceiling as his keen eyes studied her. Charlotte smiled. "You're amazing. You can understand me, right?" Jude squawked again. "As thrilling as your Gryphon is, I'd really like to see your Lion again. Please?" Jude flicked his tail, and within seconds, he transformed into his feline. Jude's chest rumbled as he sat back on his haunches.

Charlotte pushed off the wall and strode to her beast. "Are you purring?" The large cat dropped to the floor and rolled to his back. His massive paws were bent at the joint, reminding her of Gibby when he wanted belly rubs. Charlotte knelt beside him and rubbed his stomach. His smooth fur vibrated, making Charlotte laugh. "I'll take that as a yes." Gibby trotted into the room and pounced on Jude's larger cat. Jude rolled to his feet and shook his massive mane. He lowered his head, and Gibby stretched his body so he could rub his own face against Jude's. Charlotte sat back, cross-legged, content to watch her two "boys" play. She had thought her life was charmed before. Now? She didn't know how it could get any better.

CHAPTER TWENTY-ONE

Charlotte

CHARLOTTE SHOULD HAVE been afraid about getting bugs in her teeth, but she couldn't stop smiling. Riding with Jude on his bike was thrilling, and it was something she would get to do whenever she wanted now that they were mated. Remembering how intense her orgasm was when he bit her sent a flutter to her belly. There wasn't a scar on her shoulder. She almost wished there were so she would see it whenever she looked in the mirror. A flutter of a different kind popped into her mind. One day, probably soon if Jude had his way, she'd have a baby kicking around. Charlotte was ready.

Too soon, they were pulling into a driveway where Jude's friend Maveryck lived. When he called Ryker, the male suggested meeting at Mav's place. Ryker's daughter, Mac, wasn't feeling up to a bunch of company, and Ryker didn't want her to have to hide out in her room all morning.

The front door opened before Charlotte could climb off, and a little boy ran down the steps barefooted. His twin waited at the door.

"Hey Spiderman."

"Hey Major Tom."

"My name's not Tom. Duh. Who's this?"

"This is Charlotte. Charlotte, this towhead is Major."

"Wow! You're a spider too. That's so cool."

"Major Lazlo! Get your butt in this house," a petite woman with lavender hair yelled.

"Uh oh." Major grinned at Charlotte before yelling, "Coming, Lolly." Major took off running. Natalia ruffled her stepson's hair as he ran past her. Her smile was brilliant and welcoming when Charlotte and Jude approached.

"Come on in." Natalia let Jude grab the door, and Charlotte walked in ahead of him, following the pretty woman who had been an assassin upon meeting Maveryck. That morning over breakfast, Jude filled Charlotte in on the mates she would be meeting. "Would you like something to drink? I've got coffee, tea, juice, and all the alcohol."

"I'm good for now, but thank you." Jude helped Charlotte out of her jacket while he introduced her to the others in the room.

Maveryck and his twin, Warryck, resembled with their blond hair and blue eyes, but they weren't identical like the younger twins. Ryker, their older brother, looked nothing like them with his dark hair and eyes. Where Major was a whirlwind, Marshall was the quieter boy. Kerrigan was a down-to-earth redhead who War had rescued from The Ministry. Natalia was nothing like Charlotte expected an assassin to be. She was friendly, loved the twins immensely, and was completely smitten with their father.

As interesting as they all were, it was Rhiannon who captured Charlotte's attention the most. It wasn't her long, dirty-blonde hair or her big, innocent eyes, but the energy she exuded. Jude said Rhiannon had a gift, but he didn't say what kind other than she had a knack for working with plants.

Jude led her to an oversized chair and pulled Charlotte down onto his lap. She started to protest, but the others were seated the same way. The boys sat down on the floor in front of their parents.

"Spiderman and spider girl. Are you gonna have spider kids?" Major asked.

"What on earth are you talking about, Son?" Maveryck asked.

Major pointed his little finger at Charlotte. "She's a spider too. Duh." She couldn't help but laugh at the exasperation on the boy's face.

Maveryck's eyes narrowed at his son. "Do you have any idea what he's going on about?" Mav asked Natalia.

Natalia threaded her fingers through her mate's blond hair. "*Charlotte's Web* is a children's movie. Charlotte is a spider."

"Duh," Major muttered, and the adults burst out laughing.

"I'm going to duh your ass." Maveryck grabbed his son and proceeded to tickle him until the boy couldn't breathe, while Natalia did her best to stay out of their line of fire.

When Major had his laughing under control, he jumped off the sofa out of his father's reach. "That wasn't my ass. This is." Major turned around and

279

wiggled his butt, then took off running through the house. The adults cracked up again.

"He's ridiculous," Marshall said, rolling his eyes before trailing after his twin.

Charlotte rested her head against Jude's. "I want one."

"Which one? The whirlwind or the calm sea?"

"Yes." Both boys had Charlotte enthralled. She had been an only child until she went to live with Ellen and Elise. Charlotte wanted at least two kids so they would always have a best friend. At least she hoped her children would be close.

The front door opened, and another gorgeous couple entered the house with a small boy. Major and Marshall ran back into the room from wherever they'd been.

Major stopped in front of the male. "Hey, Hay."

"Hey, Little Dude. What's shaking?"

Major turned around and wiggled his butt again. "My ass." Major jumped out of the way as his uncle tried to swat it. Marshall grabbed the dark-haired boy's hand as if it were the most natural thing in the world, and the three kids ran off to presumably play.

"That's two dollars out of your swear jar," Natalia informed Major.

Major threw his arms in the air, huffing. "What? Ass isn't a bad word."

"You want to go for three?" Natalia arched a dark eyebrow, and Major took off down the hall again.

"I thought you put money *in* swear jars," Jude said.

Natalia squirmed against Maveryck's lap, getting resettled after the tickle fest. "We put money in the jar every time they help around the house. Whenever one of them – Major – curses, he has to take a dollar out. Marshall's making bank. Major? I think he owes us money."

When the newcomers stepped closer, Jude introduced them. "Charlie, this is Hayden and Sadie. The boy Marshall hijacked is their son, Mateo."

Sadie, a curvy Latina, was one of the most stunningly beautiful women Charlotte had ever seen, and that was saying something considering how gorgeous Wynter was. She smiled and gave Charlotte a wave as Hayden greeted Charlotte. "Pleasure to meet you, Charlie. You've had a rough couple of weeks. How are you holding up?" He sat down in another one of the oversized chairs, pulling Sadie onto his lap. Charlotte wondered if that was a Gryphon thing.

"I'm good for the most part. Physically, I'm all healed up, but mentally..." Charlotte wasn't sure how much to say. Having someone try to kill her hadn't truly sunk in. She figured the nightmares were coming though.

When Charlotte didn't elaborate, Rhiannon spoke up. "That's the hardest part about trauma. Physical wounds heal much quicker. Sometimes the brain is reluctant to let go. Always reminding you of the crap you've been through." Ryker rubbed a hand over his mate's belly and kissed her temple. It was then Charlotte realized Rhi was pregnant. "It's even harder when family is involved."

Charlotte looked at the other woman. Really looked at her. For someone so young, she had an aura of being wise beyond her years. "It really is. My cousin is like a sister to me. I have admired her forever, but she's willingly gone to live with and be part of The Ministry knowing they tried to kill me."

Rhi smiled softly. "I feel you. My father implanted trackers under my skin. Ones that would cause me to black out. He then took me to live with those same people your cousin's living with. Not the same compound, but another faction of The Ministry. My grandmother is the wife of the preacher where your cousin lives."

"Is Elise in danger?"

Rhiannon titled her head to the side. "Not if she truly wishes to be part of their world. They have strict rules and archaic ideas about men and women living separately. If she's gone there hoping to find a husband, she will figure out it's not like dating on the outside. If she's there seeking peace?" Rhiannon shrugged.

"She's been lost ever since—" Charlotte clamped her mouth closed. She couldn't explain without mentioning Michelle.

"Ever since her ex-boyfriend tried to kill her but killed my sister instead." Jude tightened his arms around Charlotte's waist. "This is something I've kept mostly to myself, but it's time I shared what happened. Especially with you, Ryot. Twenty years ago, my sister and Elise were friends. Michelle asked me to keep an eye on Elise's ex-boyfriend. He had been threatening Elise. I did. I followed him for a couple weeks. Long story short, he went to confront Elise. I got stuck in traffic, and when I finally got to her apartment, I was too late. He pulled the trigger, but Michelle stepped in front of Elise."

"That's why you freaked out at the gun range?" Ryker asked.

Jude nodded against Charlotte's cheek. "The panic attacks lessened over the years because I wasn't around guns. When Havyk and I were in Texas, they started up again after the shootout. Michelle's death is why I hate guns. When Warren came after Charlie, I froze. If it hadn't been for..." It was Jude's turn to stop talking.

"If it hadn't been for what?" Hayden prodded.

Charlotte rubbed Jude's arm holding her stomach. She couldn't tell the truth without spilling Wynter's secret, so she gave them part of the story. "My best friend, Wynter. She dove at Warren, distracting him. It gave Ace time to get inside and detain him. It all happened quickly with no damage to my shop. We got lucky there were no customers there when it happened."

"After talking it over with Sutton, we decided to have Warren turn himself in and admit to who all was involved. We now know where Abraham's compound is located. Sutton's hoping this will distract Abraham enough we can move in and take the man down."

"Did Ace ask this Warren if Josiah is hiding out at their compound?" Natalia asked in a slight accent. Charlotte found the other woman fascinating. According to Jude, not only had she been an assassin but also a Russian mafia princess.

"He did, and according to Warren, Abraham is pissed at Josiah. Thinks he's a liability. Their compound isn't as heavily guarded, but those who patrol do carry weapons and have been ordered to shoot Josiah on sight."

"Wow, there really is no love lost between these bastards," Hayden said.

The three boys ran full speed into the room, interrupting the conversation. Major sang, "Lolly," then Marshall added, "Tolly," and Mateo finished with, "Lollipop." Together, they announced, "We're hungry." The three boys giggled, falling into one another.

Natalia grinned. "You're always hungry. Would you like your Daddo to grill burgers and hot dogs?"

"Hot dogs!" the boys yelled together. Major did a cute little butt wiggle, Marshall pumped his fist in the air, and Mateo watched his friends with a huge smile. Charlotte guessed the adults probably considered the kids cousins even though Mateo wasn't family by blood. Taking after his mother, Mateo was going to break some hearts when he got older.

"I guess I have my orders," Maveryck said. He kissed Natalia's neck before pushing her to her feet. Like there was some unspoken code, the other males did the same. Maveryck ruffled Major's hair. "You stay out of trouble while I get lunch ready."

"Okay, Daddo," Major yelled. Charlotte wondered if the boy had ever heard of an inside voice. He grabbed Mateo's hand and dragged him from the room.

Marshall walked over to Rhiannon and kissed her belly. Rhi's hands cradled the little boy's face as he smiled up at her. When Marshall said, "Love you, Rhi Rhi," Charlotte's heart melted.

After Marshall walked off, Ryker pointed at the other couples. "One of you needs to hurry up and have our child a cousin to play with."

"Believe me, we're working on it," Hayden said, nuzzling Sadie's neck. "As often as we can." Sadie blushed, but she nodded in agreement.

While the others left to help get lunch going, Rhiannon pulled Charlotte to the side. "Has Spyder told you about my gift?"

"He mentioned you have an affinity for plants, but that's all."

"Let's sit down. Since you are family now, you should know about me." Once they were seated, Rhi turned sideways, curling one leg beneath her, and placed her hands on her lap. "I'll give you the short version. When I was young, I healed a dying bunny using the earth's energy. My mother swore me to secrecy, but my father found out. After my mother died, he inserted trackers under my skin before taking me to live at Josiah Talbert's compound. They kept me indoors, away from everything that gave me joy. Plants. Trees. Flowers. What I didn't know was the trackers also worked as a sort of zapper. If one of them was engaged, I became amenable to doing as instructed, and in this case, it was using my gift to heal people without knowing what I was doing. I would wake up later with no knowledge of what happened."

Rhiannon twisted her hands in her lap and took a deep breath. "My father also lived at the compound, but he all but forgot about me. Josiah used my father and his expertise with computers to make the cult money. To purchase weapons. To find people down on their luck and send recruiters out after these people. Say someone had cancer. Josiah promised them a cure in return for their money. He would zap me, send me in to 'heal' them, and I never knew it. Not too long ago,

I was being courted for marriage. James, my 'suitor', was a recruiter. Josiah allowed me to accompany James into town. He blindfolded me so I wouldn't know where we were. The last time he took me to town, I managed to escape, and Ryker found me. My father, using his computers and the trackers, discovered my location and kidnapped me, but I escaped again using my gifts."

Rhi reached out and gently held Charlotte's arm. A soft glow appeared, and Charlotte's arm warmed beneath the other woman's touch. "I told you all this because I wanted to offer to help out in your shop part-time. Being around flowers and plants is important to me, and I would love to learn from you. If you would be willing to teach me, that is. I'm not asking to be put on your payroll. The experience would be payment enough."

"I'd love to teach you, but you don't have to do it for free. I've planned on hiring part-time help anyway. This could be a win-win for both of us."

"How about a compromise? You teach me for a month, and if I do a good job, then you put me on the payroll."

Charlotte liked the younger woman already. Rhiannon would be a great fit. "Deal. I have two employees. Margie is like a mother figure. She mostly works in the front, answering the phone and dealing with customers. Kristoff is closer to my age and helps with bigger arrangements and some of my wedding designs. My bestie, Wynter, is a wedding planner. When she isn't dealing with brides, she hangs out and helps with the phone too. We're closed on Sundays. Margie is off on Mondays, Kristoff on Tuesdays. I'll leave it up to you how many days you want to come in."

"Thank you so much, Charlie. This means the world to me, and if you see me talking to the plants, now you'll know why."

"What does talking to them do?"

"Helps them grow. They are living things, and they, too, need love."

Charlotte reached out and squeezed Rhi's hand. "Makes sense. You know, I think you'll be able to teach me a thing or two."

JUDE WALKED OUTSIDE with the other males. Hayden passed around beers, then held his aloft. "I'd like to propose a toast. Here's to Spyder and his new mate. May Zeus forever look upon you with favor and fortune, and smile down upon you with lots of Gryphon babies."

"Cheers!"

"Hear, hear."

"I'll drink to that."

The five males clanked their bottles together. After taking a long swig, Jude rubbed the back of his neck. These were his friends. His brothers. He could be honest with them. "I'm going to find a therapist. I've tried for twenty years to get past Michelle's death. I thought I had a handle on my emotions, then we had that job in Texas, and it all came rushing back. The nightmares have returned, as have the panic attacks."

Ryker set a gentle hand on Jude's shoulder. "If you like, I can give you the name and number of the one Rhi and the kids go to." Like Rhiannon, Ryker's daughter, Mac, and her boyfriend, Elijah, had been victims of The Ministry.

"I'd appreciate that." Jude's phone rang, and seeing Sutton's name, he put it on speaker.

"Hey, Sutton. I'm here with Ryot, Mayhem, War, and Havyk. You're on speaker."

"I wanted to let you know the police have arrested Roland and John. I sent Ace, Ripper, and Locke to the compound to scope it out. They got some good intel. Abraham's setup is much like Josiah's but without a heavy guard presence. The Hounds were there when the police showed up. Roland vowed his innocence, stating John and Warren acted of their own accord. He claimed to bring Elise to the compound because he loves her and would never harm someone in her family. That might have worked if Bishop hadn't located Elise's car. He and Zander went to investigate, and they found it at Vickie's mother's place. Vickie was long gone, but her mother, after being voiced, explained that Roland paid Vickie to do some breaking and entering. The female has prior experience with both theft and simple hacking. She broke into The Blooming Boutique and got into Charlotte's computer. Vickie isn't as dumb as she let on."

"But without proof, it's Roland's word against Vickie's."

"Like I said, she isn't dumb. Vickie secretly videoed all her interactions with Roland, making sure to keep her face hidden from the camera. She manipulated her voice with some kind of modulator. The recordings show Roland offering her a lot of money for the information on Charlotte's computer. Vickie asked him why he needed Charlotte's schedule, and Roland admitted he had a problem to eliminate. Vickie had several copies. One she hid at her grandmother's when she took her back home, and another she dropped off with her mother to hand over to the cops should anything happen to her. Marla didn't know where Vickie was headed other than out west. Bishop's going to keep searching for Vickie, but with the recording, at least Roland won't walk."

Jude should be grateful, and he was, but he wanted to find Vickie and make her pay for her part in everything. "With Vickie's experience as a thief, I bet it was her who came out with the shotgun wearing a disguise. I'd like for Bishop to keep looking for her."

"I'll pass that along. I'm having a few Hounds keep an eye on the compound. As of now, we don't have proof anyone is there against their will. Abraham and his wife were suspiciously absent when the cops arrived. We're going to closely monitor Abraham, and Bishop is working on things from his end. Spyder, Rory wants to meet your mate. Indigo said she's a wonderful young woman."

"I'll be sure to bring her by."

"We'll expect you Sunday with the rest of the family, Son. Your mom will be there too."

"Yes, Sir." Jude looked away so the others didn't see how Sutton's words affected him. Their families had always been close, but it had been too long since someone besides Indigo called Spyder "son."

A strong hand clamped down on Jude's shoulder. "You've always been like a brother, but now it's official. Welcome to the family." Ryker squeezed once before his hand dropped away.

Feeling Charlie's presence, Jude turned toward the door. She was standing in the kitchen with the other mates, laughing at something Natalia said. Both he and Charlotte had lost most of their family, but now, they had more family than they knew what to do with. Jude tipped his bottle to the sky, raising his beer to Zeus, thanking him for their blessings.

CHAPTER TWENTY-TWO

Charlotte

JUDE STERLING IN his bad-boy biker gear was the stuff dreams were made of, but Jude in a suit? That was one-hundred-percent porn material. They were finally going on their date to Jacques'. If Charlotte hadn't been looking forward to eating at the upscale restaurant for the first time, she would have dragged Jude into their bedroom and ripped his clothes off. When she didn't say anything, Jude looked down at himself. Charlotte's brain finally came unstuck, and she grabbed him by the lapels and jerked him forward, kissing him hard. Lipstick be damned.

"Damn, Sweetness. I should wear a suit more often if this is how you greet me."

"Yes. Definitely. All the suits," she said between peppering his mouth with kisses. Charlotte took a step back, letting him in. Jude had run to his house to swap out his bike for the car and had dressed while there.

"I knew that dress would be fire." Jude raked his gaze down her body. He had taken her shopping a few weeks back for her birthday. Charlotte could have gone by herself and been done in under thirty minutes.

Shopping with Jude took hours. He wanted her to try on every single little black dress they came across plus some in different colors. Then he insisted she have new shoes to match. Charlotte promised she didn't need that many new things since she worked so much, but he insisted. She now had a new dress for every date night in the foreseeable future. But this one? It was her favorite. And by the way Jude's eyes flashed golden, it was his too. She loved it when his shifter came out to play.

"Your carriage awaits, My Queen." Jude bowed low, and Charlotte giggled. She loved her mate's playful side. She loved all sides to Jude.

Charlotte paused to dote on Gibby and his new baby brother Raffie, who was named after the rare Rafflesia flower. Once outside, Jude led Charlotte outside to where her new car sat waiting. Trixie would always be Charlotte's first love as far as vehicles went, but Roxie was magnificent. She was a Sebring Orange Z51 Corvette Stingray, another birthday present from Jude. It was a good thing her mate was rich because it was impossible to keep the car close to the speed limit. At least for Charlotte it was.

A kitchen fire had closed Jacques' for a while, so they were only now getting to their date. Jude made up for it by cooking supper most every night. Charlotte took over kitchen duty on her days off, but Jude always helped. They made an excellent team.

The last couple months had flown by. With Roland and the others in jail, Jude no longer needed to watch over Charlotte twenty-four seven. They were still finding their new normal together. They had searched for a house, but when they didn't find one that suited them both, Jude suggested building one. He bought a couple acres halfway between New Troy and New Latham, and after going over house plans, they chose one which they both loved with plenty of bedrooms for future children. Charlotte put her foot down at five spare rooms, though.

Life with Jude was perfect, and her shop was busier than ever. Rhiannon started work at BBs the week after Charlotte met the younger woman. She hit it off with Kristoff, and Margie had another adopted daughter. In Rhi, Charlotte found the sister she'd never had. Not in Elise, and not in Wynter. Rhi's energy was warm and soothing, and everyone she came in contact with felt it. She caught on quickly, and soon, Charlotte was able to leave the shop in the hands of her employees and not worry about taking random days off here and there.

The only dark spot in her life, if she could call it that, was that Elise had stayed at the compound, even after Roland had been arrested. Charlotte could almost understand. Elise had struggled for twenty years trying to find her footing after what happened with Greg and Michelle. She sold the house, sending Charlotte half the money along with a lengthy letter explaining how she was happy. She didn't mention Roland or apologize for not believing Charlotte, and that was the one thing Charlotte couldn't forgive. Charlotte had said she didn't want the money, but she accepted the funds, putting it in hers and Jude's joint account to use toward furnishing their new home. Their new home which would have its very own playroom in what normally would have been an attic.

Charlotte and Jude split their time between his house and her apartment. When they were at Jude's, Charlotte begged to be bound. Jude incorporated more elaborate designs each time they played, and Charlotte began stretching every morning, getting more limber so he could manipulate her legs easier. Having sex while suspended had been interesting, but Charlotte preferred when Jude focused on wrapping her so she felt like he was hugging her. Those were the moments she was able to free her mind and be at complete peace.

Dinner was exquisite. The owner, another Hound, had seen to it they had the best seat in the place. A live jazz band played softly in the back corner next to a small dance floor where the two of them spent as much time as they did at their table. Jude was an excellent dancer, and he wasn't afraid to grab Charlotte at random times, waltzing her around the living room, swaying to a slow beat, or strutting to a faster pop song. He may have been born that century, but his love for music and dancing went back farther. Jude introduced Charlotte to all types of bands and genres. One day at the shop when they were cleaning up, Kristoff caught Jude re-enacting a disco number, and the younger man had to get in on the action. Charlotte may have videoed the whole thing on her phone.

"Are you ready?" Jude asked, tugging on one of her curls. They were going to Dominion where Charlotte was going to bottom in Jude's demonstration. That was one reason she had insisted they play so often at home. She was his mate, and there was no way she would allow another woman to be bound in his ropes ever again. Not that she didn't trust Jude. She did. But to her, his rope work was personal. After going to the club and having to watch as Mistress M partnered for him, something inside Charlotte snapped. Mistress M met with Charlotte beforehand, introducing Charlotte to her husband, and as the two of them watched their partners together, Charlotte knew it would be the last time Jude had someone besides her as a bottom.

"I am." Charlotte took his outstretched hand, and Jude pulled her to his chest, kissing her passionately in the middle of the restaurant. His mouth on hers never got old. Next to making love, it was her favorite thing in the world.

After saying goodbye to the owner, Jude led Charlotte to the door where the valet had their new car waiting. Charlotte used the ride to Dominion to get in the proper headspace for their demonstration. While she wouldn't be nude, she would be in a sexy black bra and panties. When Jude had likened it to wearing a bikini, Charlotte's nerves settled. After seeing the various body shapes and sizes of the other women who frequented the club, Charlotte wasn't worried she wouldn't look good enough.

The club was already filling with members by the time they arrived. Ace was working security, and after chatting with him a few minutes, Jude led Charlotte inside. Both Ace and Ripper had joined them for dinner along with Wynter and Hawk several times, and Charlotte considered the two males good friends. Ace even stopped by the shop to purchase flowers several times, remaining tight-lipped about who they were for.

Once inside, they were met by Wynter and Hawk as well as Master K, who Charlotte now knew to be Kyllian Lazlo. She had met quite a few Hounds, but Kyllian was the most guarded. He and his older brother Ryker, Rhi's mate, were both intense with their dark hair and eyes. Tonight, he was dressed in leather pants and boots. His chest and arms were on display. He had more ink than Jude, and that was saying something.

Wynter, thank god, wasn't dressed like a hooker. She had on a red dress that hugged her curves and looked like a million bucks. "Hey, Boo. You ready for this?" she asked, pulling Charlotte in for a tight hug. *This* was Roger being confronted by his wife, Tina, not the demonstration. After some further digging by Bishop, it came to light that Roger lied about his past experience. He had been banned from several clubs after conduct unbecoming. Silas had agreed to the plan, and tonight would be Roger's last night at Dominion. After watching the man interact with the women at the club, it was clear he had a type – long, blonde curls and bodies on the thinner side. Kyllian had taken photos of Roger with several different women, and those pictures had been hand-delivered by Zedra to Tina when Roger was at work. The female Gryphon had sat with Tina while the woman processed what she was looking at. According to Zed, Tina had cried, denying the evidence before shoring herself and getting pissed. By the time Zed left, a plan had been formed.

"Showtime," Kyllian said, pointing to the front of the building. Roger entered the room alone. Jude led Charlotte to the women's locker room where she stripped down to her underwear. He met her at the door after changing out of his suit into his leather pants. Together, they strode through the club to the demonstration stage. Jude helped her onto the slightly raised platform. A crowd had already gathered.

Wynter stood next to Tina who had donned a wig for the night.

Charlotte knelt at Jude's feet as he went through his speech about Shibari, its origins, and the safety protocols. Charlotte relaxed, letting her mate's soothing voice wash over her. She didn't focus on Wynter and Tina standing front and center. Not on Hawk and Kyllian standing at the edges of the crowd. She cleared her mind as Jude had taught her. Unlike when he and Mistress M did the demonstration, Jude lovingly trailed his fingertips down her arms, bringing her hand to his mouth for a touch of his lips on her knuckles before wrapping the first length of silk around her wrist.

Charlotte closed her eyes, getting lost in the sensations of being bound by her lover. After he secured her wrists, Jude started on an elaborate chest harness. His fingers slipped between her skin and the rope, gauging the tightness. At home, they rarely spoke during the process, but with the demonstration, Jude explained each configuration.

"Check in, Sweetness."

"Green, Sir."

Jude hadn't asked Charlotte to give him the honorific, but she did so freely. She had read up on BDSM protocols, wanting to learn more about the lifestyle. The first time she called him Sir, Jude had rewarded her with the second-most intense orgasm of her life, calling forth his sharp teeth, biting her shoulder.

Charlotte was so relaxed that she almost missed what happened next.

"Red."

Charlotte's eyes snapped open when she realized the safe word had been used in the crowd. Roger towered over his wife, not realizing who she was. When Tina turned around, Roger sneered at the woman. "For fuck's sake, you're wearing a green band." It wasn't until she removed her wig that Roger realized the woman's identity. "Tina? I... Jesus Fucking Christ. What are you doing here?"

"The same thing you are." Tina held her head high, glaring at her husband.

Kyllian and Hawk moved in, escorting the couple away from the demonstration. Wynter followed as planned. Tina would need a friendly face by her side as she confronted Roger in the privacy of Silas's office.

Once the commotion was removed from the main room, the crowd returned their attention to the stage. Jude concluded the demonstration by explaining aftercare as he unwound the ropes. He opened the floor for questions as he sat on the platform, cradling Charlotte on his lap, feeding her sips of water. That part was also different from when he partnered with Mistress M. Her husband had provided the aftercare for her instead of Jude.

After all questions had been answered, Jude stood and helped Charlotte to her feet. They returned to the locker rooms and changed back into their regular clothes before making their way to a booth where Wynter and Hawk were waiting.

"Roger's an idiot," Wynter said as Charlotte slid into the booth opposite her best friend. "He tried to convince her this was his first time being here. She handed him an envelope and said, 'Don't bother coming home,' then sashayed her ass out of the office.

Roger opened the envelope to find photographic evidence of his lies along with divorce papers and a pink slip."

"What did he do then?" Charlotte asked.

Kyllian walked up, chuckling. "Not much he could do with his father-in-law waiting at the back door. The man just lost his wife and his job. Plus, Silas revoked his membership and promised he would never be allowed in any BDSM club within a thousand-mile radius. When Roger threatened to sue because the photos were taken here at Dominion, Justin got in his face and voiced him. Roger Smithson is on his way to New Mexico." The usually broody Hound propped his hip against the edge of the booth next to Hawk's shoulder and crossed his arms, scanning the club. His body tensed, and his eyes narrowed.

"Godsdamnit." Kyllian pushed off the booth and stormed across the room.

"What was that about?" Wynter asked.

After seeing who Kyllian approached, Jude wrapped his arm around Charlotte. "One of his subs being a brat. He'll handle it."

"One of? As in he has more than one?" Wynter craned her neck to see who the sub in question was.

"Yes. Kayos has a particular skill set that's quite popular. He is clear in his contracts that he is not an exclusive Dom."

"But that's a guy," Wynter pointed out.

"Not all BDSM is sexual, Muffin. Like Spyder said, Kyllian's skill set is popular. One needed by men and women alike."

Charlotte was intrigued by the way Kyllian didn't say a word, yet the other man bowed his head and followed. "And what is this skill set? I've seen his demonstrations with a whip... Oh."

"Oh, what?" Wynter asked.

Charlotte leaned over and whispered, "Pain, Muffin. He inflicts pain." Wynter glared at Charlotte who gave her bestie a cheesy grin. "Payback's a bitch, bitch."

Wynter lunged across the table, but Hawk pulled her back. "Easy, Muffin. Don't make me take you home and —"

Wynter slapped her hand over Hawk's mouth. "I think it's time for us to go."

Hawk nodded behind Wynter's hand, his eyes flashing yellow. When she removed it, he turned to Jude. "You two staying?"

"What the hell's he doing here?" Jude asked, turning all their attention to the male striding toward their booth.

"Have you seen Kayos?" Ryker asked.

"Yes, he's dealing with something. Why are you here, Ryot?"

"I have a job for him."

"And you couldn't call?" Hawk asked.

"I tried, but he didn't answer. Where is he?" Ryker looked around the room.

"As I said, he's dealing with something. Can someone else not take the job?" Jude's tone was a cross between tense and mirthful.

"No. Quinn's in trouble, and Kyllian's the only one available without a..." Ryker glanced at Wynter. "Without a wife or girlfriend."

Jude tensed the hand resting on Charlotte's shoulder. "When has that ever mattered?"

300

"This isn't a regular job. It's security, and I have no idea how long it will require his absence. If you aren't going to tell me where he is, at least go get him. Never mind. There he is." Ryker strode off across the floor to where Kyllian was standing with the sub.

Hawk slid from the booth and held his hand out for Wynter. "I guess we'll catch up with you two later." They said their goodbyes, leaving Charlotte and Jude alone.

Jude tugged one of Charlotte's curls. "What do you say, Sweetness? Do you want to stay here or get in Roxie and see if you can get another ticket?"

Charlotte pushed Jude's shoulder. "As if you have to ask."

The End

A Note from The Author

Thank you for reading Jude's book. If you enjoyed the story, a review is greatly appreciated. I have to admit, Spyder is one of my favorite Hounds if not the favorite. There's something about his wounded spirit that calls to me. I am a little jealous of Charlotte for getting to spend her life with him. Shibari has always intrigued me, and although I didn't dive into the art form too much in this book, I hope it was enough to convey the beauty of it.

This book took on a life of its own, more so than others. I am not one who plots the whole book beforehand, because whenever I do, the characters always have a different idea. The whole Roger/Roland arc was in place from the beginning, but there was also someone else I had in mind for being behind Charlotte's troubles. After talking it over with my Alpha reader, Kerstin, we decided there were too many bad guys. I like bouncing ideas off others. Kerstin, Candy, and Nikki keep my stories on the right path. I couldn't do this without them.

I want to say a big thank you to Michelle Sewell for stepping in and creating a gorgeous cover.

As usual, I have to give a shout out to the man. The life of a writer is rarely a nine-to-five job, and more often than not, my weekends are spent writing, marketing, editing, or planning the next epic story. So thank you for putting up with my silence when you'd rather have my attention. I love you.

CAST OF CHARACTERS

Sutton Lazlo – Patriarch, former cop, former Pres of the Hounds Mc
Aurora Rose "Rory" Lazlo – Matriarch

Ryker "Ryot" Lazlo – MC Pres, Leader of Mercs
Rhiannon Spencer – Witch
    McKenzie "Mac" Colins – Ryker's daughter
    Elijah McLean – Mac's boyfriend

Warryck "War" Lazlo – former Professor, current Merc
Kerrigan O'Shea – Bartender
    Lucy Ball – War's daughter, Computer Hacker
    Tamian St. Claire – Lucy's mate, Gargoyle

Maveryck "Mayhem" Lazlo – MC Vice Pres, Merc
Tatiana Volkova/Natalia Jones – Russian Mafia Princess
    Major Lazlo – Mav's son
    Marshall Lazlo – Mav's son

Kyllian "Kayos" Lazlo – Merc

Hayden "Havyk" Lazlo – Bike Designer, Merc
Sadie Rodriguez – Mom
 Mateo Rodriguez – Sadie's son

"The Girls"

Poppy & Holly, Aster & Laurel, Dahlia & Iris

Poppy & Daniel Ellis
 Devon (son) & Nora
 Theo (son)
 Jericho – grandson

Holly & Alexander Carter
Aster & Dylan Roberts
Laurel & Tucker Williams
Dahlia & Linus Parks
Iris & Brooks Nelson

The Hounds

Jude "Spyder" Sterling – Merc
Charlotte Fanning – Florist

Roman "Hawk" Hayes
Zareck "The Reverend" West - Doctor
Bethany West - Nurse
Ripley "Ripper" Davidson
Asher "Ace" McMurray

Zander Andino – Security Company Owner
Farrah Andino – wife
 Erik – son, works security

Jacklyn – daughter
Katie – daughter

Zedra Andino – Zander's Sister, works Security

Patrick "Tank" Murphy
Martina Murphy – Restaurant Owner

Locke McCloud
Bishop McCloud – Locke's son, Hacker

Sultan
King
Judge
Shadow
Legend
Brick
Maximus

Quinn Shepherd – Handler
Wynter Edgars – Wolf Shifter/Wedding Planner

About the Author

Multi-genre author Faith Gibson began writing in high school, and through the years, penned many stories and poems. As her dreams continued getting crazier than the one before, she decided to keep a dream journal. Many of these nighttime escapades have led to a line, a chapter, or even a complete story.

"Love is love, and there's not enough love in the world." This belief she holds strongly, and it's the prevailing theme in her works, all of which come with a happy ending.

Faith believes her purpose in life is to entertain the masses, even if it's one person at a time. Living just outside of Nashville, Tennessee, with the love of her life and her pit bull pup, when she's not hard at work writing her next adventure, she can often be found playing trivia while enjoying craft beer, listening to live music, or off on an adventure of her own.